Angus staggered up to safety, and stood for an instant, holding his burden and gasping for breath.

Sheila lay in his arms, limp and inert, her long dark hair streaming down like a wet garment, her sodden clothes clinging to her quiet form. Grandmother's heart gave a great shudder as she looked at her.

Was she gone already? Had Angus been too late?

Tyndale House books by
Grace Livingston Hill
Check with your area bookstore
for these bestsellers.

Grace Livingston Hill

RAINBOW COTTAGE

LIVING BOOKS®
Tyndale House Publishers, Inc.
Wheaton, Illinois

This Tyndale House book
by Grace Livingston Hill
contains the complete text
of the original hard–cover edition.
NOT ONE WORD
HAS BEEN OMITTED.

Printing History
J. B. Lippincott edition published 1934
Tyndale House edition/1990

Living Books is a registered trademark of Tyndale
House Publishers, Inc.

Library of Congress Catalog Card Number 89-50877
ISBN 0-8423-5731-0

96 95 94 93 92 91 90
7   6   5   4   3   2   1

GRANDMOTHER lived down by the sea in summer, with a lovely stone sea wall all about the garden, and pillar roses climbing over it in pink riot.

The cottage was long and low and thatched, like Ann Hathaway's, and there was ivy growing thick on the gable toward the sea, even climbing courageously up the great stone chimney and trailing down on the thatch.

Over against the back wall there were hollyhocks thickly massed, and all around the kitchen wall were morning-glories, mostly blue and white. There were borders that blazed with portulacca and quieter ones of forget-me-nots and sweet alyssum and candytuft. There was a whole corner where the soft yellow of "hose-in-hose" cowslips shimmered in the spring sunshine and lit up the delicate tint of blue phlox, and a little later blazed with the brilliance of great oriental poppies; a long stretch of gay shirley poppies shot here and there with bachelor buttons; farther on a mass of larkspur, pink and white and blue against the ivy on the back wall. Tall pale blue delphinium and madonna lilies stood near the house, with the tea rose beds just across the path, and down beside the walk that led from the house to the arched gateway and the sea there was a great drift of blue flax as blue as the sea itself. It was a wonderful garden in a marvellous setting, and happening there so unexpectedly just on the edge of the great rock-rimmed beach itself, was all the more astonishing.

Grandmother was a brisk little old lady with a face that had survived many troubles, and wise bright eyes that would not be too sympathetic for one's good, yet could twinkle with the youngest.

Grandmother stayed in her nest by the sea till the waves began to beat high above her sea wall, and the garden had gone into shrouds for the winter. Then she made brief bright visits to her sons and daughters and grandchildren, and returned to get her house in order as soon as the first hint of spring came.

Grandmother wore simple pretty gray dresses, and her hair was white and curled of itself into the loveliest "permanent" that Nature knows how to make. Sometimes the fine sea air painted a rose on her soft old cheeks and gave her an air of worldliness, but no one ever accused her of using make-up.

Grandmother still put up fruit in the old fashioned way, pound for pound, and made jams and jellies enough for a hotel. She stocked her two deep cooky jars, one with molasses cookies, the other with big sugary caraway cookies, whenever a chick or a child was coming to visit her. She had a little maid to help her, but she kept her skilled hand firmly over every bit of cookery that was concocted in her wide white-tiled kitchen.

Grandmother had fine old engravings and oil paintings on her walls, pictures of other days, each one with a story to it, and many a child had sat at her feet and heard the stories over and over again, learning history, geography, political science, yes, and religion at her feet.

Grandmother did not play bridge. She had never had time. And when anybody suggested her learning she would say:

"Pooh! What would I want to waste my time like that for?"

She could knit, even the new intricate stitches. She had recently knit her oldest granddaughter a wonderful three piece sports suit in delft blue and apricot colors for a gift toward her wedding trousseau, proving she was up to date to the last minute. Yet she still had a big print Bible on the little marble topped stand that always stood by her own deeply cushioned resting chair. There was a rare old antimacassar crocheted of finest thread in intricate pattern, covering the marble of the little stand, and on that the Bible rested. Yes, and she read it too; morning and night, as she sat in her softly cushioned corner with her eyes far away on another world.

The youngest grandson called her "Gram" and considered her a chum. The youngest granddaughter called her "Babbie" and sat at her feet learning how to use a thimble. The oldest grandson called her "Grand," and said she was a good sport. The middle-sized granddaughter called her "Gwannie" and wheedled the very eyeteeth out of her. But every one of them adored her and delighted to have her come and visit, or better still to go down to the sea and spend the summer with her as they often did.

One day in the early summer a little pilgrim arrived at the wicket gate that swung in the rose-trimmed arch of the garden wall. A little battered, tempest-tossed soul, wayworn and weary and half afraid. Shyly, hesitantly, half defiantly she lifted the latch, opened the gate and stepped within; gazing breathlessly about on the riot of joyous color, blinking her eyes and staring, unable to believe it was all true.

"Great God!" she said under her breath in a reverent awestruck voice, "I never knew there could be anything as lovely as this!"

Then after an instant, with conviction,

"This can't be the place of course, but maybe they wouldn't mind if I just stood and looked a minute, and perhaps they'll be able to tell me where to find the right place; but I just must look at this while I'm here. I'll never see anything like it again on earth, I'm sure. I've heard of heaven on earth! This must be it!"

She set down the cheap antiquated little suitcase that held her worldly goods, and yet had room to sag with an emaciated air, and gazed around, her shoulders drooping from weariness, her fingers slowly unbending with relief from long carrying the burden.

She was a forlorn little creature, dressed in a shabby serge suit of a long ago vintage, obviously sponged and pressed recently by an amateur hand. A little faded felt hat was pulled down over dark hair that rioted out in places and caught the sunlight in little rings and waves, and framed a face of delicate loveliness, whose fragile beauty was only the more startling perhaps because of the great dark rings under the sea blue eyes. Even the sweetly curved lips drooped with weariness, and her whole slender figure sagged with exhaustion. She had walked all the way from the station, six miles away, and the heels of her shabby little slippers were worn crooked so that her feet were thrown out of balance. Besides it was hot walking in the blazing sun, even on the hard smooth beach, for her serge coat was thick, and the drabbled little white blouse she wore beneath it, besides being soiled with the journey, had acquired a great rip under one arm, and would not do to appear in.

She put up the back of a small hand garbed in an old black kid glove much too large for it, pushed back the hair from her damp forehead, drew a deep breath and stared off at the beauty spread before her. Over the waves of the flax bed, blue as the sea beyond, and blowing like real waves in the breeze, over the blaze of the portulacca borders, up to the lovely old house, the green cool darkness of the ivy covered walls, the gay riot of the flowers, her gaze lingering tenderly on the lilies in their blue setting, on the curves of a great pale rose in the rose bed, on the gray of the stone wall with its garland of roses, and then beyond to the blue sea itself with the fitting white sails here and there. From inside this safe sweet enclosure, somehow the sea looked better, more restful, more wonderful to look at than when she had been walking all alone on that great empty stretch of shore with the sea like a monster who might approach at any moment and swallow her up.

Just a step farther inside the wicket was a rose-trellised seat. Would it be any harm to sit down for a minute and rest? It was cool in here, and she was so faint, so tired. She had not eaten yet that morning and it was nearing high noon.

With a stealthy step she slid over to the seat and sat down, watching the house furtively. If anyone came out she would ask her way and go at once of course. If it was a pleasant person she might find courage to ask for a drink of water. How good a drink of water would taste!

She dared to lean her head back against the arbor, and close her eyes for a moment. How good the breeze felt on her hot cheeks. She pulled off her shabby little hat and smoothed her hair back. She must look very disheveled, and if she was to venture to the door to ask the way she must not look like a tramp.

She fitted her hat carefully on her head again, tucked in the soft tendrils of hair till they were demurely smooth, and then sat back looking off toward the sea. She could just get a glimpse of the blue with one sail at a place where the wall dipped down to meet the lower level of the front. Oh, it was lovely here. It was like resting in Fairyland. It was almost like coming into a deserted island. Was there nobody at home?

She turned her eyes cautiously toward the house, Yes, the front door stood open, disclosing a wide hall, or perhaps it was a living room, with a glimpse of low stairs in the dimness, and the outline of a stone fireplace under the stair landing. A lovely house. Of course they would not go off and leave such a beautiful house alone with the front door wide open. There must be someone there, and eventually whoever it was would appear.

Yes, there was the unmistakable slam of an oven door in

the region of what must be the kitchen, the clatter of a hot pan upon a table, and an instant later the delicious odor of something hot and crisp and sweet and spicy wafted on the air. Cookies, or it might be gingerbread! And homemade! How wonderful it smelled! How hungry she was!

What if she should dare to rush in and grab a cooky? How ravenous she felt! Probably if she should ask for something to eat they might give it to her, but she would rather starve than do it. She laughed quietly to herself, a trifle bitterly, over the thought of following out her hungry desire and rushing into that strange kitchen to grab something to eat. How terrible to have come to such a pass. She ought never to have started to come here with so little money. To think that she was down to the last five cents!

And when she arrived at her vague destination, suppose she found it just as impossible as the place she came from? How was she to get back?

Well, that would be to settle if the time came. At least she was so far on her way, but with only five cents left for emergencies. How long would five cents satisfy a hunger and a weariness like hers?

There! There was that sound of the oven door and that delicious wave of spicy fragrance again, that brought on another wave of sickening hunger. Another pan of cookies put in to bake! It smelled as if there were raisins in them.

This would not do. She was growing maudlin. She must get out of here or she would go to pieces. This was too nice a place to spoil by collapsing. She would go to the door, enquire her way, and get on. If she were going to pass out it would be more decent to do it out there on a lonely stretch of sand than here in this lovely home entrance.

So she rose with a deep breath to draw courage, and one more wistful glance around the garden where butterflies were circling in droves above the poppies, and a green and gold humming-bird was spinning pin wheels over a great white lily. Ah, to get a glimpse of heaven and to have to leave it!

Grandmother Ainslee had come down to Rainbow Lodge rather late that year on account of having had to wait on the multitudinous festivities attending the marriage of the oldest granddaughter. She had been at the shore only a couple of weeks, hardly time enough to get everything going for the summer. She never had come down so late in all the summers that had gone before. She still was regretting having missed the cowslips and blue phlox.

But the cottage was in order from top to bottom, not a thing out of place. They had got in a fisherman's daughter for three days to scrub and wash windows, and now everything was in shining order. For Grandmother was expecting company.

"She should have been here half an hour since," she said to Janet the little maid, as she stepped to the sea door and looked out toward a dim ship on the horizon, as if that should be bearing the guest. "I told her to take a taxi," she soliloquized, "and there hasn't been a taxi by this morning. She must have missed her train. Her telegram said this morning train. I hate people missing trains. It shows they have no order. One should never miss a train." She said it sternly as if the little maid were arguing otherwise, as if against her will she wanted to believe that it was all right to miss trains.

"But mightn't the train have been late?" argued Janet, as Grandmother had known she would.

"The train is very seldom late!" said Grandmother severely. "It is usually the traveler, not the train, that is late. Have you got that pitcher of lemonade in the refrigerator, Janet?"

"Yes ma'am, it's been in this half hour. It's frosted nice by this time, all over the crystal of the big round pitcher. I like that pitcher M's Ainslee. It looks like a big rock of ice."

"That's a very old pitcher," said Grandmother with a dreamy look in her eye, as Janet had known there would be.

"I had it when I was married. I'd feel it, Janet, if anything was to happen to that pitcher. I've always been so fond of it."

"Yes ma'am you would! And so would I, M's Ainslee! I jus' love that pitcher. I got two glasses like it on the little silver tray like you said. Jus' ta think you had 'em all these years, an' ain't one o' the twelve broke yet. My I'd hate it ef anythin' was ta happen to 'em when I was washin' up."

"You're always very careful, Janet," said the mistress softly.

"Thank you, M's Ainslee, I try ta be. There! There's a knock. Would that be Miss Sheila? Sheila, my that's a pretty name! Want I should go ta the door, Miss Ainslee?"

Grandmother cast a quick apprehensive look at Janet, almost assenting, then shook her head.

"No, Janet, I'd better go. If it should be Sheila it wouldn't seem very hospitable. But—I didn't hear the taxi, did you Janet?"

Grandmother was patting her soft curls into shape and taking off the big print apron that covered her pretty gray muslin.

"No, M's Ainslee, but then you 'n I ben talkin' a lot. Mighta ben."

Grandmother handed Janet the apron and darted away to the door. Janet sidled to the crack of the kitchen door and fixed a fine discerning black eye where she could just get a glimpse of the front hall, and the cookies winked at each other and took occasion to burn with a fine sweet odor like incense.

When Grandmother saw the little-girl-tramp at the door she almost turned back and let Janet go in her stead. Janet was much more successful in dealing with tramps and salesmen of all kinds than kindhearted Grandmother Ainslee. But something in the tired sag of the girl's slender body, something in the shy wistfulness of the great blue eyes that peered anxiously in at the screen door, drew her in spite of herself.

"Would you be so good as to give me a drink of water?" The girl's voice was sweet and clear. It was not the voice of a tramp-girl. It sounded almost cultured.

"Why, of course," answered Grandmother briskly. Then raising her voice as she came on toward the door with the intention of looking up toward the road to see if a taxi was in sight, she called:

"Janet, bring a pitcher of water and a glass, will you?"

But she brought her eyes to meet the blue ones of the girl first before she sought the road, and something haunting in those eyes caught and held her attention, something that stirred an old memory with a sweet bitter stab of pain. Those eyes! Who did they remind her of?

"I'm so sorry to have to trouble you," said the sweet voice again, "but I've walked a long way and the sun is very hot. I think I must have turned the wrong way at the village, and I just couldn't go all that way back without a drink of water."

"You poor child!" said Grandmother pityingly. "It's no trouble at all. Here, Janet, I'll take that and you run back to your cookies. I smell them burning!"

The girl drank the water eagerly, draining the glass, and handing it back with a grateful smile.

"Oh, that is so good!" she said with a quiver in her voice, "I felt almost as if I was going to faint if I didn't have some water."

"Won't you sit down out there in the shade and rest awhile before you start back?" said Grandmother a shade hesitantly. It wasn't exactly what she liked to plan for to have a little tramp-girl sitting under the trellis when Sheila arrived, but—well one couldn't be inhuman, and it was a hot morning in the sun.

"Oh, thank you," said the girl with that wonderful lighting up of her tired young face that gave a stab of haunting memory to the old lady again. Who was it she looked like? "I'd love to stay a little and just look at those wonderful flowers and that sea. It seems like heaven here. I never saw such a lovely garden. But I must be getting on. I may have a long way to go yet. I wonder—" and she hesitated and looked shyly at Grandmother, "I suppose it wouldn't be at all likely that you would know the people living up the other way, would you? I suppose I must have come in the wrong direction, for it seems as if I had walked about ten miles since I left the station."

"Why, yes, I know most of the people around this vicinity. I ought to. I've lived here around forty years," said Grandmother briskly, running swiftly over the names of the winter settlers thereabouts. "What was the name of the people you wanted to find? Are they fishing people?"

The girl looked startled.

"Why no, I don't think so," she said thoughtfully, "I really don't know, but I don't think there are any men in the family now, at least not at home. It's a Mrs. Ainslee I'm hunting. Do you happen to know anyone by that name?"

"Ainslee!" exclaimed Grandmother looking at the girl with a puzzled frown. "Why my name is Ainslee! But I don't know anybody else in this region by that name. What are the initials?"

"Mrs. Harmon Ainslee," said the girl with a wondering look at her.

"Well, that's my name," said Grandmother with a grim, almost startled look at the girl. "What was it you—who told you to come to me—? That is, why did you—?" Grandmother stopped short in a kind of dismay, not knowing just which question she wanted to ask. This girl didn't seem like either a beggar or a book agent. Perhaps she wanted to hire out for housework or something. Well, she must get this business over quickly before Sheila arrived.

"But—I don't understand!" said the girl wearily, giving a wondering look around that included the garden and the sea and the humming bird by the lily, "it just couldn't be a place like this. There must be some mistake."

The girl swayed and caught hold of the pillar by the door, and a sudden dazed look in her eyes pulled at Grandmother's heart strings.

"You'd better come in and sit down and rest a bit anyway," said Grandmother opening the door and putting out a hand gingerly to the shabby serge sleeve.

But the girl swayed again and leaned against the pillar.

"I have a letter here," she said, fumbling in the worn little leather hand bag she carried.

"A letter?" said Grandmother, half closing the door again. Then she was a beggar or an agent. They always carried letters, dirty tattered letters that one didn't want to touch.

"Yes," said the girl bringing out a crisply folded letter.

"I'm sorry," said Grandmother almost curtly. "But I really haven't time to read letters this morning. I'm expecting a guest any minute. If you could just tell me in a word what it is you want—"

The letter suddenly fell from the girl's nerveless fingers and fluttered down on the brick pavement.

"Please excuse me," she said with a frightened look in her eyes, "but I've just got to sit down for a minute if you don't mind," and she suddenly collapsed to the step, her head swaying back to rest unsteadily against the pillar, and her long lashes sweeping down across her pale cheeks.

Grandmother pushed wide the door in consternation and knelt down beside her, calling "Janet, Janet, come here quick."

But even as she knelt she had that strange feeling tugging at her heart that she had seen those long lashes before somewhere lying on a round baby cheek.

Janet slatted the last pan of cookies down on the marble topped kitchen table and came, gave one look and dashed out beside her mistress.

"We better get her inside outta this sun," she said briefly. She gathered the frail girl into her strong arms, lifted her and bore her in, laying her gently on the floor.

"I'll get the aromatics," she said efficiently. "Don't you go to worry, M's Ainslee, she ain't bad. She's jes' passed out fer the minit. She'll be awright!"

She was back in a trice with the aromatic spirits of ammonia and a clean rag, wafting the pungent odor in front of the girl's face.

"Here, you hold that to her nose," she commanded Grandmother, "and I'll fix her a dose." She handed over the restorative, and went to get a glass of water and fix the drops.

"Now," she said coming back with the tumbler and spoon, "I'll lift her head up and you get some of that inside her lips."

A moment more and consciousness returned. The girl opened her eyes slowly and looked up puzzled, gazed about on the strange ceiling, the walls, then gradually focussed her eyes on the two women bending over her, and intelligence came back to her face.

"The letter!" she murmured, fumbling feebly about for her bag.

"Your letter is all right, dearie," said Grandmother solicitously. "Janet will pick it up for you. Just lie still a minute until you feel better."

The long lashes fluttered on the pale cheeks again, but opened wide in a minute or two and the blue eyes looked steadily at the kindly old face bending over her. Then the girl lifted her head and struggled to rise.

"I'm all right now," she said feebly, trying to smile. "I'm sorry to have made so much trouble. You've been very kind. I didn't think I'd go to pieces like that. You see, I—"

"There, there, child, don't trouble to explain now. Wait till you feel better. Here's your letter. Now Janet, let's get her up on the couch where she can lie more comfortably."

Janet stopped and swung a strong young arm under the slight girlish form and got her to the couch without trouble. Grandmother came and stood over her, feeling her pulse with a practised hand.

"You are so good and kind," murmured the girl with another attempt at a smile. "I'm quite all right now, I really didn't mean to arrive this way, I really didn't. But it was just the smell of those heavenly cookies that did it I think. It kind of overcame me."

"You dear child!" said Grandmother quickly. "I'll get you some. You've had a long walk and must have been hungry. You probably had your breakfast early."

"I—didn't eat any breakfast this morning. I guess that was it."

"You didn't eat any breakfast? That's no way to do. You never should do that! Try to walk on an empty stomach! It's never wise especially in hot weather. Why didn't you eat your breakfast?"

"Well, you see, the train got in early,—at least I thought it was going to, and I didn't think it was worth while to go into the dining car. But then the train was late—"

"Oh! Late, was it?" said Grandmother with a quick look out the door still in search of the missing taxi. "Which way did you come from? South or West?"

"West," said the girl drawing a long trembling breath.

"Oh!" said Grandmother going over to the door quickly and giving another long look up toward the road from the village. "That explains it then. You see I'm expecting my granddaughter from the West this morning and I couldn't understand why she didn't arrive. But—" with a quick look at the girl, "if you walked all that distance she certainly ought to have got here before you in a taxi. She was to take a taxi. Still, perhaps she came on another section. They sometimes have two sections on those through trains I know."

The girl on the couch lay very still for a minute with her eyes closed. Then she slowly opened her eyes and looked at the old lady and spoke, hesitantly:

"I guess, perhaps, she's here," she said in a grave reserved voice. "I couldn't believe it would be such a wonderful place as this, but if you say you are Mrs. Harmon Ainslee then it must be true. I'm Sheila Ainslee!"

2

GRANDMOTHER whirled about and gave one long penetrating look at the threadbare little waif who had drifted to her door. Then she swung around to the kitchen door and called:

"Janet bring the pitcher of lemonade and some hot cookies right away."

She said it in the tone in which one might have said: "Bring forth the best robe and put it on him, and shoes on his feet!"

Then she whirled about to the girl again. "So that's whose eyes you've got, my little Andy's eyes, and his long bright lashes. I might have known, poor fool I!"

And she was down on her knees beside the couch working with the buttons of the shabby blue coat, pulling off the dejected felt hat, and smoothing back the waves of hair from the white forehead.

But Sheila put up her hands to protect the coat from being unbuttoned, and reached shamedly for her hat.

"No, please," she said feebly. "I'm not fit to be seen until I've cleaned up a little. I've had five days and nights in the common car, and I'm a sight! My blouse is fairly black! And, please, I can't get fixed up nor anything until I've said what I've come to say."

Janet came in just then and Grandmother rose regally and took the tray from the reluctant Janet who did not want her cookies and carefully prepared drink wasted on a little tramp-girl.

But Grandmother thoroughly understood Janet. She placed the tray on a small table beside Sheila's chair, poured her a glass of the tinkling frosty drink and pressed it to her lips, till she drank eagerly, set a plate of cookies in her lap, and then in a voice that conveyed both rebuke and command to the little serving maid she ordered:

"Janet go up and see that everything is all right in Miss Sheila's room, and draw the water for a bath. She has had a hard journey and will want to rest. You might open the bed and draw the shades down, for the sun will be shining on that side of the house by now perhaps."

Janet stared and turned hastily to do her mistress' bidding, half sulky that things had turned out this way.

But when Grandmother turned back to her guest she found her sitting up and putting on her hat again, a grave reserve in her manner.

"Grandmother, you are very kind," said Sheila, "and this is a wonderful place, far lovelier than I had ever dreamed any place could be, and not at all the kind of place I thought I was coming to. But I can't take off my things, nor accept any of your hospitality, until I find out how you feel about one thing."

"Why, child!" said Grandmother aghast, sitting down suddenly in the nearest chair.

"It's about my mother!" said the girl. "I've grown up feeling that you hated my mother, and if that is so I couldn't stay here even for a short visit."

"I never hated any living soul!" defended Grandmother pitifully. "I certainly do not hate her. How could you get such an idea?"

"You wrote my father long ago. We found the letter in an old coat pocket after he went away. You said something about his having married beneath him."

The blue eyes rested accusingly upon the old lady and she sat up bravely under the challenge.

"My son wrote me that he was marrying a girl who sang in a cabaret," she answered with dignity. "That was all I knew about her. In my experience girls who sing in cabarets are not usually well brought up, nor rightly educated nor cultured. I felt that my son would only add to the sorrow that he had brought to us all, by marrying—" Grandmother hesitated for a word—"out of his class," she finished lamely.

A white flame blazed into the eyes of the girl, and her lips grew hard and thin with anger as she answered.

"That's it. Out of his class! You thought she was out of his class when you knew nothing about it at all. You knew only one thing about her and you judged her out of his class. Well, she was. She was in a class far *above* him. Don't misunderstand me. I loved my father, but my mother was as far above him in every way as the stars are above the earth. You did not know that my mother's mother was dying without the proper food and medicine when my mother began to sing in the cabaret, and that she had to sing there even the day her mother died because she had not enough money to bury her. And that she had to go on singing there afterward because there was nothing else in the town that she could get to do while she paid the honest debts she had had to make while her mother was dying!"

"No! I did not know that!" said Grandmother meekly, her eyes filled with a dawning trouble. "I only knew that my son wrote me he was going to be married and wanted money to finance what seemed to me a disaster to his life, which had already gone far toward ruin."

Sheila's cheeks were burning now with excitement, and a new strength had come to her.

"You did not know that my mother belonged to an old and honored family in Ireland once. There is a great castle over there where my mother's mother used to live before their money was used to further what they felt to be a righteous cause."

"No," said Grandmother sadly, "but it was not of things like that I was worrying. Money and castles and an honored name. I would have been satisfied if he had married a poor obscure girl who was decent. But it did not seem to me that a girl—"

"No," said Sheila, "you did not ask questions. You did not know that my mother came over to this country with her father and mother when she was a young girl because her father thought that he had a chance to retrieve their fortune and save the castle to the name; and that he was killed in a train accident before he ever succeeded in making much. My mother brought her mother out to the west to save her life because the doctor said it was her only hope. And they took every cent they had and spent it to save my grandmother's life, and still she died. Then my mother was left alone and had to keep on at the only job there was. She hadn't anybody, not *any*body, to help her, and she hadn't a cent. So she sang in that cabaret. And you hated her for it!"

"No, child, no! I am not as bad as that. I did not hate her! I didn't understand!"

"No, you didn't understand! Well, I came here to tell you. When your invitation came for me to visit you I wouldn't answer you. I didn't want to come and see you. I'm afraid I even hated you. I knew how much you might have helped us in our trouble and you didn't, and I felt I never wanted to come near you, not even if it could save me from starving to death. But afterward I got to thinking. You wrote a very nice letter to me. If it hadn't been that you never suggested that you would like to know my mother, or to have her visit you, perhaps I would have thought it was loving, for I hadn't found that letter in Father's pocket then that showed how you had been against her from the first. That was before Mother died and—"

Grandmother lifted a shocked face.

"Your mother is *dead?*"

"Yes," said Sheila fiercely, and suddenly bowed her head with a great overwhelming sob that shook her slender shoulders. "Yes, she is dead. She died six weeks ago. Worn out! It was after that I found the letter in an old coat pocket of Father's when I was packing up to move to a cheaper place."

"My dear!" said Grandmother heart brokenly. The tears were coursing down her wrinkled cheeks now. "Oh, my dear! I am so sorry! I did not even know she was sick! Your father has not written me in a long time. He was always remiss in so many things. My poor bad boy! My Andrew! But I would have thought he would have written me when his wife died!"

"My father does not know," said Sheila in a colorless voice, a full apathetic look coming into her eyes. "He has not been home in three years. That was what killed her. She loved him through everything."

"He had not been home?" The mother's voice was filled with horror. "Not been in his home for three years! Why, where was he?"

"I don't know."

"You don't know? Why, what can you mean?"

"He often went off," said Sheila drawing a weary breath. "He used to get tired of having us always needing things. He used to get tired of Mother being sick, and not having good meals, but how could Mother get good meals when there wasn't money to buy anything to cook? And he used to go off. The first time he went I was almost four years old. I remember he said he wasn't coming back till he had money enough to live comfortably on."

Grandmother put her face down and wept silently into her hands. Sheila went on with her story in a sad little hopeless voice as if she had gone over it all so many times that the pain was all drained out of it. As if it were merely a ceremony she was performing.

"It was then that Mother had to get a job," she said it desolately, "and there wasn't anything else she could get but to go back to the cabaret where she had been singing when Father found her and married her."

Grandmother made a sad little moan.

"She had to take me with her," went on the girl. "I remember there was an old couch in the dressing-room where my mother changed into the costume she sang in, and I used to curl up with an old coat over me and go to sleep till she was ready to go home."

Grandmother lifted her tear-wet face and spoke earnestly.

"But surely your mother could have written me then. For her child's sake she could have written me. She knew I had plenty."

"My mother was a proud woman," said the girl with a little haughty lifting of her chin. "She was as proud as you are. She knew that my father had asked help of you at first, had told you that he was turning over a new leaf, and that marrying my mother was a part of it, and that if you would help him get a start you would never regret it. And all you did was to urge him to go away and never see her again."

"Oh," groaned Grandmother, "I thought I was doing the right thing. I asked advice of several friends and they all said that was what I ought to do. I did not trust my Andrew. He had made promises before and not kept them."

"Well, maybe they were right," said the girl in a toneless voice. "Anyway you can see why my mother did not write to you. And somehow we made out, and my mother managed to keep me in decent clothes and send me to school till my father came back again. And the first time he came back he brought a lot of money with him."

"Oh!" said Grandmother hopefully.

"But it didn't seem to bring happiness with it. My mother

gave up her work and stayed at home, and we had a nicer place to live in, a nice little cottage with three rooms downstairs and two bedrooms. But Mother cried a great deal. And once in the night I woke up and heard them talking. Mother wanted to go away to another place and get away from all the old surroundings, but it seemed that Father was tied up in some way. He told her he didn't dare. It had something to do with money, and he seemed to have to go around with a lot of men that my mother did not like. Men she thought were bad. They gambled a great deal and they drank. I am sure my father gambled for our money sometimes would all be gone in a night, and Mother would suffer so, and cry so. And I know he drank. He would often come home drunk. I used to wonder if he wasn't ashamed to come sober because I know he loved Mother, and hated to hurt her."

Grandmother sat with bowed head as if wave after wave of sorrow were passing over her. She seemed to have aged in that few minutes. Suddenly Sheila looked up and her eyes which had been hard and hopeless softened, and the tears began to come down her face too.

"I'm not doing this to hurt you," she said sorrowfully. "I just thought I had to come and tell you about my mother. I didn't come here to sponge on you nor to touch your sympathy and get you to help me. I came because I couldn't stand it not to have you know what a wonderful mother I had. Why, she has been father and mother both to me, and she has gone to work night after night I know when she was almost too weak to stand up. No, please don't stop me yet. I must tell you all."

Grandmother had lifted her hands in protest and opened her lips to say something but she dropped her hands again in her lap submissively and sat still, with the tears flowing, and a look of utter humiliation on her sweet old face.

"My father went away several times," went on Sheila in an obvious struggle to get through with the story, "and every time he came back we had prosperity for a little while, but it never lasted long, and my mother always had to go back to her singing. They liked her at that place and were kind to her. I always thought the proprietor was mixed up with Father in some sort of deal. But as I grew older Mother wouldn't let me go near the place and she made me promise I would never go there even if she were taken away. She wanted me never to let people know I could sing."

Grandmother's face kindled at that.

"But this last time, when Father went away," went on Sheila, "Mother didn't find it so easy to get her place back again. There was a young girl who sang jazz and danced and was more familiar with men. Mother wasn't like that. She was always very distant to everybody, just did her part gorgeously and went off to her dressing-room. Some of the new people didn't like that, and if it hadn't been for the old proprietor she would have been dropped at once, but he insisted that Mother had to be kept on too. But there was a new manager, the old man had had a stroke and couldn't do much, and the new manager was hateful to Mother. Made her sing twice as much, encores and things, and cut down her pay. I was working evenings too at the Junction Hotel waiting on table and washing dishes. Mother hated it for me, and I was still in school you know, so it kept me pretty busy, but it was the only way to make ends meet."

"Oh!" groaned Grandmother, "to think that I—"

"You don't need to feel that way," said Sheila pityingly, "I knew how to take care of myself. My mother taught me to keep away from everybody as much as possible and not let anyone get familiar with me. No, don't stop me yet, Grandmother, I must tell the rest. I'm almost done."

The old lady wiped away the tears and set herself to listen again.

"That last winter was a hard one. I knew Mother was sick, but I didn't know how sick till afterwards." Sheila took a deep breath and held her lip between her teeth to keep it from quivering.

"I tried several times to keep her from going to sing, but she would do it. She said if she stayed away just once the new manager would have something to complain of and she would lose the job entirely. But that last night it was raining and she was very weak. She had been lying on the bed all day, too sick to eat, but she *would go*. I begged her to let me take her place. She knew I could do it. I could sing all her songs. But she rose right up as if she were frightened and began to dress."

Sheila paused to close her eyes and take a deep breath as if the memory hurt her too much for words. Then she hurried on.

"I got off from my work that night, because I was worried about her. But I could not stop her. Then I begged her to let me go with her, but she grew so excited I was frightened. I think she dreaded that place for me worse than anything she knew. So, when she started out in the rain I followed her. I dared not let her go alone. The wind was blowing a terrific gale, and she was like a willow wand in its power. How she ever got to the hall I do not know. It was all I could do sometimes to keep my footing. And once she reeled and almost fell, but caught hold of a tree and went on when the blast was over."

Grandmother had lifted her face now, and her eyes were bright with excitement as she listened breathlessly to a tale that was cutting her soul with anguish. But Sheila had forgotten her listener perhaps. Her face was tense, her eyes were far away as she went rapidly on.

"After she had reached the door and gone in I hovered about in the shadow by the side entrance until I got a chance to steal in when no one was looking. I knew the way around of course, for I had been with her so much when I was little. I slipped into the end of the hall back of her dressing-room where I knew people seldom came. There was a closet near by where I could hide if it became necessary, and I watched, and listened. When she came out of her dressing-room I watched her from the dark and saw her totter. I was afraid she would fall before she got on the platform, and I stole out to keep near if she needed me. But I was amazed when I heard her voice. It was rich and clearer than it had been for years. It seemed as if she had put all she was and all she ever had been into that song. It was an old Irish ballad and it seemed to me I could see the castle where she was born, and the shamrock gleaming like emerald. She had told me about Ireland, and it always seems to me that I have been there, it is so real to me."

Sheila's eyes were large and filled with tears but she went on with her tale without stopping to wipe the tears away.

"The audience went wild. They cheered and cheered, and called her back again and again. And each time instead of growing weak her voice seemed stronger and clearer than the last. I couldn't believe my ears, and she so sick all day! But then after she had sung over almost her whole repertoire I heard her speak, sweet and clear, and there was something in her voice that I had never heard before, a kind of command and confidence, and a great tenderness. The clapping stopped and the room was so still it seemed as if I could hear people breathe, almost hear them think. She said:

"I can give you only one more to-night. I am very tired. Listen! It is an old song I love. I leave it with you!"

"And then she began to sing,—it was slow and sweet and tender, but so clear that every word reached out into the far shadows of the room:

> *Jesus, Lover of my soul,*
>   *Let me to Thy bosom fly,*

"I had never heard her sing like that. Every word seemed as if it were a cry from her soul to God.

> *Hide me, O my Saviour hide,*
>   *Till the storm of life is past.*

"It broke my heart to listen, but I was drawn closer and closer to the door just behind the stage till I could see her standing there in her little old white dress, with her face so white and sweet, and her eyes looking up as if she saw beyond the gaudy garlands of the place."

Sheila's voice broke and she buried her face in her hands for an instant, then lifted her head once more and hurried on:

"As I watched her I seemed to know that she was not singing any more, she was praying, really praying to God. I think the people in the room all felt it too for some of them were crying. Even the rough men stopped drinking and the common painted women stopped laughing and listened and had tears in their eyes. But she wasn't thinking of them any more, she was singing right on:

All my trust on Thee is stayed,

"She sang all through the verses and no one spoke nor moved:

Thou, O Christ, art all I want;
More than all in Thee I find:

"Her voice grew with each line into a great crescendo:

Plenteous grace with Thee is found,
Grace to cover all my sin,

"Her accompanist at first had just struck chords here and there. He was used to following her, just wandering into her key and improvising, but when she came to the last verse, he broke into great triumphant strains, as if he sensed for an instant how real it all was, and then he suddenly died away and left her to sing those last four lines alone:

Thou of life the Fountain are,

"She sang it so triumphantly, so pleadingly. I saw the pianist suddenly look up as if he half expected to see God standing somewhere above.

> *Freely let me take of Thee;*
> *Spring Thou up within my heart,*
> *Rise to all eternity.*

"There wasn't a waver of her full wonderful tone to the last word sustained to the end, and then, suddenly, as the sound died away to a whisper, I heard a great sob come from somewhere down by a table back by the door, and Mother dropped softly down in a little white heap—

"Even before I started to run out there to her I knew she was gone, and it seemed to me as if God had somehow let her sort of glorify the awful work she had to do, the work she hated so, and only did for my sake."

Sheila was still for an instant, looking out the open door down toward the lilies where the humming-bird was glancing here and there with green and gold flashes. Then she raised her great blue drenched eyes and said quietly:

"I think she is in some place like that over there, now, for that's as near to heaven as I could ever dream, and I'm sure if there's a heaven she is in it."

She said the last words defiantly, and looked at her grandmother sitting there so silently, weeping great tears down upon her withered clasped hands.

Then the girl suddenly closed her eyes and lay back wearily as if the effort of talking had been too much for her, and for an instant the old lady's tears dropping softly on her hands was all that could be heard in the room.

3

"I wasn't going to come here at all," Sheila's tired voice took up the story again. "I was going somewhere and find some work. Even after I'd sent you the telegram from Chicago saying what train I would take, I almost backed out. But somehow I had to come and tell you about my mother once — let you see how mistaken you were — before I did another thing. But — I — guess — maybe — it wasn't any use. I suppose — you'll go right on — thinking what you've always done — !"

There was a catch in her voice like a sob as it trailed off into silence again, and the grandmother sprang up as if she had been struck, and went over to kneel beside her.

"Oh, my dear!" she said in a little catchy voice full of tears. "It *is* of use. I *don't* think so any more. I think your mother was *wonderful!* And I wish so much I'd known her and could have helped her in her hard time. Oh, I was a fool, a *fool!* I knew my boy was a black sheep, but I kept right on blaming outside influences and I was afraid of everything that came in his way that might lead him farther astray. Oh, forgive me, forgive me, little Sheila! I'm a poor silly old fool of a grandmother. I shall never forgive myself that I did not help her. It was all my fault, dear child! Can you forgive your wicked old grandmother?"

They were both crying now together, their arms locked about one another, their tears mingling. Grandmother drew her new found girl close and kissed her, and Sheila's lips answered to the tender pressure of the soft ones.

Then a great weakness came over the tired girl again, her arms dropped away from about her grandmother, her head fell back on the pillow of the couch and her breath came feebly.

Grandmother sprang up, conscience smitten.

"Child!" she said in great concern, "you aren't able to talk. You need a good hot bath and then a long sleep. Come, we will go up to your room—"

Sheila roused again.

"I couldn't really," she said with a sweet dignity that made her grandmother marvel. "I didn't come here to work on your sympathies. I came to tell you that you need not be ashamed of my mother, and you need no longer think of me as a disgrace. No, please, I really understand. You didn't know of course, and I have no hard feeling about it now that you know it all. I am content to go. Just let me have another taste of that wonderful cold drink and I can go on."

"Go on?" said Grandmother with dismay in her voice. "But you have come to stay with me! I have invited you! Dear child, if I ask you to forgive me for the ignorance and unkindness, the mistaken notion I had of your mother, won't you believe me that I had no ill-will against her?"

"Yes," said Sheila giving her a clear steady look. "You look as if you were a good grandmother and told the truth. I'll believe you. And sometime later if you still want me I'll come back and visit you. But I've got to find a job now somewhere and get some decent clothes first. I wouldn't want to come back to you even to visit this way."

"Dear little girl!" said the grandmother letting the tears flow down unheeded. "Do you suppose I care about your clothes?"

"Perhaps not," said the girl wearily, "but my mother would

not have liked me to come to you this way. I must not disgrace her. If I hadn't been afraid of that man I would not have come even to talk to you until I was fitly dressed. But I had to leave suddenly."

"Sheila, dear child, don't you know that it will be my greatest pleasure to get you all that you need? Don't you know that I shall never feel that I can do enough to undo the terrible mistake I made when I did not help my poor misguided boy to make a good home for your mother? Oh, child, I shall never feel that you have forgiven me unless you stay with me now, and let us get to know each other and heal all the hurts of the years! Sheila, my baby Andrew's little daughter, don't you see my heart is hungry for you? Maybe I've been wrong and proud, but don't you be proud too. Two prides never make a right. It's been all wrong. Let's begin again, will you, little girl?"

Grandmother's arms were yearning around her again, her dear old eyes wet with bitter tears, pleading, her white hair fallen in little soft silver waves about her flushed eager face.

Then at last Sheila's pride broke and she bowed her head upon the frail old shoulder and gave herself up to the tender arms that encircled her.

Suddenly Grandmother came to herself:

"Child! You are roasting alive in that hot coat and hat! There's a land breeze to-day and it's unusually sultry. Get it off right away. No matter how you look. There's nobody here to see, and nobody shall ever know even if your blouse is soiled. Get up, dearie, and come right upstairs with me. Where are your things? At the station? Did you order them sent up?"

Sheila laughed wearily.

"Oh, Grandmother!" she said almost hysterically. "All the things I own in the world are out there at your gate in an old suitcase that is just ready to drop to pieces."

"I'll call Janet to bring it in—" began the old lady.

"No, please," said Sheila springing up, "I wouldn't have her see it for anything! She'd never forget it. Please, I've carried it all the way from the station and I guess I can carry it a few steps farther," and Sheila fairly flew out the door and retrieved her decrepit baggage.

The old lady held the door open for her, and watched the sag of the young shoulders as she lugged the old satchel into the house.

"And you carried that all the way from the station! Why, child, it's a good six miles! Oh, my poor little girl!"

"It's not so heavy," panted Sheila feeling a great weakness suddenly steal over her again. "Now, where do I take it?"

"Right up the stairs, dear, the first room on the right," and Grandmother trotted excitedly up after the girl.

The old lady gave one glance, aghast, at the oilcloth satchel.

"Put it in the closet, dearie," she said. "Don't try to unpack now, you're too tired. I've got a nice little cool nightie in my room that I bought for your cousin Jessica; but I never gave it to her. I found she had taken to wearing outlandish pajamas, so I never even told her about it. I'll get it."

She was off on her excited old feet and came back in a moment with a wisp of pale pink and lace, over her arm, and a soft silk kimono of pale green crêpe.

"There! Those were just made for you," she declared throwing them down on the foot of the bed. "Now, there's your bathroom!" and she threw open the door into a white-tiled sanctum that looked like a corner of heaven to the soiled, travel-stained girl. "You take a good hot bath and then a cold shower. You know how to work the shower? It turns on here. Now, I'll run down a few minutes and see to having your lunch on a tray. Yes, you're going to get right into that bed and eat your lunch and then you're going to sleep! There's no use protesting. I'm boss here now, at least till you get rested. After that we'll let you have as much of your own way as is good for you anyway. Now, be smart and mind me! And when you're done washing get right into that bed and lie still till I come back. Now, will you be a good girl, or do I have to stay here and see that you are?"

Sheila laughed wearily with a great relief in her voice.

"Oh, I'll be good. For to tell you the truth I'm so absolutely all in that I don't believe I'd get farther than that lovely wicket gate even if I tried to run away and have a decent self-respect."

So Grandmother trotted away downstairs to the kitchen almost gleefully and gave exulant little commands to her small sullen maid.

"Get the tray, Janet, no, not that one. The silver one from the dining room. And yes, the lace dollies! And the Dresden china!"

There was a "this-my-son" lilt in her voice.

"A bowl of the hot soup with plenty of rice, Janet! Yes, hot! Not frozen. She's worn out with a fearful journey and needs stimulating! And the breast of a chicken, Janet, the whole half! And isn't there a potato roasted yet? A small one would be done, wouldn't it? When did you put them in? That will do nicely, Janet. You have a pan of hot rolls up in the warming oven, haven't you? And plenty of butter. Roasted potatoes take a lot, you know, and so do rolls."

Janet went about with a disapproving air still, but Grandmother ignored it, talking as if Janet were as eager as herself, as indeed she had been but a short hour ago, before she saw the shabby little stranger that was turning out to be the expected granddaughter.

"You had better get a dish of those big red raspberries. We'll have the ice cream for dinner to-night. And a glass of milk — make it mostly cream, Janet. Yes, a cup of coffee. She needs all the stimulant she can get!"

Janet obeyed silently.

"You know she walked all the way from the station, Janet, in the hot sun."

Janet said nothing. She had walked all the way from the station herself many times in the hot sun. A girl with a shabby old serge coat like that ought to expect to walk in the hot sun and not mind it, she thought.

"You know, Janet," said Grandmother, stooping over the sideboard drawer to select one of her very finest napkins, "she's had a very, very hard time. Her dear mother died only six weeks ago!"

"Oh!" said Janet, sudden sympathy in her voice. "Now, ain't that too bad! Whyn't she let you know? You didn't know it, did you?" There was just a shade of suspicion in Janet's voice and Grandmother felt it. It hadn't occurred to Grandmother that Janet would think of that. In fact she hadn't thought of it herself till Janet mentioned it.

"No," said Grandmother in a confiding tone, thinking fast and using her imagination, "no, she didn't tell me. She was all alone out there, very far out from town and nobody to help her with things, and I guess she was so stunned she didn't really think of it. Besides she is very proud, Janet. She was afraid I would think I had to help. You know her father—my—my youngest son—had gone away some—months before—" Grandmother was feeling her way through her explanation, trying to have it all true, and yet not give a queer impression to Janet who was all agog now, listening. "Yes, he's gone away—on business—up in some of those wild places out there—" her voice trailed off vaguely—"and he hadn't come back, and they couldn't get trace of him."

"You don't say, M's Ainslee!" said Janet dropping a hot potato on the speckless linoleum so hard that it burst open and sent up a white film of steam and a shower of fluffy flakes. "Didn't he even know his wife was dead?"

"No," said Grandmother firmly, realizing that it must have been so. "No, and they're—they're afraid—well—they aren't sure he's living—!"

"Oh, M's Ainslee!" said Janet. "Your son? Your youngest son? Now ain't that awful?"

"Yes, Janet, it's pretty awful!" sighed the old lady with a

tremble in her voice, "but now Janet, we mustn't stop to talk. This child is just worn out with all she's had to do, and we must nurse her up and get her strong again as fast as we can."

"But ain't you going to do nuthing about your son, M's Ainslee?"

"Oh, certainly, we shall continue to do all that can possibly be done," said Grandmother with dignity. "Now, Janet, just a couple of cookies. I'll take the tray up and you can bring the coffee. No, I won't fall. Well — all right. Have it your way. I'll run up and see if she's ready, and you can bring the tray up. It's ridiculous the way you treat me, like a baby! I'm not so old but I can still carry a tray I hope." Grandmother started gaily up the stairs, Janet discreetly waiting for a minute or two till summoned.

Sheila had come from the wonder of her bathroom and was standing, attired in the pink nightie and the floating green kimono, gazing out the open window at the sea. She had thrown a big full bath towel over her shoulders and her rich dark hair fresh from a thorough shampooing rippled down in waves and ringlets a little below her waist.

Grandmother stood for a second looking at her, the sweet profile just outlined against the distant blue of sea and sky. The likeness to her boy Andrew was strong. Grandmother's heart almost turned over at the sight. Yet there was something stronger about this young face than there had been about that boy Andrew's face. She recognized it at once. Andrew had been like Grandmother's only spoiled brother. She had always known it, and yet she had never been able to resist him. His fatal beauty and his winning ways had been the cause of his downfall.

Sheila felt her presence at the door and turned smiling.

"It's so wonderful, Grandmother!" she said shyly.

"You feel a little better already, don't you?" said Grandmother, practically, to keep down the sob in her throat. "Now get into bed quick! Or no, perhaps you'd better sit in this chair till you've eaten. I'll draw up this little table. And here, I'll get you a pair of slippers. There's a pair of silly ones with feathers on them that Jessica brought me for my birthday. I'll never wear them. Wouldn't I look like an old fool wearing pale green slippers edged with white feathers? Here, sit down. Janet is coming with the tray."

"Oh, but Grandmother!" protested Sheila, yielding to the gentle push and dropping down into the big wing chair, "you make me feel like a person in the fairy tales my mother used to tell me. All dressed up in silk things with feathers on my feet! And that sea out there, and those flowers down in the garden — and *you!* Such a wonderful dream-grandmother! I can't think it's true. I believe I've just fallen asleep out there under that trellis and dreamed it all, and pretty soon I'll wake up and find I have to travel on."

"You precious child!"

"But I mustn't sit down in this lovely flowered chair with my wet hair. I just had to wash out the cinders you know. I wasn't fit to have around, not even for a day, as dirty as I was."

"We'll just put the towel over the back of the chair and spread this lovely hair out to dry. How pretty it curls!" said Grandmother handling it like a child with a doll.

"My mother's hair was like that," said Sheila. "It was so black it had blue shadows in it."

"Have you a picture of her?" asked Grandmother softly.

"Only a little tintype that a traveling photographer took," said the girl sadly.

"I want to see it, sometime," said Grandmother tenderly. "Perhaps we can have it enlarged somewhere."

"Oh, could they do that?" asked Sheila. "I didn't know it was possible."

"Yes, they do wonderful things with old pictures now. Some day we'll go to the city and see what can be done."

Then Janet knocked at the door and brought in the tray. Grandmother noticed that she had waited to run out to the garden and pick a great pink rosebud and put it on the tray.

"That's right, Janet," she said with a grim old twinkle, and Janet set the tray down on the little table and cast a respect-ful smile of deference at the lovely girl who looked no longer like a little tramp.

Then Janet went away and Grandmother busied herself fussing around, getting water in a clear crystal bud-vase for the rosebud.

"Oh, how good this soup is!" said the starved child, swal-lowing the last delicious drop, and fishing out the last ker-nel of rice from the bowl. "And all this chicken for me? It's a great deal more than one person ought to eat in a meal. Why this tray would have kept Mother and me for two or three days."

"Oh, little girl, I'm so sorry!" sighed Grandmother.

"Please, I didn't mean to hurt you," said Sheila lifting ear-nest blue eyes. "I just couldn't help thinking how wonder-ful it was, and how glad Mother would have been for me. But, Grandmother, there is something that troubles me very much. You wrote about other grandchildren. Father used to tell us there was one before he came away. There are others too, perhaps, and what will they think of my being here?"

"What will they think? Why, welcome you of course. What would they do? But not just at present, for they're all away. Jessica was married last week and has gone on her wedding-trip around the world. She was my son Robert's daughter. They live in Boston. Her brother Donald is four-teen and he's at a camp in Canada. Rosalie and Annabelle Van Dyke, the twins, are sixteen. They and their twelve year old brother Horace have gone with their father and mother to Europe for a couple of months. They are my daughter Anna's children. They live in Washington. Damaris Deane is Mary's daughter. Her father died when she was only three years old. Damaris is studying music in Germany and her mother is with her. They won't be home for another year. That leaves only Dana and Gregory and Jean, the children of your father's oldest brother, Max. Their mother is dead and they are quite grown up. Dana is in a bonding house with his father in New York, Gregory is studying architecture abroad and Jean is married and living in Mexico. So you needn't worry about your cousins running in right away. I'll get out the album by and by and show you their pictures. Then you will feel more at home with them. Now, little girl, get into that bed and sleep all the afternoon. I'll call you when it's time for dinner."

Grandmother took the tray and slipping out closed the door and Sheila nestled down under the thin summer blanket and the soft percale sheet, and wondered how she could possibly waste the time going to sleep in a wonderful place like this, with a lovely sea breeze blowing now, and lifting the crisp snowy curtain, waving it like a flag, revealing white flitting sails against a blue blue sky and a blue blue sea.

And then before she knew it she was in the soundest sleep she had known for weeks.

When she woke the sea was a simmer of pink and gold and green, and the little white sails on the horizon seemed to slant eagerly as if they were striding home hastily before the night caught them and detained them from their goal. The rose in the crystal bud-vase had opened its leaves half way and was sending out a delightful fragance, and just at the very first Sheila wondered if it wasn't heaven after all that she had inadvertently stumbled into, and wouldn't Mother be hovering around somewhere? Then she remembered that she was still on earth and must live out her life and meet a lot of problems before she got there, if there really was a heaven anywhere.

She drew a deep sigh, and brushed her hand softly, appreciatively across the fineness of the sheet. What would her grandmother think if she knew that the only sheets she had known for years were made out of flour sacks pieced together carefully! But they had been clean and sweet even if they were coarse and rough, and the memory of the bed her mother had always furnished for her was precious and brought the tears.

Then she saw Grandmother coming in the door, after a gentle tap, with her arms full of bright garments.

"I've been rummaging!" she announced. "I thought maybe it might rest you to have something new to put on that you had not worn before. I don't want you unpacking to-night and getting your memories all stirred up and sorrowful. I want you to get rested first. And I found several dresses and some under things that Jessica left here. She said they were too short for her and she didn't want them any more. I think one little dress hasn't even been worn. Jessica is wasteful that way. She buys a thing and then if she doesn't like herself in it she won't wear it, no matter how much it cost. But I really believe you could wear this, you are so tiny. See!" Grandmother spread out a little blue hand-made voile on the bed. It was scattered over with blue embroidered butterflies. It had a smocked yoke and skirt, and little smocked puffed sleeves.

"Oh, isn't that lovely!" said Sheila, rising up to look at it and feel of the butterflies. "Why, that's the prettiest dress I ever saw!" she said happily, reaching over to lay an awesome finger on one of the silken butterflies. "Do you mean I'm to put it on?"

"Yes, if it fits you. Here are several others. You might use anything you like. There are some under things too. And over in the closet across the hall there are several pairs of shoes. Some are Jessica's, some belong to Rosalie and Annabelle. I don't know whether any of them will fit you, but you might try them. There are blue ones and white ones and silver ones and black. Take your choice, wear any you can. I've got to give them away to someone. They are just cluttering up the place. I meant to get rid of them before, only it was lonely here and it seemed kind of nice to leave them around. It seems as if some of the girls might run in any minute when I see their things, only of course I know they can't this summer."

"Oh, Grandmother, how wonderful!" said Sheila. "It gets more and more like a story book."

"Well, are you rested enough to get up for dinner, or would you rather just have a tray up and then go on sleeping till morning?"

"Oh, I'm very rested!" declared the girl. "I want to get up. I've missed a whole afternoon of the wonderful sea, and the flowers. I want to see the sun set. But I really don't need any dinner. Why I had a great dinner before I went to sleep! I had more than I ever had before in one single day in my whole life."

"Well, you've got to eat some dinner too. It's time you made up on some of the lost meals. I'm sure your mother would want that for you. You are as thin as a breath of air and I don't want you to blow away now I've found you. Come, be brisk and come down or the sun will be set and you'll miss the prettiest sight of the sea that comes in a day. It's changing every minute now."

So Sheila arose and plunged her hands into the pile of soft pink silk things, each one a wonder in itself to the girl who had never had any of the pretty things that modern girls count as common necessities. She presently selected with awe an outfit.

"They all fit!" she declared breathlessly as Grandmother appeared at the door again just as she was slipping the blue butterfly dress over her head.

Her hair was dry and rippled about her head like a purple grackle's plumage. She had combed it out hastily and braided it in two long ropes pinned about her shapely head, and she looked like a sweet little girl as she turned to go downstairs with Grandmother, her feet in blue kid slippers that looked as if they had been chosen just for her.

"Those are Rosalie's," smiled Grandmother, looking at

them. "Rosalie is a little hoyden and her feet are growing rapidly. She cried the night she tried them on and found they were too small."

"They are lovely!" said Sheila. "But I'm sorry she couldn't have had them. It must have been very hard for her to give them up."

"She has plenty more," said Grandmother. "Her father gets her anything she wants. More than she ought to have I think. And now, come out on the porch and watch the last colors on the sea till the supper bell rings."

So Sheila sat on the terrace overlooking the garden, watching the sea over the garden wall, as it changed from green and gold and crimson to purple and yellow and silver, and then dropped down into mother-of-pearl shot through with all colors. A little quick star twinkled out, forerunner of all the train of heavenly lights, and far on a jutting point of land that darted out into the sea, a light house blazed forth on duty.

Reluctantly she followed her grandmother at last into the big dining room, big enough to feed all the children and children's children when they came home, and yet cosy with bright lights and flowers, and fragrant foods. Festive for her coming she realized with a strange glad thrill.

So she took her seat, a grandchild of the house, in a gay little butterfly dress, and in shy wonder bowed her head with Grandmother when she repeated the evening grace, a thing that Sheila had never heard before.

"Lord, we thank Thee for these Thy bounties, and we thank Thee that Thou hast brought at last dear Sheila, the child of my dear lost Andrew, to be one of us here. Amen."

Sheila felt her heart thrill that Grandmother should have said that, and when she lifted her head she gave the old lady a sweet loving smile, that, had she only known it, made her look the perfect image of her dear lost mother, Moira.

Grandmother noticed with relief that her new granddaughter ate her food daintily. Even though she had been a waitress for rough workmen at a railroad junction hotel, she yet had been trained in the niceties of a cultured world. That would make the way ahead much easier than if she had been rough and boorish. Yet Grandmother told herself that even if she had not been trained she would have loved her, for she was so like her lost Andy in many ways.

They had finished the ice cream and angel cake and were just getting ready to leave the table when there came a rap on the door, and Sheila looking up across the living room saw a young man standing at the front door outlined against the luminousness of the night. Just a dark silhouette, but there was a look of strength and fitness about it that interested her. So many of the men she had met in her isolated home in the west had been rough unmannerly fellows, men of the hills who had sloughed off the refinements of the world, if they ever had any. The railroad Junction House had not been a place to meet what one would call gentlemen. Tourists and men of culture seldom stopped at the little Junction House where there were few of the comforts of life to be had.

Even Sheila's own father, on the rare recent occasions when he had been at home had assumed rough ways and unmannerly speech. Sheila remembered remonstrances and even tears on her mother's part, but her father had only laughed and there had been no change in his demeanor. So perhaps the look of the stranger made more impression on Sheila than if she had been accustomed to men of gentler breeding.

Janet showed the caller into the living room and came back to Grandmother just as they were rising from the table.

"It's a Mr. Galbraith," she said. "He's brought a message from your son, Mr. Max, in New York."

"Oh," said Grandmother looking pleased. "Come on in with me Sheila. He's an old friend. I want you to know him. They have a beautiful place up on the cliffs, a little above us near the beach."

So Sheila, suddenly shy and frightened, went in with the old lady to meet the stranger, who was standing by the fireplace, his hat in his hand, looking interestedly at a picture over the mantel.

He turned quickly as he heard them enter, and Grandmother seemed suddenly startled.

"Oh, why,—I thought it was my friend Mr. Hugh Galbraith," said Grandmother looking at the stranger questioningly.

The younger man smiled pleasantly.

"I am his nephew," he said, "My name is Angus Galbraith. My home is in London. I met Mr. Ainslee in New York today, and when he found I was flying up here for dinner and returning to-night he asked me if I would bring you this note and some papers to sign. He said they had been mislaid and should have been sent you last week."

Grandmother smiled affably.

"That's like Max," she said. "He always was scatterbrained. But I thought he had a good secretary. I was wondering where those papers were. I almost telephoned him about them. It was most kind of you to bring them. And now, let me present my granddaughter, Sheila Ainslee. If you'll sit down just a minute I'll get my pen and sign these right away."

So Grandmother went her way into the library and left Sheila alone with the first really educated cultured young man to whom she had ever spoken. Sheila was suddenly overcome with embarrassment.

4

BUT the young man was not in the least embarrassed. He looked at the sweet girl in her childish little butterfly dress, with the glow of the firelight flickering over her delicate features, making purple shadows in the black waves of her hair that banded about her head so symmetrically, and he was filled with delight. Did they have girls like this over here? She seemed the kind one read about in old, old books of days long since gone by.

She had none of the assurance, the sophistication, the poise, the impudence, the impertinence, of the girls he had been meeting since he came over this time. She seemed not to be ashamed to be a woman, nor to keep in the background.

"You live here with your grandmother?" he asked eagerly as he pushed forward a chair for her to be seated.

She lifted shy eyes of uncertainty under those wonderful dark curled lashes.

"I—why—you see I have just come to-day," she answered, settling down in the chair, crossing her small feet in their laced blue slippers, and letting her hands lie quietly in her lap with a shy stiffness he could not quite understand. "Grandmother has asked me to stay—" she finished with a sweeping glance that yet held not the least bit of coquetry.

"It seems a delightful place to stay," he said with a quick look about that included the whole room with its vistas to dining room, stairway, and moonlit porch. He sat down beside the fireplace and looked at her again with clear eyes full of admiration.

"Oh, it is wonderful!" she said eagerly, her face flushing with pleasure, just like a child's, her eyes starry. "Have you seen the garden? There are lilies and a humming-bird, a green and gold humming-bird!"

"I only caught a glimpse of the garden in the moonlight as I came in," he answered. "The lilies were like silver spectres trying to look over the garden wall to the sea."

"Oh, do you think of them that way too?" she asked earnestly. "I fancied they were little people. They are so lovely they must have thoughts. Flowers are always half human to me. But I've never dared speak about it to anyone but my mother."

"Is your mother here with you?" he asked, just to have opportunity to watch the play of light and shadow on her speaking face.

It was like an April cloud coming in the sky to see the sudden sadness his question brought.

She shook her head slowly.

"No, she is gone!" she said sorrowfully. "She is in heaven!" she added almost defiantly. "I'm *sure* she is."

"I should think of course," said the young man thoughtfully, and added in his heart "Since she was capable of bringing up a girl like you."

The tension in her face relaxed and she gave him a faint sparkle of a smile.

"Your home was far away from here?" he asked.

"Yes," she said quickly, almost as if she were glad, "*very* far. Almost to the California line."

"That is not far," he said with his pleasant smile, "not when you fly. I've just come back from there. I might have passed over your house. Who knows? What was the name of your town?"

"It wasn't a town," said Sheila reservedly. "It was only a few little houses and a railroad junction. You wouldn't be able to find it on the map. It was too small. There was nothing but wild land about there. A few ranches, all far apart. I went to school three miles away at a little settlement called Coburn, but there weren't a dozen other houses there and it was off the railroad."

He looked at the shy grace of her and marvelled. Then spoke his thoughts.

"You must have had a marvellous mother."

"Oh, I did! She was *everything!* I don't know how I am going to live without her."

His eyes flashed tender sympathy.

"I wish I had known I was to meet you when I flew over that part of the country. I would have liked to look down and see where you lived."

Sheila gave a little ripply laugh. Her face was full of sparkle. Then she sobered and submitted a subject of conversation on her own account.

"It must be wonderful to fly," she mused. "Planes used to go over us there sometimes, very far up. They never stopped. They did not come often either. But I always ran out to watch them if I could. I used to wonder what kind of people dared to go up there above the clouds with so much confidence. I never thought I would meet one of them."

"Well, now that's interesting," he said. "I wish I'd known you were down there when I was flying over you. You know I've been out in California part of the winter and all the spring. I often took short trips down into Mexico and in fact all about in that region. I would have loved to drop down and call upon you. Perhaps I might even have had the pleasure of taking you up for a little ride, if I had only known you then."

Sheila's eyes grew large and dreamy, startled too. She was

trying to vision what it might have been to have had a young man like this call upon her at the Junction. She visioned the people he would have had to see, the threadbare garments she would have been wearing, the dance hall where her mother had to sing, the whole unkempt tawdry appearance of the straggling settlement called the Junction, and then she looked up and shook her head.

"You wouldn't have liked it," she said soberly. "I don't believe you would have liked me. I had to work hard and I wasn't dressed up." She gave a quick glance of respect at the simple little blue dress she was wearing.

"You don't think friendship consists in the clothes we are wearing, do you?"

Sheila looked thoughtful.

"Perhaps it oughtn't to," she answered, "but,—I should think it might make some difference—right at the beginning, anyway."

"Well," said the young man with friendly smile just the least bit daring perhaps, "you're wearing delightfully right ones to-night anyway. And I'm hoping you are going to stay here this summer, because I'm planning to be here awhile myself a little later on. I'd like to be seeing you some more if you don't mind."

Sheila gave him a wondering smile. She didn't quite know what to say to that. But she didn't have to answer for Grandmother came trotting back in a business like way waiving the paper she had just signed.

"My pen was empty of course," she said. "It's always empty when I need it in a hurry, and I had a time trying to find the ink. Janet has been writing a letter in the kitchen and she borrowed it. It certainly was kind of you to take all this trouble! I hope I haven't kept you waiting too long, Mr. Galbraith?"

"No indeed!" said the visitor rising as if he were loth to leave. "I've been enjoying it here and I wish I could stay and get acquainted with you both. This fire feels good even though we did have a pretty warm day, for the breeze off the sea has come up strong since sunset. I wonder if you'll let me come back sometime soon? I'm going to be at Uncle Hugh's off and on all summer."

"Come soon and often," welcomed Grandmother. "There was a note from Max in there saying you were one of Gregory's choice friends. That's introduction enough for me. You'll always be welcome."

When he came to shake hands in leaving. Sheila looked up with her eyes shining and managed a shy question.

"Did you say you were *flying* back to-night? Do you go over this house?"

"Why, yes," said the young man. "I will. Leave the porch light on for me, will you, Mrs. Ainslee? I'd like to look down and think of you two sitting cosily together beside this nice fire."

"I'll leave the porch light on all right," said Grandmother with a twinkle. "But we two'll not be sitting cosily by the fire while you fly over our heads. We'll be out in the garden yonder watching you fly. I always like to see my friends off, whether by land or sea or sky."

"All right then, look for my card out somewhere in the garden to-morrow morning," he said, smiling at Sheila. "You'll find it I fancy, unless the humming-bird gets there before you. I'll be passing over here in a little less than an hour, I should think."

They all stood together a moment on the porch with the moonlight making a halo behind his head, and then he was gone through the wicket gate and they could hear his footsteps for a moment padding briskly along the hard wet beach.

"The Galbraiths are very nice people," quoth Grandmother as she turned back into the room again. "This must be one of the Scotch nephews his uncle Hugh is always talking about. He seems a nice sort. We'll have to invite him down."

"And now, child," she said, dropping into her big rocking chair, "tell me about the man you ran away from. What was he like?"

"Oh, Grandmother!" said Sheila in dismay, putting a hand involuntarily over her heart. "You wouldn't like to hear about him. He was dreadful! He was like a—a—snake!"

"Maybe not, child, but I guess I need to know about him. I might meet him sometime and I'd want to recognize him at once, you know."

"Oh, but Grandmother!" There was fright in the girl's voice. "He wouldn't come *here!* So far!"

"Maybe not, child! I don't suppose he would. But I want to be prepared. How did he look?"

Sheila gave a little shiver, and clutched her hands together nervously.

"He was tall, and bold, and had shining black hair, just as if it was varnished. He had thick lips that sneered, even when he smiled, and showed a lot of big white teeth. People thought he was handsome but he always made me shudder. I hated his lips. Once he tried to kiss me! Oh! It was awful! I got away, but I never went where he was if I could help it after that. He had eyes like—well, you'll laugh, but they were like little white boiled onions. They were sort of full for their places. I heard people in the hotel say they were stunning eyes, but they looked wicked to me. And when he smiled it was like a dart of lightning."

Grandmother was listening, wide eyed.

"Did he have a laugh like a horse, Sheila?" she asked in a startled voice, "and was he a friend of your father's?"

"Why, yes, Grandmother! How could you know?"

"And they called him 'Buck'?"

"Why, Grandmother! How could you know?"

"I know!" said Grandmother. "I suspected. That was Bucknell Hasbrouck and he was always a bad boy. Even when he was in the Primary School he was a bad little boy. He used to do the most devilish things. When he was only five he took a little fellow out to the swimming pool down in the woods and pushed him in. They didn't find his body until the next day. But another boy told he had seen him pushing him in, and finally he owned up he had because the other boy had candy and he wanted it. He took the candy and pushed him in. He said he didn't know the boy couldn't swim. They let him off of course because he was only a baby, but he went right on doing things and not getting caught, till one day he helped to hold up a freight train with some other bigger boys, and they sent him to jail. Then when he got out he seemed to be a great hero to the rest of the boys. Your father was somehow under his influence. I never understood why. And when your father went away it was the same night that Buck disappeared. And Buck was proved to have broken into the bank and taken two-hundred and fifty thousand dollars worth of cash and bonds that they couldn't get back."

"Oh, Grandmother!" said Sheila her eyes big with trouble. "You don't think Father was in a thing like that, do you?"

"I never believed he was," said Grandmother sadly. "He had always been honest. At least I never had any cause to suspect him. He was a real bad boy, and had to be punished a great deal, but I never knew him to be dishonest. But it did look bad for him, dearie. It almost broke your grandfather's heart. He was a director of the bank and had to make good of course, and he did, but it rankled in his heart that there was any possibility of suspicion attached to his son. Of course there were finger prints to show that Buck had been there, and Buck had been in trouble before; and there was nothing to prove that our boy was mixed in it, only that he was always thick with Buck in the old school days, and that he went away. I used to think maybe he had had some minor part in the affair without knowing how far Buck was going, perhaps, and got frightened when he saw how the thing had turned out. But we never knew. I often thought that hastened your grandfather's death."

"But didn't my father write to you, Grandmother?"

Sheila had drawn a little footstool close to her grandmother's knee and was sitting with her elbows on her knees, her troubled eyes looking up into the old lady's, a new terror in her countenance.

"Yes, he wrote," said Grandmother. "He wrote and said he had a good job out in Chicago, and we sent out there and had him watched and found he really was going pretty straight, working every day, and boarding at a respectable place, and not spending a lot of money anywhere, as he might have done if he had profited by Buck's robbery. But he didn't write often, and by and by he disappeared again for a long time, and then he wrote from away out west telling me about this wonderful girl he had met, and how he was going to keep straight now if I would only help him out. But — do you wonder, Sheila, that I thought it was only one more trouble he was getting into?"

"No, Grandmother! I don't blame you at all now," said Sheila with a trembling lip.

"Well, I blame myself. I should have gone out there myself right away and found out about everything. I shouldn't have been so taken up with my new grandchildren and my own life. I had got used to thinking my Andy would never be any good. And then he disappeared again and I didn't know where to find him. Not for three or four years did I hear from him and then he wrote that he was getting on nicely, and told about you. But he still seemed hard and bitter at me, and said things that hurt. I used to lie awake at night and cry about it. I used to blame myself, too, for not having done something when he was younger. But the next day all the children would blame me for worrying about a good-for-nothing and I would shut my teeth hard and try to bear it. And I prayed for him every night always. Oh, my boy, my boy! He always went wrong, Sheila, from just a little fellow! Such a pretty little fellow! I suppose it was my fault somehow, but I didn't know it at the time."

"Don't—*dear* Grandmother!" said Sheila her own tears flowing now. "Perhaps he couldn't help it!"

"Don't ever say that about any living soul, child!" said Grandmother sharply. "He may not have been able to help it himself but there is always God. And my Andy knew about God, from a little child he knew. When a man goes wrong it is always because he wants to go that way, not because he can't help it. But I never knew that man had followed him, or was with him. Or perhaps he followed Buck, I can't tell which."

"Grandmother, I've sometimes thought Buck had some kind of a hold over my father. I heard several things that made me think so. He hadn't been around us long. Only a few months ago he came to the place and had something to do with the dance hall where Mother sang. He was the one who made trouble for Mother, cut her pay and made her work so hard. He didn't like her because she wouldn't be friendly with him!"

"My dear!" said Grandmother, "You *must* have had a most unusual mother!"

"Oh, I did!" said Sheila in a new burst of tears.

Then suddenly there arose a murmur which grew into a distant whirr, gradually differentiating itself from the steady murmur of the sea, until it sounded very near.

Sheila looked up, startled, and Grandmother sprang to her feet.

"That'll be Mr. Galbraith. Let's go out and watch him. He's coming this way just to salute us. The planes usually go a little to the west of this spot. Hurry! He'll be over us in a minute!"

Grandmother snapped on the porch light as she passed the switch, and together, hand in hand, like two children the old lady and the girl hurried out into the garden.

They were just in time, for they could see the great plane skirting the sea, circling out over the water in a wide loop, and rushing on over the house and garden.

Sheila looked up and marvelled. She had never seen a plane so close. It was swooping down right over the garden which lay bathed in a silver sea of moonlight, and even as it came a clean bright ray of signal light shot out from it, and searched the ground below. Then the ray was shut off again and down from the plane as it dipped something bright and burning, a smaller ray of light, burning in itself, like a tiny ball of fire, came hurtling down straight as a die, and dropped among the lilies, where its little ray kept shining on, making the lilies stand out from the other flowers with a strange lovely incandescence.

"Oh!" breathed Sheila. "What is it?"

They hurried down the garden path toward the lilies, Grandmother guiding, for Sheila's eyes were up in the sky watching the curve of the great bird as it swept upward. Grandmother as eager as Sheila.

"There it is, child, pick it up! Right at the foot of that largest lily! My old bones can't bend to reach it!" cried Grandmother.

Sheila brought her eyes down to earth for a moment and picked up the bright thing. A small metal flashlight, with the light turned on.

Sheila looked at it in wonder.

"What is it?" she asked again. She had never seen one like it before.

"A pocket flashlight," said Grandmother giving it a quick glance. "It's a wonder it didn't break in falling. That's his card tied to it. See, Sheila, he's coming back again to give us another greeting. Answer it this time. Move that little button back and forth. That shuts off the light and turns it on again, see? Now, he's sending down his search light again, isn't that pretty where it strikes the lilies and delphinium? Now, hold yours up and move the button back and forth."

They were like two children as they stood there among the flowers with heads lifted, hands raised waving, the little light answering the big one. Sheila never had had such a sweet time in her life, not since the days when her mother used to make strings of tiny paper dolls out of the paper that came around the sugar package, and then blow them into the air, while Sheila would burst into gales of laughter.

It was so wonderful to have a great plane flying overhead, a handsome friendly face looking down above that shaft of light. She could not discern the good looks, but the friendliness was there in the trouble he was taking to show this courtesy and greeting. Of course the most of it was for Grandmother. He knew her cousin too. He was just being nice. Sheila had no foolish notions about it. But it was so lovely to be a part of this little play in the air above the garden.

Three times the great plane circled out over the sea, and returned. The fourth time, with the shaft of light making big circles in the sky, it sailed away toward the southwest, and presently was a mere speck of red light in the distance, a mere rumble in the night for a minute and then was gone.

Sheila stood still in the garden path where the sky had become a mere distant haze of night expanse, and looked down at the little thing in her hand, feeling its smooth nickel sides, snapping it off and on again just to watch it come and go, then turning it into the cup of a lily and out again.

"Well, that was nice!" said Grandmother briskly. "He is a nice young man. He treated me as well as if I'd been a girl too. There don't seem to be too many nowadays that bother with an old woman."

"Oh, Grandmother, he liked you! I could see it at once!"

"We must have him down to dinner when he gets back. Now, child, let's walk around the garden, and then we must go in. You need to get to bed again. There still are dark circles under your eyes."

So they walked around in the moonlight for a few minutes, Grandmother introducing her new granddaughter to the different flowers and giving their pedigrees.

"I think it is the most beautiful place I have ever seen — or even thought could be!" said the girl ecstatically.

"Well, it is pretty," admitted Grandmother. "especially

sometimes. You know we call it Rainbow Cottage, don't you?"

"No," laughed Sheila. "What a pretty name! Is it because of the rainbow colored garden?"

"No, though that might fit sometimes," answered Grandmother. "It's because we have a real rainbow here sometimes. Wait till you see it. Sometimes when the sun is just in the right position, and there's been a storm, a great lovely rainbow will suddenly bloom out with one foot in the garden right among the flowers, as if it drew its colors from the flowers, and one foot out there on the sea, as if they belonged together, the garden and the sea, and there were no sea wall to separate them. It is a wonderful sight. It doesn't come often but when it does you just can't do a thing but stand and watch it. It almost seems as if you could go out there and put your hand in the separate colors. I actually tried it once myself when no one was watching me, but all I found of course was misty sunshine, for I couldn't handle the rainbow at all. It almost seemed as if it must have moved, run away laughing to hide when I came too near, you know, but when I went back to my window where I saw it first there it was as clear as ever in all its bright colors! If I were an artist I would like to paint a picture of it to keep, only no artist could ever mix those clear, transparent, sparkling colors with the mystery of the sea and sky both in them, for if they tried the paint would be too dull to hold them."

"Oh, Grandmother!" said the girl looking at the lovely little old lady with the silver of the moonlight on her white hair, and the delicacy of her cameo profile against the blue blackness of the night. "I think you are a poet anyway, if you are not an artist. I do wish my mother could have known you!"

"Well, I wish I had known her. It's to my everlasting shame that I neglected to do so. Now, let's go in. To-morrow is the Sabbath. We can't go to church because they haven't started the services in the little summer chapel yet. But we'll have a service by ourselves, and take a good rest day, and then if you are feeling quite rested, we're going to run down to Boston for a couple of days' shopping. How is that?"

"Wonderful!" said Sheila. "I've always wanted to see Boston. But, won't that cost a lot Grandmother, to take me along? I could quite well stay here while you are gone."

"Stuff and nonsense!" said Grandmother. "Just please remember I owe you a lot for my stupid actions in the past, and don't mention money to me again. Now, run along to bed!"

5

THE night that Sheila left her western home so precipitately Buck Hasbrouck had come in to the Junction House a few minutes before train time and ordered a piece of apple pie and a cup of coffee while Sheila was hurrying around getting ready for the evening rush.

He had done that several times lately, always making it necessary for Sheila to wait upon him, usually managing to come when she happened to be alone in the serving-room. Several times he had tried to be familiar, and she avoided him on all occasions possible.

This time however Mrs. Higgins called to her from the kitchen to wait on him and she had no choice.

When she set down his pie upon the pine counter and turned to go for the coffee he caught her wrist and held her with a fierce grip.

"You meet me to-night outside, down by the water tank, as soon you get done here, see? No more monkey shines. I've got something important to tell you. If you don't come on time you'll be sorry. There are plenty more girls I can put on this job at this counter in your place if you don't do what I say. Then where would you be? You can't be so choosy. You have to be nice to the one that gives you your job, see?"

Sheila's heart stood still in horror. Her lips turned white, and she felt suddenly cold all over. It seemed to her that the earth was giving way under her feet. She looked the man straight in his wicked eyes for an instant, trying to steady her thoughts, trying to think what to say, trying to keep from trembling. She seemed to know by instinct that she must not let him see how frightened she was.

His grip on her wrist was hurting her. There would be a cruel mark there to-morrow she knew, for her flesh turned black and blue very easily.

"You're hurting me," she said coldly, steadily, without struggling, and wondered at herself for being able to do it. She thought, "This is the way my mother has had to go through hard things sometimes. I shall have to be brave as she was. Somehow she was protected. Somehow I will be."

"I'll hurt you worse!" laughed the man setting his fingers deeper in her frail young flesh. "Do you understand? I shan't let go till you answer me!"

"I understand!" said Sheila, still in that cold steady voice, though inwardly her spirit was quailing with fear.

Then, just as she felt that she should sink down on the floor and cry out with the pain if it lasted another second, she heard Mrs. Higgins' voice calling her, her footsteps coming to the doorway.

With an oath the man flung her hand from him, and called after her as she vanished into the kitchen, "Remember! I mean it!"

As she entered the kitchen Mrs. Higgins demanded a platter for the meat she was frying. Mechanically Sheila brought it to her, and then turning, swiftly sped up the back stairs on feet that were as silent as they were swift.

"Where you going?" called Mrs. Higgins. "It's almost time for the train." But Sheila was out of hearing.

She was mounting the second story stairs to the little back cupboard of a bedroom, the only place in the world now that she could call her own. She had glanced at the clock as she left the kitchen. Could she make it? Ten minutes to the train, her only hope now!

For days she had been getting ready to go away sometime, but she had not intended to go until she had earned a little more money. She wanted to be able to stop somewhere and buy decent clothes. Not since her father went away over three years before had she had any new ones. She knew by the people who stopped to eat at the restaurant that she was very shabby and out of date, and people who stopped off at such an unpromising junction were not themselves likely to be overstylish.

But now there was no time to think about clothes.

As she sped up the stairs her thoughts flew lightning fast. Her suitcase, an old valise of ancient days that her father had discarded, was ready as far as necessities were concerned. She had always put away everything including her comb and brush when she went down stairs to work because there was no lock on her door and she dared not trust Mrs. Higgins' ten year old daughter. She did not like to have her hairbrush used, nor any of her things handled over, therefore she had carefully put them away, and been thankful that her mother had saved the rusty key to the valise.

A box of books in the corner, for the last few days nailed shut, was all the rest of the wordly goods that she possessed. There would not be time for her to open it and get out even the ones she most prized. Her father's name was on the box. Perhaps some day she could send for it, if she ever dared. Not if Buck were in those parts she was sure.

She was thankful that she had taken out the little sandal-wood box containing the few things her mother had said she must never part with, papers and letters of her father's, and put them in the satchel, before she closed the box of books. She would not have dared to leave them behind.

All this went through her mind as she mounted to her

room tearing off as she went the big calico apron she wore over her neat gingham dress. Mrs. Higgins' voice was ringing petulantly behind her, but she must not listen to it, or her sense of duty to Mrs. Higgins would perhaps make her hesitate until it was too late.

She slipped inside her room and shut the door softly. There was no key. There was no one to come up for her except Mrs. Higgins and she could not leave the meat she was frying. Unless — horrible thought! — what if she should ask Buck to come up and get her? The thought filled her with terror and sent her to working frantically.

It was dark in the room except for the light that came into her little attic window from the luminousness of the sky after sunset, for the window faced the west. But she did not need light. It was all the better in the dark, for then anyone seeking her would see no light from the crack under the door and would think she was not there. She would not even light the candle. She knew exactly where everything was. She groped to the nail on the back of the closet door where hung her hat and an old blue serge coat and skirt of her mother's, the only decent thing she owned to travel in. She flung on the skirt over her gingham dress, put her arms into the sleeves of the coat, pulled down the old hat over her head and was ready to leave.

Back of the box of books in the corner was a clothesline, saved from the wreckage of home, intended to strengthen the weakness of the box that held the books when she came to the point of moving somewhere. But now there was no time to think of books.

She felt behind the box and unrolled the rope, thankful that it was a new strong one. Would it be long enough to reach? But there was no time to think of such hazards now. She was desperate. She had seen enough in the eyes of the man who threatened her to make her take a last risk.

So she felt for the handle of the old valise. There was another thing, that handle might break. But that too could not be reckoned with now. There was no time to cut the rope and reinforce it.

She slipped the rope through the handle and drew it in a long loop, until the rope was half way through the handle. Then she tiptoed to her window and carefully, breathlessly swung the valise out, letting it down slowly to the roof of the second floor annex. When it touched and seemed to rest firmly, she drew a breath of relief, and then began to pull the rope up again gently, hand over hand. If it should catch and refuse to come out of the handle what should she do? But it came easily back into her hand the full length. She gave one swift mental glance about her room. The bed was next the little window where she meant to make her exit. Was that the train she heard in the distance? Oh! Swiftly she flung the rope about the stout little bedpost of the old cord bed, glad that it was strong, wondering if it would hold, and then carefully crept through the window, both ends of the rope knotted about her waist lest it slip from her frightened, un-accustomed hands. At last she was out, and trembling on the edge, her fingers gripping fearsomely the window sill.

It was only the distant sound of an oncoming train that gave her courage to let go her hold one hand after the other, and grip the rope instead, and then slowly, tremblingly, let herself down to the roof below.

It wasn't a long distance but it seemed mountains high, and at the last the rope went so swiftly though her tired fingers that her hands were bruised and burning.

The roof she was on was steeply sloped. If she dared sit down and slide it would not be far to drop to the ground from the lower edge. But she must let her valise down first.

Her fingers shook as she untied the rope and began to pull it again. Oh, suppose the bed had got too near the window frame and the rope would catch? There was no knot in the end. It ought to come free.

It seemed a long anxious time, and once the rope did hitch,

but her vigorous pull got it loose, and the last end came cavorting down like a lash and struck her in the face.

But there was no time to nurse the stinging cheek. The train was distinctly nearer now, and in the clear evening atmosphere sounded even nearer than it was. She must get down from the roof in the next four or five minutes or all was lost. A vision of the ugly face, leering eyes and fulsome lips under the hateful black mustache nerved her on.

Creeping carefully over to the north edge of the lean-to, dragging the valise cautiously with her, inch by inch, she slipped the rope again through the old handle and let the valise down to the ground. Her heart beat widly when it was safe in the grass and weeds, just under Ma Higgins' bedroom window. Nobody was in that room now she was sure, so nobody would have seen it.

Quickly she drew the rope up again, and applied herself to the final problem of how she was to get down to the ground herself. There was a chimney at the south edge of the roof but its girth was so great that she feared her rope would not be long enough to span it and yet swing her low enough to drop. Besides, she would have to pass the kitchen windows and door if she dropped over there, in order to get back to her valise. Then, too, how would she ever swing the rope around that wide chimney and get hold of the other end? She couldn't put it over because its top soared up almost as high as the top of the main house. There was nothing for it but to drop from the lower edge of the roof and risk a sprained ankle or worse.

So, with the rope quickly coiled over her arm she half slid, half crept down the steep incline.

Three feet from the edge she was startled by the whistle of the train only two miles down the track. There was no time to waste in caution. She must get that train or all would be lost. It was her only hope. She knew it would be of no use to appeal to Mrs. Higgins for help because Buck was her overseer, and could turn her also out of the job at the restaurant if he chose. There was no one nearer than ten miles upon whom she had the slightest claim, and that was a woman who had once been kind to her mother. She was old and poor. She could do nothing to protect her. Since the teacher of Sheila's school had died two years before, Sheila and her mother had been strangely by themselves. The people about there who would have been friendly were not to their taste and they had held aloof. Those whom they would have liked to know looked askance at them because of Moira's singing at the dance hall. So they had kept apart from human kind and Sheila had no friend to turn to now in her distress. She *must* get this train.

Desperate, she slid down the rest of the way to the edge, swung herself hurriedly over, holding on with a nervous grip, gave one dizzy look at the space below her, unable to calculate the distance, in the dim twilight, told herself she must remember to bend her knees and spring on her toes to break the jar of the fall, as they used to tell them to do in school jumping, then she closed her eyes and dropped.

There was an instant of dizzy fright, and the ground came much sooner than she had expected. She gave a weak little spring from the ground and then dropped again in a heap, stunned for a second or two, strangely weak and trembling, stupid with fright and the shock of the fall. But the steady oncoming of the train brought her back to her senses again and she stumbled to her feet. She had a bruised feeling all over and felt queer and dizzy. She wondered vaguely if she could have struck her head against the house as she dropped. But she managed to crawl around the corner to the lean-to to where her valise lay, and then dragging it softly, crept on under two more windows and down behind some great bushes that bordered the track. If she could only get across to the other side before it was too late! For people would be coming out on the platform and might even be that Buck would be there now awaiting the coming of the train. He often did that. And she could not hope to escape notice if she tried to cross close to the house.

Breathless, she rushed along through the weeds and tall grass, carrying the valise that seemed to her shaking arms to weigh a ton. She dared not look behind toward the Junction House till she was under shelter of the bushes. Then a quick glance told that she had been right. There were people out there. Mr. Higgins with the mail bags. Tony the man from the nearest ranch. A woman from over at the cabaret, her mother's old rival! She would tell Buck at once if she saw her. No, she dared not risk going across in front of the train even though there was plenty of time, for the brightness of the headlight from the engine would show her clearly in silhouette, and all eyes were turned in that direction with nothing else to do but look.

No, she must wait till the train had passed, and then rush across, and back along the other side of the track behind the train. She remembered that there was a pretty steep bank on the other side of the track built of cinders. It would be hard to climb up with her baggage. Perhaps she would have to tie the rope to her valise again and swing it up after she was on the step of the train. Oh, she would have to hurry, hurry! The train stopped only ten minutes for supper. She was not safe even yet.

The train swept along, blinding her with its brilliant light, taking her breath with its near swiftness, and pelting her with a tornado of dust, cinders and stinging particles of hard earth. She had to stand with down-bent head and closed eyes till it was past. And then it seemed to have gone so much farther up the platform than usual to-night, and she had all that long way to go back to get to it.

As soon as she could get her breath she scrambled up the steep embankment, crouched a moment and then gripping her valise dashed across the track like a shadow and slid down the other side getting her shoes full of big, painful cinders.

She dared not run up the track, for then she would be in full sight of everyone, and there seemed to be many passengers to-night, more than usual.

But when she reached the firm ground she found the going hard, for there were little unexpected hillocks and twice in her haste she fell and bruised herself.

When she reached the train and looked up at its forbidding length hopefully, she found to her dismay that not a single car had its doors open on that side of the track. Her heart sank. She would have to enter from the other side, no matter what happened, or stay behind.

There was nothing for it but to climb that bank and drag her satchel up after her, which she did, slowly, painfully, on hands and determined feet, her shoes hurting cruelly with the invading cinders.

Standing close behind the train she pulled up her valise after her, and then flung the rope far down into the darkness of the ditch. If anyone found it there in the grass it would tell no tales now, for no one knew she possessed such a rope.

She turned blindly and rounded the end of the train, dashing madly for the first entrance open. But there was no welcoming door either at the first or second cars. They were all closed and sealed against invasion. There was an open door at the upper end of the third car with a little carpeted step on the platform before it, but that was the door to the diner, and Sheila shrank from parading through that brightly lighted place of tables and well dressed people carrying her shabby baggage. It would attract too much attention. Someone on the platform might see her and call attention to her. On to the next car she dashed, where was also a velvet carpeted step, but a burly porter in white linen prevented her with a big while linen arm.

"Parlor cars, Miss, take the fourth car up for the day coach!"

"Oh, but I'm afraid the train will start," pleaded Sheila, lifting frightened eyes to his imposing grandeur, "couldn't I just walk through the cars?"

"No, Miss. Plenty of time! Just walk up front there. We got four minutes yet!"

Two men and a woman obviously out from a parlor car for a walk while the train stopped, turned and looked curiously at her. Sheila fled down the platform, keeping close to the train, her face turned away from the house. Her breath came in quick gasps now. Her shoulders sagged under the weight of her valise. Her knees threatened to buckle under her. She felt as though she were going to cry. Oh, if she should stumble and fall and somebody have to pick her up and make a disturbance! Oh, this was cruel, cruel! Now at this last minute to have to fail, and have Buck come out and take her in, and look at her gloatingly with his awful eyes.

At last, a pair of steps with nobody guarding them! It wasn't a day coach. There were still two more sleepers, but Sheila dashed up the steps and inside the narrow passage out of sight, drawing a deep breath and swaying against the paneled wall for an instant, closing her eyes and battling back the tears. Thankful! Thankful! Just to be inside shelter. Just to have a car floor under her feet instead of the prairie. A paneled wall instead of a mesquite bush.

But some people were coming up the steps, a man and two women. They were coming into this car.

"Fancy living in a desolate spot like this!" one of the women said, and her laugh rang out disdainfully.

Sheila started and dashed on through the car which was almost empty save for fur coats and overcoats on the backs of chairs. Everybody had gone outside to get a little exercise. Sheila gave thanks again for that, and hurried on through the next car. A porter eyed her askance but she flashed him a frightened smile and hurried on, so obviously trying to get out of his car that he forebore to say anything to her.

Her arms ached, and her legs trembled, but she was at last within a day coach. She knew it by the lack of upholstery and the crowded human life within.

A glance outside the window showed this car to be headed about on a level with the west end of the house, and her window from which she had so recently descended, showed a square of candle light and a figure moving about within! They were looking for her. That was Buck up there looking for her! Mrs. Higgins wouldn't have the time! She would have to take her place serving! Poor Mrs. Higgins! But there hadn't been any other way!

Sheila's heart seemed to turn completely over, and her feet grow like lead. Wildly she hurried on, dragging her heavy feet, her heavy, heavy arms with their burden! She must get farther ahead, as far front as she could. She might easily be seen from the windows of the restaurant. Buck had eagle eyes.

So on she went through several more cars, wondering how long the train was, not daring to look behind, resolved that if at the last minute she should see Buck coming after her she would simply swing herself down into the darkness and hide somewhere. Even if the train were going fast she would do it. Even if it killed her she were better dead than in his hands!

But she came to a car at last that had a whole seat without a sign of occupant, and two children in the seat behind it asleep in each other's arms. A woman across the aisle was nodding, with her head on a gingham pillow, and another old lady was snoring up in front. The rest of the travelers were likely out getting supper.

Sheila settled down in the vacant seat as quietly as her taut nerves and strained muscles would let her, slid her old valise in after her, crept close to the window, pulled her old hat down over her face, hunched her back up toward the aisle, put her head on her arms, with her face mostly hidden and pretended she was asleep too. Fortunately her seat was on the left side of the car away from the Junction House. That helped.

Presently, when she could breathe normally again, she

bethought herself of her fare. She would probably have to pay it as soon as the train was in motion again, and she must have it ready so that she would not attract attention to herself. Some of these conductors and trainmen knew her, at least might recognize her and ask questions. Well, she must be ready for questions.

So she whipped her tired brain to think it all out. She slid her old valise up on the seat beside her, next the window, turned her back still more to the aisle and got out her mother's little worn purse. She had been paid that very morning for her past month's work, and she hadn't had time yet to sew this money inside her garments with the rest of her savings. But there would be enough in the purse to pay her way to the next big city, she was sure of that for she had made enquiry, and studied a map. She had been thinking for a long time of going away. Indeed her mother and she had often talked over together how much it would cost for them to go. Yet they never would actually consider starting because of Father, not till they were sure he was never coming back. For if he should come back how would he find them?

So Sheila plucked out her purse, fastened up the old valise, slid it back as far as possible from the aisle, and once more adjusted herself as if taking a quiet nap, with her face turned as far out of sight as possible.

The people were coming back to their seats now, wiping their lips and settling down for another long ride. They laughed and joked, and apparently no one took note of her.

Incredibly at last after what seemed like centuries of perilous waiting, the train lurched and started on. They were really moving, and moving rapidly.

Sheila opened one eye and looked into the night. She could see the familiar landmarks hurrying by in the darkness. Far to the east there were signs in the sky of the moon that would soon rise, and over there against the darkness she knew they were now passing a crude cemetery, unfenced and forlorn. Two or three simple stones, a few rude crosses here and there, and one dear grave over in the far corner that was her mother's, set about with stones that she herself had carried one by one to mark the spot. She was going off to leave that poor little grave all alone.

But it did not matter. She could do nothing now for the beloved mother but to get to safety herself. She lay still with her head pillowed on the window sill and watched that dark place of the graves out of sight, and then became conscious again of her immediate future, and her fear lest after all she had not escaped. Buck might have somehow sensed that she was on the train and boarded it before it left the station. He might turn up any minute. She must lie quite still and not attract the least attention.

6

BUCK sat at the rude pine counter waiting for his coffee and when it did not come he called loudly for Sheila. And when Sheila did not come, nor answer, he got up and stamped up and down the shallow room in front of the counter and cursed.

When that had no effect he got himself over the counter by placing his hands on its top and vaulting over, and thundered out into the kitchen cursing loudly at Sheila and Mrs. Higgins and the coffee, and at Sheila again.

Mrs. Higgins lifted a flushed face beaded with perspiration from her work over the hot stove. She was turning small pieces of steak and a savory steam was going up.

"What's the trouble?" she asked sourly. "Seems zif you're always round about this time makin' a fuss. Zif I didn't have enough t' do 'thout you mouthin' round."

"Where's that hell-cat of a girl?"

"Girl?" said Ma Higgins poising one bit of fried meat on her fork as she looked at him. "That's a nice name t'call *any* girl, let alone such a nice little thing as Sheila. She's hard workin' if she does look kinda pinklin'. I don't know what I'd do without her."

"Where is she?" demanded the man with another curse.

"She was round here a minit ago," said the woman turning back to her meat. "I reckun she'll be back."

"Well, I ordered coffee, and when I order coffee I want it," said the man setting out his ugly jaw at her.

"Look ahere now, you there, you don't have any call ta come out in my kitchen an' give me words like that. I don't havta take 'em an' I won't!"

"You don't havta, don't ya?" said the man angrily. "Well we'll see about that. Who is it pays ya I'd liketa know? Mebbe you don't know, an' if you don't I'll tell ya. I do. I've bought over the concession to this place. It's upta me ta say who gets your job of cooking, see?"

"Well, it ain't so much of a job," said the woman with a weary grimace. "I'll quit right now ef you say so. I ain't pertikiler abot this train load of folks gettin' any grub er not. They ken go on ta the next stop an' eat, ef you say so."

"Shut up!" said the man. "Where's that girl, I say?"

"I don't know'n I don't care!" said the woman wearily. "I guess likely she's sick. She's been kinda peaked all day. She might uv gone up ta her room fer suthin'. There's yer coffee settin' right 'afore yer face an' eyes! Take it an' git outta my kitchen ef I've gotta go on an' cook."

Buck took up the coffee cup and drained it in one gulp.

"Where's her room?" asked the man.

"Top o' the third story stairs," answered the woman apathetically. "But don't you keep her. Tell her I see the headlight of the train comin' round the curve an' she oughtta be right on the job this minute! Tell her I can't cook an' wait both."

But the man was already on the way up the stairs.

He didn't stop to knock on the door. He pushed it open roughly and stared around in the darkness. Only the square patch of western sky, where the window was, relieved the darkness, and that merely served to blind him. He blinked into the dark for a moment, and just in that instant the headlight of the train swept around the curve, and the light curved about the room like a search light, making visible one corner after another.

Buch saw the empty bed, the stark washstand, the chair, and the wooden box nailed up in the corner.

He strode to the tiny closet which was not more than an alcove under the eaves, and lighting a match flashed it in the corners.

There was nothing there but a little pair of worn out shoes, with big holes in them, huddled shamedly in one corner, to tell that the girl had occupied the room.

He looked at them thoughtfully, frowning a moment, then turned and strode over to the box in the corner and lit another match.

"ANDREW AINSLEE" flared out at him in big clear letters. He started and lighting another match stooped nearer.

The boards across the top of the box were not nailed tight. They seemed to be put in only temporarily. There were cracks between the boards and he could see books between.

He arose and looked around, found the old candle almost burned down to the socket and lighted it. Then he put a strong cunning hand on the box and inserting his fingers between the boards in the largest crack wrenched off a board. Then another. He took out the books one by one, and in the uncertain light of the flickering candle examined each one, holding it by the two covers and shaking it out. Sometimes a frail pressed prairie flower fluttered down to break in dust as it touched the floor. Sometimes a paper. When it was a paper he eagerly picked it up and examined it, holding it near the candle flame to study every line upon it.

But they were not the right papers. Most of them had pitiful little sums of figures scribbled down. Once it was a Bible verse and the man cursed under his breath and held it in the flame of the candle till it flared up and fell in ashes. Avidly he searched each book, page by page, twice over, then turned the box upside down and searched every crevice.

If that box could have spoken it might have told a tale of the paper for which he was hunting and how only five brief hours before it had been packed here with the books, wrapped in cotton, carefully concealed in an old silver pen holder and in a fine old carved sandalwood box. But the box could not speak and the man was angry. Giving the books a kick that scattered them across the floor, and leaving the candle to sputter itself out where it stood beside them, Buck tramped downstairs. Just as he reached the top of the first flight he heard the train pull out of the station. He had been so engaged in hunting for that paper that he had not even noticed it pulling in.

"I can't find that dratted girl!" he said as he stormed into the kitchen. "Where is she?"

"What's the difference now?" asked the tired old woman dropping down into a wooden chair and brushing back a straggling lock of gray hair from her hot tired face. "She couldn't do any good ef she did come. Gracious! All them people and only me to cook and serve. I hadta set Tony takin' the money. Dear knows how much he kep' himself! But what could I do? I couldn't be in three places 't'oncet could I? Two is all I ever hope ta be able ta occupy. Ef you was anxious about servin' yer passengers why'n 'tya come down an' hep yerself, steada huntin' after a girl that don't wanta see ya, no ways? I'm all beat out, an' I'm servin' notice right her an' now. I don't serve another train-load alone, not if I lose the only job between here an' heaven."

"Heaven!" said the man with an oath. "A lot you'll see of heaven! Now, you tell me where that girl went or I'll lame you!"

Ma Higgins looked up with her tired eyes into the bright cold eye of a little repeater, but she didn't waver a hair.

"Lame ahead!" she said drearily. "I couldn't be no worse off'n I am. Ef I'm lame I couldn't do yer cookin' fer ya, could I? Well, shoot ahead. There's no loss 'thout some gain. I'd about as soon die one way as another!"

The man lowered his gun and swore at her, went to the shelf over the sink and gathered up two candle ends, then turned and slammed out the kitchen door, walking away into the darkness of the night. He was on his way to the little shanty, a couple of miles through the woods, where Moira and her daughter Sheila had eked out a scant existence for the past three years alone.

And out over the dark prairie, a long train wound like a bright scaled snake along through the night, carrying a tired frightened girl who was afraid to show her face lest he should appear to menace her.

Buck was never one to regard other people's property. When he reached the shanty and found it all dark, he listened a minute, gave a thunderous knock, and then when no one responded took hold of the door knob with a mighty wrench, kicked the heavy door, and the latch gave way.

He stumbled into the dark room, his hand on his gun, ready for any possiblity, listened an instant, then struck a light and looked around. He lighted a candle from his pocket and looked around more carefully. There were only three rooms to the shanty, and it did not take long to go through them all. They were bare and clean. A bedroom, a kitchen and a little living room.

The shelves in the kitchen were bare and clean as a whistle. Not even a broken saucer to tell of the former inhabitants. Sheila had cleaned the whole house before leaving it.

He poked around in the corners of the shelves, ran his hand back into any cracks, even the ledges over the rough doors, he felt in every one.

The bedroom had sheets of wrapping paper neatly tacked over the rough uprights, sealing it clean and tight. He poked his finger through a place and tore off the paper in great jagged pieces, peering behind each piece. He did his work thoroughly.

But it was in the living room that he did his best searching. On one wall there were shelves across the whole end from floor to ceiling, and by the marks on the old boards he could see there had been rows of books there. Books! Where did they get all those books and what did they want of them? Books! Where were they? The paper might be in any one of them.

Carefully Buck climbed up and searched the top shelves. It was possible the woman and the girl did not know the value of that paper. Perhaps they did not even know of its existence. Andrew Ainslee would be out in a few months. If he could only find that paper beforehand he would have Andrew right where he wanted him. He could put him back again to stay, where no word from him could ever reach the outer world to upset the lowest schemes he might devise, if he only had that paper.

So Buck searched every cranny, far back. But nothing came to light. Then he turned his attention to the rough ledges over the windows and doors.

Once, when Andy was first put in, when he was tossing in fever, and Buck had gone to see him, he had cried out in his delirium to some imaginary presence, perhaps his wife or daughter. "It's in that old pencil, over the door! Don't let him get it!" Buck's eyes had narrowed and he had remembered.

Now he drew himself up by his hands, chinning himself in the doorway, feeling along the ledge above the door. A great spider crawled out of its creepy nest and grimaced at him, its eyes like black, wicked stars in the candle flame, and the man yelled nervously and dropped back to the floor. There were creepy strands around his fingers that made him shudder, and he could see the spider's eyes shine even when he shut his own.

He stood a moment in the flickering light of the empty room and shuddered. Then he strode outside and brought in a box he had seen standing by the door. Mounting it with the candle in his hand he glared at the ledge above the door. The spider hastened away to some far inner recess in the wood, leaving its mysterious shuddery house behind it, but close by the thick gray web there lay an old tin pencil holder such as a child carried to school.

With a gleam of triumph in his eyes Buck seized upon it and jumped down. The pencil case after all. Why had he not thought to search for that before?

He set the candle on one of the shelves and tried to open the case, but it seemed to be rusted shut. The cap would not turn.

Impatiently, Buck twisted it and broke it in two. It was not hard to do. Yes, there was a paper inside. A bit of yellowed paper, and there were tracings on it, figures, and lines, and a scribbled name signed. Buck studied it for a long time. A date, there was a date, and at the top just the lower half of printed letters. He could not make them out. But it was not the paper he had come to find.

At last impatiently he stuffed the old tin tube with its crumpled paper back in his pocket again. It might be of some value sometime, though he could not see how. But put up this way it must have some significance. Perhaps there was another tube.

He mounted the box again and held the candle high, but there was no other. He took a long, sharp, cruel-looking knife from his pocket and unfolded it, poking back behind the wood to see if anything had fallen down between the timbers. The spider hurried out of his hiding-place and darted away into the shadows, spinning a line swinging to the floor, and disappearing into the dimness, but nothing else was revealed behind the old door frame.

Suddenly there came a sound outside the door and Buck sprang down from his box, his candle in one hand, the other going to his pocket.

"Who's there?" he called, and flung the door back to face a gun aimed straight at him. The gun wavered however as the candle light was flung between the men.

"Oh, it's you!" said the intruder. "I seen a light over here and as I knowed the place was locked I thought I better investigate."

Before the speech was finished the man was facing Buck's gun.

"Put down that gun, Spud, I got a better one than yours, an' I can shoot quicker—you know that."

"Oh, sure," said the mild defender, "but being as I seen a light you know. What you doin' here? Lookin' fer gold?" and he gave an uneasy cackle of a laugh.

"Always lookin' for gold," said Buck with a hard grin. "I come over to-night to get a paper fer the little girl that lived here. Somepin' she forgot when she moved. Who cleaned up here, Spud? You?"

"No. I never. I reckon she must have did it herself."

"What's come of all her books?" Buck waved toward the bookcase. "Those shelves useta be full."

"Yes they did, in her ma's time. The school ma'am over ta Coburn left 'em to her when she died. Leastways she left 'em to the gal."

"Well, where are they?" asked Buck, menace in his voice.

"Why, she sold 'em. A few here, an' a few there. My wife bought some. We got 'em on a shelf in our shack."

"Well, I wanta look in 'em," said Buck with determination. "The's a paper lost that might mean a lot ta the girl, and I promised her I'd find it for her. She thinks mebbe it got left in some book. Come on, le's go to your house and look 'e over."

"I don't think there's no papers in the books we bought," protested the man with fright in his eyes. "My wife looked 'em over careful fer that very thing. She thought there might be a letter ur sumpin'. But there wasn't a blame thing."

"Come on, le's go!" commanded Buck, and leaving the candle wavering where it was he went out with the little man.

For three more hours Buck tramped on from house to house, searching out every place where Sheila had sold her precious books and bits of furniture to gather together money enough to get away somewhere. And he went through every book he found in the same thorough and disastrous manner, disastrous to the books, and disturbing to their new owners.

Always everywhere he asked if they had seen Sheila that evening, and was told by each that they had not seen her since they bought the books.

Late in the evening he stormed back to the Junction House.

Ma Higgins had washed her mountain of dishes alone, had shaken down her fire for the night, had combed out her straggling old gray locks, and betaken herself to her lumpy bed. Pa Higgins was over at the cabaret playing dominoes and drinking poor whiskey.

"That girl come in yet?" demanded Buck.

"I ain't seen her," said Ma. "I was too tired ta climb up those stairs. I 'spect it's your fault. You ben up ta some deviltry and druv her away."

"Where would she go? I gotta see her. It's important."

"Well, I don't know. It's important I gotta get some sleep ef I've gotta git breakfast fer the early passenger train. You go on up ta the cabaret an' fergit the gal. Mebbe's she took ta her ma's job, an' is singin' up there. Anyhow, git out. I'm sleepin'."

Ma Higgins shut her door with a slam and locked it, and Buck shouting uproariously. "Well, I'll find her, if I have ta go ta hell ta do it," whirled on his heel and went up to the cabaret.

Slouched in a corner under the gallery, far back from the platform where Moira's successor would be singing the latest croon, he sat before a pint of the best they served there and glowered, trying to figure out what had become of Sheila.

"Yes, I'll find her ef I havta go clear back ta the home town ta do it," he murmured under his breath.

Presently he got up and walked stealthily out of the place, a wicked look in his small black eyes, a look of determination on his hard, cruel mouth.

7

AT first when Sheila awoke that Sabbath morning she heard the rythmic beating of the waves along the shore, and she could not tell where she was. It seemed to her the sound of the train was dimly in her ears.

Yet the sweet air that came in at her window, the soft twitter of some little birds in the eaves, were not reminders of her long train trip; and with a growing sense of peace and rest it presently dawned on her consciousness where she had found haven.

When she at last opened her eyes the world seemed made anew, and she lay there looking about on the quiet of the lovely simple room, the blowing muslin curtain showing glimpses of that wonderful blue sea, clothed in its morning mystery. A shimmer of light as if joy were dancing afar on the waves, a mist of sun and sparkle mixed at the horizon! A curtseying sail appearing and then dipping out of sight! It seemed to her like waking up in a kind of heaven.

Then her mind went back to the evening before and the stranger who had come to the door, grown so friendly, and sailed away in the sky. How wonderful it all was. Just like a dream.

It was all so quiet there by the sea, and all so quiet in the house, she hadn't an idea what time it was. Perhaps they were keeping still to let her sleep. Or perhaps it was early and they were still asleep.

But she felt as if she had slept long enough, felt more rested than she had for years, and stealing from her bed she slipped to the window and looked out far to the glorious blue sea, letting the breeze blow full in her face, drawing in deep life-giving breaths of salt air, then catching a view downward of the garden in its morning dewy freshness, its maze of newly opened flowers.

Presently she tore herself away from the window and went about her dressing, tried the lovely new bath room again, exulted in the refreshment of the shower.

She hesitated about the new garments, wondering whether to wear them again early in the day. But when she surveyed her old ones, even the clean things she had brought with her for changing, they were so very few and shabby, and her standards even in these few short hours had changed so radically, that she felt she could not put them on. They might make her grandmother ashamed. So, doubtfully, she arrayed herself in the butterfly dress again. It was Sunday, anyway, and people always dressed up on Sunday if they could, especially if they did not have any strenuous work to do like waiting on table.

When she finally ventured downstairs there was little Janet in a new pink gingham with a lace collar about her neck. Of course. It was right. She had been expected to dress up on Sunday.

Grandmother had not yet come down. Janet explained that she always slept late mornings when she came down here. She thought it helped keep her young.

Sheila offered to help Janet get breakfast, but Janet only laughed at the idea, and beamed on the young guest. This lovely girl in the blue butterfly dress was an entirely differ-ent proposition from the draggled little tramp-girl in the hot, rusty blue serge of yesterday. This was Grandmother's own flesh and blood, and Janet was ready almost to bow down and worship.

"You run out and walk in the garden, or down on the beach and watch the little sandpipers catching crabs. It's a real pretty sight if you ain't seen it," suggested Janet. "It'll be a good half hour yet before M's Ainslee's down, and you might's well enjoy it before the sun gets hot. I'll ring the bell out the window for you when it's time for breakfast. Run along and get an appetite. I'm having blueberry muffins for breakfast."

So Sheila, clothed and rested, stepped through that rose-wreathed wicket gate into which she had first entered so weary and discouraged, out onto the broad expanse of white sand, and down toward the sea. The little white kid sandpipers were strutting in the edge of the waves, stopping now and then to yank up a sand crab from the water. Sheila followed along the edge of the water, watching them and crying out a gay little trill of laughter now and then at their funny antics.

She had walked some distance down the beach and was on her way back again when she heard a pleasant voice behind her speaking:

"They are queer little creatures, aren't they?"

She turned and saw a young man standing just behind her watching the small birds amusedly. He wore white flannels, and looked so very like the young man who had called last evening and then sailed away through the sky that she thought at first it was he. Their voices were alike also, yet there was something lighter in his manner, a little look about his eyes that checked the smile with which she was about to greet him, and gave her manner more constraint.

"Oh," she said, "why,—I thought it was Mr. Galbraith," and then was annoyed with herself that she had spoken out her thought.

"And so it is," said the stranger laughing. "I'm Malcolm Galbraith from The Cliffs. But I don't know who you are. You must have lately arrived."

"It is Mr. Angus Galbraith whom I have met," said Sheila trying to be a bit more formal. Somehow she did not quite feel at her ease with this informal stranger.

"Oh, so you've met Angus, have you? He's my cousin. We do look a little alike perhaps. Some people seem to think so. I believe the resemblance largely ceases at looks. But where in the world did you meet Angus?"

There was something so breezy and informal about this man's questions that it seemed impossible to stand aloof; but Sheila was ill at ease. Her mother's training had been most strict on that one point at least. Sheila was not to have anything to do with strange men. This man hadn't been even introduced.

"He called at my grandmother's last evening," she answered gravely.

"Oh, he did!" said the young man, studying her mischievously. "Well, and how am I to know who your grandmother is?"

"My grandmother is Mrs. Ainslee of Rainbow Cottage," said Sheila pleasantly, with a little distant lifting of her chin, a little coolness in her voice.

"And *you* are?" persisted the young man.

"I am Miss Ainslee," she answered simply.

The man laughed with a twinkle in his eyes.

"No first name?" he asked winningly, "I told you mine you know."

"Oh," said Sheila naïvely, "I have no cousin who looks like me!"

The young man stared, and then laughed again, narrowing his merry eyes and watching her.

"No, I guess you're right," he said. "You haven't a cousin that resembles you in the least, and I think I know them all."

Sheila was a bit disconcerted. She realized she didn't know those cousins herself, and perhaps she was being absurdly distant. If this man was a friend of Grandmother's and knew all her cousins, why of course she mustn't be too formal.

"Oh, do you?" she said in a small voice. Then after an embarrassed pause she said:

"I must be going back. They will be looking for me."

The young man wheeled and fell into step with her, studying her curiously as they walked along.

"I think I will go with you, *Miss* Ainslee, if you will permit it," he said with emphasis on the Miss. "If for nothing else than to learn your given name. We don't use much formality in our life down here at the shore."

Sheila wondered if she ought to let him go, yet he did not look like a young man who could be stopped very easily if she should attempt it. She felt more ill at ease than ever, for her life in the west, while in some ways exposed to rough conditions, had been greatly sheltered by her mother's fears. Yet this man was a gentleman in looks at least, and seemed to be a friend of the family, why should she hesitate?

But the young man began to talk now, freely and pleasantly about the sandpipers, about the sea and tide, and about the little white sails that curtseyed on the horizon. The mock merriment had disappeared from his manner. He had become grave and impersonal, and now she liked him better, and began to wonder why she felt that instinctive drawing away from him.

When they reached the cottage he swung back the gate with what seemed like an accustomed hand and took the initiative, walking in at the door as if he felt quite at home there.

Grandmother had just come downstairs and Janet was tinkling the breakfast bell out of the dining-room window.

"Splendid!" cried the caller, "I haven't had a bite to eat yet. Won't you invite me to breakfast, Madam Ainslee?"

"Why of course," said the old lady, "if you want to leave the nectar and ambrosia of your home on the cliff and accept of our humble cottage fare you are quite welcome. Janet, bring another plate and cup. The gods are going to breakfast with us this morning."

"Ma'am?" said Janet perplexedly.

"Set another place!" said the mistress. Then turning to the self-invited guest she said, "You'd better go to the telephone and call up your wife, Malcolm, or she will be wondering where you are."

"Not she," laughed the young man gaily, pulling out Grandmother's chair for her. "She won't be awake for another hour or two and when she is she'll breakfast in bed. Don't worry about her."

Sheila's face relaxed. The young man was married then. That was why he was so free and easy. Perhaps it was foolish of her to have been so stand-off-ish.

She sat down at the table, relieved, and let herself enjoy the pleasant chatter between the guest and her grandmother. What delightful people these Galbraiths were. How nice he was to Grandmother. How merrily the little twinkles came about his eyes, how crisply his hair curled away from his forehead, how blue his eyes were. Not the same blue as her own and her mother's, not Irish blue, but a warmer Scotch blue. There had been a Scotchman out at the Junction working for a few months. Sheila remembered her mother saying his eyes were Scotch blue, and that hers and her mother's were a colder, Irish blue.

This was a golden young man like his cousin who had been with them the night before, golden brown hair, a sunny look in his eyes, a golden look when he smiled. A bit older than his cousin Angus was he? Or no? Perhaps not. Sometimes he seemed even younger. But always that gay, blithe air about him.

For some reason she felt she liked his cousin best. But how silly. Of course she liked them both. They were Grandmother's neighbors and friends. Why shouldn't she like them? And why think about them anyway? She wondered what this one's wife would be like, and would she be friendly as he was? Perhaps the Angus one was married too. Who knew? Just a nice, friendly person. Perhaps his wife would come to see them, and they would have pleasant times together. Sheila had never had nice times with anybody but her mother, and a sudden stab of pain came to think that she could never again talk things over with that beloved mother and ask her what she thought of these new friends, and get her reactions to everything that happened. What for instance would Mother have thought of her informal meeting with that gay young married gentleman down on the sand? What had Grandmother thought of it? Perhaps Grandmother had thought she was one of those girls who were bold enough to scrape acquaintance with strange young men. Mother had talked a great deal about that. Whatever Grandmother thought, Sheila meant to stick to her mother's standards.

Sheila studied her grandmother's face all through the meal. She was gay and pleasant to the stranger, yet there was a spice of reserve in some of the things she said that the girl could not quite understand. A gay line of banter went back and forth between them while Sheila sat quietly and watched.

Malcolm Galbraith had easily discovered Sheila's first name and adopted it without ceremony, with the compromise of a prefix.

It was a sweet breakfast, with the breath of the sea and the breath of the flowers coming in at the window. Luscious melons in crushed ice, cereal cooked so perfectly that it seemed like ambrosia, with rich yellow cream on it; amber coffee, an omelet light as a fluff, and blueberry muffins, piping hot, tucked under their linen cover.

When the meal was concluded the young man pulled back Grandmother's chair and said with a sweet deference,

"Now, Grandma, may I have your lovely granddaughter for a little while? I want to show her all the charming spots along our shore. Miss Sheila, will you come along with me? I'm going to take you up to the cove. It's the prettiest place around here, and you must get acquainted with it at once, for it's a land mark."

Sheila turned astonished eyes upon the questioner, but

Grandmother spoke up quite firmly before Sheila could open her lips:

"No, young man. This is the Sabbath day, and seeing there's no service to go to Sheila and I are having one right here of our own. You're welcome to stay to it if you like, but we can't have any upsetting of our plans."

The young man smiled indulgently and consulted his watch.

"How long will it last, Grandma? Ten minutes? Then could I take your little girl?"

"It will last till twelve o'clock," said Grandmother firmly, looking at her tall Grandfather's clock by the chimney corner. "Time enough to see the cove when you can take Betty along!" Grandmother gave the young man a significant smile. "I want to have my girl to myself this first Sunday. But you'll bring Betty down to see her, won't you? I want her to know Betty."

"Why, surely!" said young Galbraith most courteously. Then he gave a twinkle of his engaging eyes toward Sheila and bowed low.

"Good bye, Princess," he said gravely, "I'll be back someday when the war is over and the stars are more propitious."

He bent low over Grandmother's hand and kissed it, and went away with a gay fling of his hand toward them both.

"He's very pleasant but always absurd," commented Grandmother with a quick glance at Sheila. "His wife is a nice girl. I sometimes think she is a little lonely. The Galbraiths have always been good neighbors. His father is an elder in our church at home, winters."

"Grandmother, did I do right to let him walk back with me?" asked Sheila. "I didn't know what to say. There seemed to be no stopping him. He came up behind me and spoke before I saw him at all. He talked about the little sandpipers as if we had known each other always. I thought he was his cousin at first."

She gave a careful account of the encounter.

"He's that way," said Grandmother non-committally. "Just keep your dignity and you'll be all right. I sometimes think the children of this generation have lost all sense of dignity and sweet reserve. It looks as if your mother had managed to include some in you in spite of adverse surroundings. I'm afraid your cousins are some of them rather free in their companionships. It isn't the way I should have brought them up, but then I didn't have the upbringing of them so I have to take them as I find them."

By this time Janet had cleared the breakfast table, and came in silently and took her seat by the door, her neat white apron off and folded away in the kitchen. She sat demurely in her chair with her hands folded on her clean pink gingham lap and her eyes drooped, with now and then a furtive look of admiration at Sheila in the little rocker next to Grandmother's big wing chair.

"Now, child," said Grandmother sweetly, looking at Sheila, "you said you could sing, didn't you?"

Sheila caught her breath and her cheeks grew pink.

"A little," she said.

"Well, there's a hymn book on that little stand by your side. Pick out a hymn and sing it. Janet and I'll hum along with you as well as we can."

Sheila took the book and began to turn over the pages uncertainly. It was a book she had never seen before, but presently she found a familiar song.

"This is one of Mother's songs," she said with a catch in her voice.

There was a little rustle of leaves while they all found the place, and then Sheila's clear sweet voice began to sing.

> Rock of Ages, cleft for me,
> Let me hide myself in Thee; —

Grandmother's quavering notes trembled in a little on the second line, and Janet murmured out a faint alto at the third, but they were both listening to the pure full voice that was leading them, and Grandmother's heart quivered with a new thrill. This *was* a voice. She knew it. Grandmother had been to symphony concerts and heard some of the leading soloists of the world. She knew there was a quality here that few untrained voices possessed.

Furtively she watched the sweet face of the girl as she sang on through the verses so simply and unaffectedly.

When it was finished she spoke her satisfaction.

"That's nice! Could your mother sing like that, child?"

"Oh, much, much better, Grandmother!" said the girl, trying to steady the tremble of her lips at the memory of her dear mother's singing. "I do wish you could have heard her. She had lessons from some of the best European teachers you know."

Grandmother was silent an instant, seeing many things she had not sensed before, and then she said in a small ashamed voice,

"No, I didn't know!"

Then after an instant, when Janet jumped up to take the bottles of milk from the milk man, she asked:

"But since that was so, why did she stay in that lonely place? Why didn't she come to some place where her voice would have been worth more to her? Why didn't she go to some big city?"

"Because Father wasn't willing to leave," said the girl, lifting troubled eyes to her Grandmother, "and then after he went away, because she was afraid if he came back he could not find us."

"Poor little girls!" murmured Granmother with a sob in her throat and a mist on her glasses. "Well, sing us another, dear!"

Sheila sang two more, and then the old lady bowed her head and quavered out a prayer.

"Father in Heaven, we thank Thee that Thou has forgiven us when we are such misguided, foolish creatures, going our own blind way when we might look to Thee and be led. Forgive us again, and help us to be yielded to Thy will. Bless this house and help us to worship Thee pleasingly even though we cannot assemble with others in Thy house. Bless my dear new grandchild and show us how to be useful to one another and to please Thee. May she find this a happy home. Bless Janet and show her how to do her part in the world wisely and well, and teach her to know Thee better. Bless all my dear children everywhere to-day. Keep us all in Thy way, for Jesus' sake."

Grandmother's voice was very quavering as she finished her prayer and there were tears on her cheeks.

"Now another song, child," she said as she wiped the mist from her glasses.

So Sheila sang again and then Grandmother opened her big-print Bible and read the thirty-fourth psalm. After another song she got out a tiny little booklet and asked Sheila to read it aloud.

It was a simple, clear direction of how to be saved and Sheila had never heard anyone talk or write on that subject. It interested her greatly. She had never known much about being saved. If anyone had asked her before she read that booklet what she must do to be saved she would have said, "Be good."

But this book made it plain that a man can do nothing at all to save himself, that he must simply accept the salvation already wrought out by Jesus Christ.

Sheila looked up when she had finished with a kind of wonder in her eyes and voice:

"Why, my mother was saved!" she said simply.

Janet had slipped out to look after the chicken that was roasting in the oven; and so they could talk freely.

"I judged as much from what you told me," said Grandmother. "Perhaps that last song she sang was her confession
of faith."

"Yes," breathed Sheila. "I'm sure it was!" and her eyes were
bright with unshed tears. Then after a minute she went on:
"Why, it's very easy," she said earnestly. "If this little book
is right, you don't have to wait till you die to be sure. I always thought you had to do the best you could and never
be sure till after you were dead."

"Oh, no," said Granmother earnestly. "You can be sure
now, just as quick as you accept Christ's atonement for your
sins."

"Then I'm saved too!" said Sheila with a new light coming into her face, a wonder of joy.

"Dear child!" said Grandmother putting up a quick hand
and brushing away a bright old tear. Then after a second she
asked, tremblingly: "And—your father?"

Sheila slowly, sadly shook her head.

"I'm afraid not, Grandmother. Father wouldn't listen to
such things. Sometimes when Mother talked to him he
swore at her. It made him angry. He simply wouldn't let her
talk."

Grandmother's tears were falling again.

"I know, he never would," she said sadly. "Even when he
was a little boy he said he didn't want to be good. He
wouldn't say his prayers."

"Maybe God will find a way to make him listen!" said the
daughter with downcast eyes. "Or, if he has gone already,
maybe He did."

"Maybe!" said Grandmother with a little quick sigh.
"Sometimes I am quite sure of that. I have prayed for him
ever since he was born. I am quite sure God hears His children's prayers if they are according to His will,—and this
surely is! And the Bible says if we know He hears us we
know we have our requests."

"Oh, does it say that? I wish I knew more about the Bible.

Mother used to make me learn verses sometimes when I was younger. But I never understood many of them."

"We'll study it together," said Granmother with a spark of pleasure lighting up her sad face.

Then Janet called them to dinner, and no more was said about it.

After dinner Grandmother and Sheila took a bit of a walk in the garden, and Grandmother told her about some of the flowers, told her also more about the rainbow that came down among them sometimes till it seemed to be drinking of their sweetness and color.

"Oh, I'd like to see it," said Sheila.

"You will," said Grandmother. "They come, but not often. And there has to be a storm first. They come only after a storm, like many other lovely things."

Sheila took that thought with her up to her room later when Grandmother went to take her afternoon nap, and thought about it a great deal. Bright things after hard dark ones! Was that the way God always worked? Was this bit of peace and home her rainbow after the clouds of death and distress that had been about her?

Late that afternoon when they were down on the open porch where they could watch the opalescent sea in its sunset dress, they saw two riders galloping along the beach, a man and a woman. The man had his hat off and had crisp golden hair that blew up from his forehead and caught the late sunbeams. The woman was slight and rode as gracefully as a feather. They went far down the beach, as far as they could see, and later turned and came back, stopping at the wicket gate and swinging off their horses for a moment.

"That is Betty and Malcolm Galbraith," said Grandmother in a guarded tone as she led the way down to the gate to greet her callers.

Betty was a slender, dark-eyed girl with a discontented, painted mouth and great dark circles under her restless eyes. She studied Sheila furtively as if she could not make her out.

Sheila gave her a shy smile, and wondered if she could ever be friendly with such a distant, apathetic looking girl. Yet she liked her, was intrigued by her.

They stayed only a few minutes, the man doing most of the talking, in a charming lingo of sparkling words. He stood by the garden path and snapped his riding whip, snipping the heads off from some of Grandmother's brightest flowers, as ruthlessly as if he did not see them at all, until Sheila had to cry out. She could not keep still.

"Oh, you are hurting them!" she said. "Don't you see you have taken their heads off?"

"But don't you see what a lovely swath I have cut!" smiled the man twinkling his eyes at her. "A flower lives only a day any way. There'll be another in its place to-morrow. It's done its work and made color in the garden."

"Oh, but not to die that way!" protested Sheila, stooping to pick up the broken flower and smooth its bright petals.

"Well, you pick it for pleasure and stick it in a vase to be looked at and to die slowly, and I snip it off and enjoy doing so, what's the difference?" persisted the young man. "I enjoyed snipping that flower off."

"You would!" said his wife coldly, and turned away toward the gate.

"But would God think that was what He made the flower for?" said Sheila, half angry at herself for continuing the argument.

Betty turned about and stared at Sheila.

"Oh, if you're going to get ethical about snipping off a flower's head I'm done," laughed the man.

"You're a strange girl. I believe I like you," said Betty, looking Sheila up and down. "I'm coming to see you myself some day."

"Do!" said Sheila, and a spark of something passed between their glances leaving a warm wonder in their hearts. Were they two going to be friends?

8

THE next morning they went to Boston.

Sheila had gone to bed with the birds, almost, because the old lady said she must rest so that they could start early.

A taxi came to take them to the train, the taxi that Sheila should have taken to bring her to the cottage. It was driven by an old man who had lived in those parts for years and was interested in everything that went on thereabout. Grandmother discoursed with him all the way to the station and Sheila had time to sit back and think of herself trudging along in blue serge so hot and tired and discouraged and frightened, but two short days before.

She was wearing a little dark blue crêpe-de-chine dress, with a red leather belt and a fragment of lovely white embroidery at the neck that Grandmother had hunted up from some of the cousins' cast off things. Janet had ripped out the hem and pressed it before breakfast, and Grandmother had achieved quickly a rolled hem in the edge which gave the proper length. Sheila had not been permitted even to help.

"Your felt hat will do," said Grandmother. "Felts are always all right, and it isn't a bad shape. Just take that whisk broom and give it a good brushing. Then dip the whisk in water and brush it again. You'll find it will make a wonderful difference."

So Sheila did not feel at all like the little tramp-girl who had trudged along on Saturday into a new life that she feared and dreaded.

There were other cottages along the roadside, but not so far out on the beach as Rainbow Cottage, and none with a garden wall against the sea, and a vine-clad wicket. Sheila wondered if she was to know the people living in those houses, and what they would be like, and wondered again if Betty Galbraith would really come to see her.

Grandmother sent the driver of the taxi to purchase tickets and chairs.

"I am afraid I'm making you spend a lot of money, Grandmother," said Sheila suddenly, waking up to the price the old lady had put in the man's hand.

"That's what money's for," said Grandmother contentedly, "to be spent. I'm sorry I didn't realize that fact sooner. One can't go back but one can go forward."

Then the train came, and Sheila followed her grandmother up the little upholstered box that the obsequious porter put down for her to step on, and reflected that clothes certainly did make a great difference.

It was very different sitting here in the luxurious chair, with cultured, quiet people all about, and a porter to open a window or adjust a screen, from the ride she had taken across the continent. Sheila sat watching the flying landscape and musing about it, and finally her grandmother swung her own chair around where she could talk without having to raise her voice.

"What are you thinking about, dear child?" she asked, a tenderness in her voice from having watched the young face full of thoughtfulness.

Sheila smiled.

"You'll laugh," she said, "but I was thinking how different I look from the way I did last time I was on a train, and

I was wondering if it will be that way when we get to heaven."

"Heaven?" said Grandmother, looking a little startled. "What could have put that into your head?"

"Well, you see, Grandmother, when I went to get on the train to come away I tried to step up to a Pullman car and the porter wouldn't let me in. He wouldn't even let me walk through the car. He said I had to walk along the platform till I got to the day coaches up ahead."

"That was because you had no ticket for the sleeper," said Grandmother, understandingly.

"No," said Sheila shaking her head. "He didn't even know if I had a ticket for the sleeper. He didn't ask me. He just judged by my clothes I'm sure. He looked me up and down and shook his head and said I couldn't go through. He was polite but very firm. And though I was in a terrible hurry, and was so afraid they would see me before I got away, especially Buck, I had to run along behind people till I reached the day coaches. And I was just thinking there won't be any question like that about me when I get up to heaven, will there? I read in that little book yesterday, the pink covered one that you gave me, that we are to be clothed in Christ's righteousness, not our own, and there will be no question about having on the right clothes. Nobody can put me out because my clothes are not good enough, because I shall have on the very best that can be had. I thought of it right away when I saw how very polite the porter was to us, and how he didn't even question me with a look. I was dressed right and I was with you, and that made all the difference in the world. And we'll have Christ with us when we go into heaven, won't we?"

"We certainly shall," answered the old lady, marvelling.

"But you see, Grandmother, you had to give me these clothes to wear. I'm pretty sure if I had on my old dirty ones this morning and tried to get into this nice car that the porter would have given me a queer look and made me feel very uncomfortable. I guess that was what the little book meant yesterday when it said that Christ is going to put His own righteousness about us, isn't it?"

Grandmother's eyes were very tender as she looked at this little new granddaughter who was learning great truths so very swiftly, and understanding what many a wise and prudent child of the world cannot comprehend.

"You are right, little girl," said the old lady with a sudden huskiness in her voice, "and I'm beginning to wish that that mother whom I seem to have despised and discounted had had the upbringing of the rest of my grandchildren, for there isn't one among them who is at all interested in such things. They think I'm old fashioned and queer when I try to tell them that they must not live wholly for this world, but must get ready for another life beyond this. But now, Sheila, tell me about Buck and why you had to hurry away. Tell me everything, child. I ought to understand it all."

So Sheila began to tell more fully the story of her life, especially through the last four or five years, ending with the details of her sudden flight from the Junction House.

The old lady was very thoughtful and troubled during the recital and when it was finished she said meditatively:

"I think there must be some reason beyond just what an ordinary bad man would want to get hold of a girl for. I think he has some hold upon your father, or upon some property perhaps, in case your father is dead. Didn't Andrew — didn't my son leave anything when he went away? Any papers or anything valuable?"

"Yes," said Sheila. "There was a little box of things. My mother always guarded them very carefully, hid them whenever she left the house. I brought them with me when I came. They are in my valise, wrapped in an old cotton nightgown of Mother's. There was one paper that he had folded very small and put inside an old hollow silver penholder. I remember the day when he put it there, just before he went away the last time. He told Mother she was never to part with it.

Not even if somebody were to bring her a letter from him asking for it; she was never to give it up."

"What was in that paper?" asked Grandmother. "Was it something about money? Property? Some title or deed or certificate?"

"Why, I never knew," said Sheila with a troubled look. "I don't think it was property. It was small and written on white paper, like a piece of your writing paper, and he folded it very tight so it would go in. I remember hearing him tell Mother that even if his life depended on it he would rather she would keep that paper, that it was far more valuable than his life, and some day when he was dead she was to send it to his mother. Perhaps I should have given it to you at once, only there has been so much to think about, and I am not sure that he is dead. I know Mother felt that he might come back some day. But now if he did he would not know where to find me."

"I think he would," said Grandmother decidedly. "I think he would know that you were with me when he found your mother was gone. But tell me, didn't you ever open that paper? Didn't you ever know what was in it? Why didn't you ask your mother what it was about?"

"I started to ask her once," said the girl sadly, "but she put me off. I think she knew herself, for she said, 'Not now. Perhaps a little later,' and I never thought of it again. It didn't seem important them, and afterwards somehow I was afraid to open it lest I wouldn't be able to get it back into its case again. I knew Father had a hard time putting it there. And besides, I had so very little time in daylight when I was sure no one would see me. You see there was no lock on my door."

"No lock on your door?" said Grandmother with a startled look. "And a man like Buck Hasbrouck in the house?"

"Oh, he wasn't in the house," said Sheila, a grey look coming over her face at the memory of him. "He stayed up at the cabaret, or somewhere around there, whenever he came to the Junction. He only used to come now and then when Father was at home, and things always went wrong when he came. I know Mother thought he had something to do with Father's going wrong. But the last week before I came away he had been around every day all the time, and he always came over at night and ordered something to eat and tried to talk with me. I had a feeling that he wanted something very definite."

"Could it have been that paper?" asked Grandmother, eyeing her keenly.

"Why, I never thought of that," said the girl turning startled eyes toward the old lady. "Perhaps he did. You see I never paid much attention to that paper. I hadn't seen nor thought of it since Father went away, until I took out the box when I was packing up and decided to put it in my valise instead of nailing it up with my books. I'm glad I did, for I wouldn't have had time to get out the box. I had barely time to jump into my suit and get out the window."

"Oh, child!" Grandmother shuddered. "To think of you in such extremities!"

"Oh, never mind that!" said Sheila laughing lightly. "It's all over and I've forgotten it. I guess God took care of me. I'm sure I couldn't take care of myself."

"I'm sure He did!" said Grandmother solemnly.

Then after a minute or two she added:

"When we get home we'll look into that paper at once and see if we can find out what it is all about, and we'll put it in some safe place, whether we understand it or not! Now, forget it all for a while and let us talk about clothes. You'll need practically everything and I want you to understand that before we get to the shops. You are my grandchild, and I want you dressed befitting your station. If you get a proud fit and feel like protesting, just remember that I'm dressing you up for my own sake as well as for your own. I like to see you fittingly dressed, and I probably know how that should be better than you do, since you've been so long a time isolated from the world."

"Of course, Grandmother. I realize that," said the girl

humbly. "As long as I am with you I must not disgrace you. And of course I don't know how things should be as well as you do. But Grandmother, I really wouldn't need many things, would I? Just a couple of morning dresses and a dress-up dress. And I'd like it so much if you would give me a chance somehow to earn them and pay you back for them."

The old lady gave a quick little protesting movement with her hand and was still a moment. Then she said:

"Child, is that the way you are going to do when you get up to Heaven? Are you going to tell God please not to give you all you really need, only just grace enough to get you into some little back corner of Heaven out of sight, and let you clean the golden streets and comb the angels' wings to pay for that much, when all the time He is offering you all you need in life and that which is to come, and glory besides?"

Sheila laughed with a tender look in her eyes.

"Is it really like that, Grandmother?"

"It really is," said the old lady earnestly. "What do you suppose God gave His only Son to save you for?"

"Oh, I know that. It was one of the first verses I ever learned when I was a little girl. 'For God *so loved* the world that He gave His only begotten Son, that whosoever believeth on Him should not perish but have everlasting life.' But Grandmother, is it like that? Do you—?"

Her voice trailed off in wonder without finishing that sentence.

"I certainly do," said the old lady. "I love you for yourself. Even if I hadn't seen you and known how sweet you were I would have loved you for my son's sake, because you are his child. And as God loves to give us all of the riches of his glory in Christ Jesus, so I love to give you of the things that you need. Can't you see it is my pleasure?"

"Oh, that would be wonderful, Grandmother, but—"

"Well I do. It is," asserted the old lady crisply. "Anyhow, here's another thing! There's a large sum of money that really belongs to your father, an inheritance from his father. It was left in trust with me, because your father was not doing right when he went away, and his father did not want him to have his money until he was sure it would not harm him. That money is waiting for your father if he comes back, and a part of it left in trust that can be used for your father's children should he have any. It was for that reason that I have been writing lately to find out about you. You know your father did not tell me you existed until about four years ago. Why, it must have been about the time he went away the last time. Perhaps he thought he might not be able to get back. Perhaps he—" And now Grandmother's voice trailed off thoughtfully, and then she added "Well, we'll see when we get back to the cottage and read that paper if there is any clue to him. But anyhow, child, there's plenty of money to clothe you in the right way for all you shall need, money that you have a perfect right to."

"Oh, Grandmother, that's like a fairy story!"

"All right, then, let's talk about what you need. Here's a pencil and a note book. You write and we'll get things set down in order so we can save time in shopping. First tell me what colors you like best."

"Oh, all colors!" said the girl eagerly.

"Very well. We'll make a rainbow out of you," said the old lady with a twinkle. "Now write down first, suit and hat. We'll take a taxi straight to the store and buy you the right kind of a dress for street wear. We might meet some of my old friends, and I want you to look well groomed when I introduce you. Don't misunderstand me. I don't put great emphasis on clothes myself, though I do believe everybody should look as neat and pretty and inconspicuous as possible, within their means, of course. You look very nice to me now. But I want no gossip about your past and it is well for you to wear the kind of things other girls are wearing."

"But isn't this dress I have on nice and right?" asked Sheila looking down at it critically. "I thought it was wonderful."

"Well, it's cool and clean, but it is a bit old fashioned to critical eyes. The skirt isn't cut according to the present notion, and I know it is weak in the under arm seams for I mended one this morning. We'll get you the right kind of dress and shoes, too. You can put them on and have the old ones sent home. But I think we had better go first to the millinery department. That will get you rid at once of that hot hat. It looks a bit tired, as if it needed a good long rest."

For another half hour they planned, and Sheila absorbed an atmosphere which would help her in the store.

Grandmother was wise in this world's ways as well as those of another world. She did not have granddaughters for nothing. She knew what the young woman of to-day considers necessary in order to be well dressed, and she had heard the younger generation talk enough to know pretty well where they went to buy what they considered the best. She did not want Sheila to be like them, but neither did she want her to be dowdy. She wanted good taste, good lines, good materials, and a degree of the present mode, not in the extreme. She wasn't sure what a girl from the wilds might choose however when let loose in a large department store, so she entered the millinery department in some trepidation.

9

GRANDMOTHER was delighted to find that Sheila's taste was most conservative. Given two articles to choose from, she invariably picked the quieter one, the least sophisticated. Sometimes Grandmother even had to say, "No, I think that one is too old for you," or "not quite individual enough."

Sheila quickly learned discernment. She went quietly from case to case at first, eyeing the hats carefully, sharply; standing off and watching one or two pretty girls who were trying on hats. She caught the exact angle at which the queer little hats were worn, and when she sat down before the dressing-table in the softly lighted gray and old rose trying-room, she took the little hat offered and set it smartly on her outer head with the same tilt that the girls in the outer room had worn theirs.

"Ah! The young lady knows just how to put it on!" murmured the French Madam who was serving them, and Grandmother nodded and wondered. Had the mother been a genius, an artist, in more ways than in music? This girl certainly was gifted. And she certainly looked as well as any other girl in the lovely new hat of deep Lincoln green. There was no denying but that this new granddaughter was a beautiful girl as well as a sweet one.

The old lady looked at her as hat after hat was set upon her dark head, and thought how very different she looked, even so soon, from the little forlorn tramp-girl who had come to her door but two days ago.

Grandmother bought three of the hats that were tried on, though Sheila looked her astonishment, and came and whispered softly: "I don't need but *one* hat Grandmother. I never had but one hat at a time in my life, and sometimes not that!"

"Don't you like them all?" asked Grandmother crisply.

"Oh, yes!" said Sheila enthusiastically, "I love them! I would hardly know which to choose, but I guess this green one is most becoming."

"Well, don't worry then. I'll look out for the need, you pick out what you like best. That green one will be lovely in the fall when we go up to town. We'll have to find a green knit suit to match. You know we've got to be prepared for the first days back in town as well as just for the summer. And then there might be trips, or week-ends."

"Trips?" said Sheila wondering. "Week-ends? What are they?"

"Never mind, child, you'll come to those things later. We've got to get as much shopping in to-day as possible. We'll take that green hat and the white one will go with fluffy summer things, and the tan one for knockabout. I guess that will do. Perhaps you ought to have one of those tight little things they call a béret for boating, too. Mercy, you ought to see the hats Jessica got just for her wedding trip! And Jacqueline. You don't know who Jacqueline is, do you? Well, she's my grandniece. My only sister's only grandchild. Both mother and grandmother are dead and Jacqueline rules her father and does as she pleases. She wouldn't think she could get through two weeks on three hats and a béret."

"But Grandmother, I'm not like that!" said Sheila in dismay. "I wouldn't know what to do with so many hats."

"Well, we'll take these this time and see how it comes out," concluded the old lady. "I'm sure I hope you won't turn out that way either, and goodness knows I don't want to be the one to spoil you. But we'll have to work these things out between us, and I want to be sure and have enough this first time. When your cousins see you I don't want them to begin to pick you to pieces right away. Not that it matters of course, only I don't choose they shall have a chance, not if a few rags more or less can prevent it. If you don't have use for all we buy this time we can return some of them, or we can find someone else who needs them. Keep that green hat on. I want to match it in a suit."

So Sheila in a wonderfully becoming little hat at whose price she would have been horrified had she heard it, went with her grandmother to the department where knitted suits were sold, and was presently arrayed in a lovely green coat and skirt with a little cream colored blouse with lacy revers. Looking in the long mirror she was amazed to find that the little girl from the prairies was no longer an odd character at whom people turned to stare, but was just like other girls.

And when new dark green kid slippers were added, and the borrowed ones of Annabelle's were discarded, the transformation was complete.

"That's very nice," said Grandmother in satisfaction. "I like those shoes. They match perfectly. You'll need a handbag and some gloves and then we can go and get some lunch."

Sheila was like a child over the dark green leather bag with its bright clasp, and the soft white gloves that completed her costume.

"We've done very well," said the old lady, sitting down at the restaurant with a sigh of satisfaction. "I really don't believe Jessica could have done any better."

"It's all beautiful!" declared Sheila. "I never dreamed of having so much."

"Much, my child, why we've just begun!"

"Grandmother!"

"Look here, child, you mustn't get the idea that I'm extravagant. Remember we have to begin at the beginning and get you a whole outfit, and we can't just buy a few now and a few some other day because we don't want to waste time and strength running down to Boston every few days. So cheer up and take things as they come. You'll need everything I'm getting you."

"But Grandmother! You're tired. It's time we went home and that you took a nap!"

"Not a bit of it!" said the old lady in a sprightly tone. "When I get my cup of tea I'll be as fit as a fiddle. You see it isn't so hard to get an outfit when you have a list all made out. And, besides, we aren't going to run around the city, we'll do everything in this one store. After lunch we'll go to the dress department and you can try on and I'll watch you. That won't be hard. We'll pick out a few dresses and have them sent up to the hotel and then to-night you can try them on again and decide definitely. You'll need a warm coat, too, for cool days. It gets quite cold at the shore sometimes. Then to-morrow I think we could finish our shopping and perhaps take a drive around, and go home the next morning, or afternoon at the latest."

"But Grandmother, what else could there be besides dresses and a coat?" asked the bewildered girl from the desert border.

"Oh, lingerie and negligees and accessories," recited the old lady glibly, recalling phrases of her other grandchildren.

"But I don't know what any of those things are," laughed Sheila. "How could I need them?"

"Well, perhaps you don't but you're going to have them," laughed the old lady as if she were a young girl. "I've never needed many of those things myself, but I've learned what they are, and I think it will be fun to have an excuse to buy some. Anyway I'm going to try it."

They had a gay time ordering lunch. Sheila just could not get over the idea that she must take the cheapest thing on the menu regardless of whether she liked it or not, so Grandmother had to do the ordering; for indeed Sheila did not recognize half the foods by the names given on the menu.

So, refreshed by cool drinks and salads and an ice, they started out again, this time to the dress department.

"That knit thing is too hot for to-day," announced Grandmother critically as they journeyed downward in the elevator. "You must have something thin and dark for coming up to town. A dark blue georgette or something."

Sheila caught her breath at the idea of considering trips to Boston as every-day affairs to be provided for.

"But Grandmother, I'm only a plain little girl," she protested. "I won't likely go to many places. You oughtn't to buy so much."

"No, child, you have a place in the family now, and must expect to be invited here and there of course."

Sheila shrank.

"But I'd rather stay with you."

"That's nice," said the old lady. "Well, here is our floor."

So they found a smiling saleswoman, and Grandmother was established in a chair in one of the fitting-rooms while Sheila got herself into various creations that the woman brought.

Sheila in dark blue georgette with lovely creamy eyeleted embroidery in the wide elbow sleeves, and at the throat. Sheila in brown satin with amber buttons. Sheila in pink chiffon, blue chiffon, yellow chiffon, green chiffon. Sheila in white: white organdy, white crêpe, white satin, white wash silk, white wool; with flowers on her shoulder or rare old lace, or bright bands of brilliants. Sheila in lustrous black like the sheen of her hair, and a rope of pearls about her neck "just to show how it would look" as the saleswoman said. Sheila in red and green and blue and yellow and pink and mauve and heliotrope.

The most elaborate ones Sheila would look at a moment and then shake her head and say, "take it off, please, that doesn't look like me," or "No, Mother wouldn't like that."

At last the saleswoman said: "Why not have this sent up, Miss Ainslee, and let your mother see how lovely you look in it?"

Sheila looked at her a moment as though she were going to cry, and then a smile came out instead and she said gently:

"Oh, you couldn't. She's up in heaven you know."

The saleswoman gave a little gasp of apology, gathered up the condemned garment quickly and took it away, and presently brought sweet white robes that Sheila liked.

Grandmother sat by enjoying the fashion show and marvelling at the good taste of the girl reared in a western shack.

Now and then the old lady would insist on sending up something that Sheila had decided against, and she always gave way with a smile. So really they enjoyed the day quite as much as a game.

Then came the choosing of coats. A white one, a heavy green one with a luscious beaver collar, and a soft velvet evening wrap which Sheila thought quite unnecessary.

On the whole they were both tired but happy when at last they tore themselves away from the wonders of the store and took a taxi to the hotel. And then wonders began again for Sheila.

She stood at the great window of the hotel suite watching the city go by, while Grandmother lay on the couch pretending to take a nap though she was really watching Sheila through the gray fringes of her eyes and wondering. Was she doing wrong to get all these folderols of the world for this little unspoiled soul? Would she presently turn out to be just like her spoiled grandchildren; wanting her own way, going a wild new way of modern times? Her heart quailed before the thought, and she prayed softly in her heart, "O, Father keep this little girl clean and sweet and humble."

They had dinner served in their room, for Grandmother was tired, and they went to bed early, not to discount the next day. Sheila, in her soft bed in the next room to her grandmother, cried softly into her great, strange pillow, now that it was dark and Grandmother couldn't see her, cried because she was having all the things that her mother had always wanted to get for her, and couldn't, and her mother wasn't there any more to enjoy them with her. It seemed somehow as if it were wrong for her to have them since Mother couldn't share them, Mother who had been born to such things and had given them all up and lived such a sad, disappointing life!

But Sheila was young, and tired with all the excitement, and sleep came soon to make her forget, and in the morning there was another day of excitement before her.

They got up early and went down to the great dining room for breakfast. They took a taxi and drove through some interesting parts of the city for an hour while the morning was fresh and cool. Then they went to the stores again.

They bought a trunk, a suitcase, and an overnight-bag all fitted with wonderful things. They bought lingerie and negligees and accessories and Sheila found out what they all were and laughed gaily as she picked out the prettiest of each kind. She felt like a princess in a book, just picking out pretty things for fun, and never really expecting to see them and handle them and wear them.

When they went back to the hotel again there were packages, packages, packages everywhere. But Grandmother insisted that they should lie down for an hour before they opened anything.

Sheila was too excited really to sleep, but she lay there in a daze of expectation, like a child at her first Christmas.

But the afternoon delivery brought still more and Grandmother said the nap time was over. So Sheila with eager fingers began to unwrap and try on again.

It was much easier, here in the quiet room, away from the array of gay merchandise, to judge just what would be the wisest purchases, and the large collection of garments was finally narrowed down within respectable limits.

The trunk was there and Sheila took much pleasure in folding her new garments and packing them carefully in her new trunk, trying to realize that all these lovely things were really her own.

"I'm sorry not to let you see more of the city and some of its attractions," said Grandmother, watching her happy face, "but next time we come, or in the Fall, we'll take some long trips around, and go to some wonderful concerts and things."

"Oh, but I've seen a lot of the city," cried Sheila. "It's a lovely city and I'd like to see more sometime if I may, but I'm just in a hurry to get back and see if that wonderful garden is there by the sea, or did I just dream it?"

They took another ride around however before they left about noon time, and then they took the train, the new trunk travelling along, with a check in Sheila's new purse by which to claim it.

They took lunch in the diner, too, a thing that Sheila had secretly longed to do ever since she had seen the first train pass the Junction House, and had watched the well-dressed ladies and gentlemen sitting there at leisure being waited upon.

While they were eating she looked around on the comfort and luxury, and thought of the poverty back on the prairie and wondered.

"What is it?" asked Grandmother, knowing there was some perplexity behind that look.

"I am wondering why my father left it all and went out there, to what we had, and *stayed!* How could he *stand* it? Why didn't he come back and try to make things straight?"

A dart of pain crossed Grandmother's face.

"I'm afraid he had gone too far to retrace his steps," she said sadly, "I'm afraid there was some reason why he thought he *couldn't* come back. He was always a loving lad, though mischievous. I've always been sure he would have come back unless there was some reason—something he couldn't undo. Something that made it impossible!"

"You mean," said Sheila with a startled look, "you mean you think he had committed some crime?" She spoke the words low and her lips were white as she said it.

"I don't know," said Grandmother tremblingly. "I never would believe that it was intentional. I always felt there might be something he was mixed up in that others got him into. Yet I never had any proof. But, there, there! We mustn't think of such things. It is better not."

"Of course!" said Sheila. "I shouldn't have made you feel bad. Perhaps it will all be explained some day. Don't think about it dear Grandmother, please."

"I won't!" said Grandmother. There was a gentle twinkle in her eye but it only showed up a regular tear about to fall.

The old taxi driver took them back to Rainbow Cottage and asked about their trip as if he were almost a part of the family, telling how he went up to Boston himself ten years ago, but it tired him all out and he came back after two days. He said there were too many people there, and too much noise.

He told them all the news since they had left, how the Billingses and the Taylors and the Havens had arrived and opened their cottages, and about the lease of the old hotel by the Point that had been closed for two years past.

Sheila found herself watching for the first glimpse of the cottage wall, the first gleam of the gay colors in the garden, as if it were the Fairyland it had first seemed to her.

And then when they finally came in sight of it, there was a long, smart, shiny red car drawn up by the side of the wicket gate, its flaming vermilion sides clashing with the pink roses clambering over the arch, and she drew her breath with a hurt feeling that someone was intruding.

Grandmother eyed it sharply, uncertainly, also.

"That's a new car," she said as if talking to herself, "I don't recognize it."

The taxi driver was engaged in drawing up before the gate. He hadn't given attention to the strange car yet. He would in a moment, Grandmother knew.

"Got *comp*'ny!" he said as he stopped with a flourish, and eyed the red car.

"Yes," said Grandmother, "friends from a distance, I suppose," and she got out spryly and handed the man his money, turning swiftly to go in away from further curious questions.

Half way up the walk Janet met them with deprecating air.

"M's Ainslee, Miss Jac'eline just come 'bout a nour ago."

"Jacqueline here!" Grandmother gave a startled look toward the smart, expensive car. "Well, Sheila, we didn't go to Boston any too soon."

But Janet was hedging in the way.

"M's Ainslee, Miss Jac'eline insisted she wanted the east room. She said she always had it. I told her there was a guest and her baggage was in the closet, but she just insisted!"

Janet was almost crying.

"Well, she can't have that room. She'll have to go in the yellow room."

"But she's in it a'ready. M's Ainslee. She done tore the bed ta pieces an' made it up all fresh, an' she pulled the things all outten tha bag Miss Sheila brought, and scattered them all over the floor, an' then she tole me ta come an' take 'em out on the trash heap an' burn 'em. An' when I said I couldn't 'nless you said so she come tuk 'em her own self, and started fire to 'em—"

At that Sheila gave a little cry like a wounded animal and fled up that garden path, through the house and out to the back door where she supposed a trash pile would be.

"Janet!" said her mistress severely, "I thought I left you to protect the house."

"I did, M's Ainslee. I went fast 's I could an' put the fire out. I stomped on it and I carried water, an' only a few things is scorched a dear little bit, but you know Miss Jac'eline, M's Ainslee. You know she will have her way an' nobody can't stop her."

"I can stop her!" said the mistress of the house, marching grimly up the garden walk. "Where is she?"

"In the east room layin' down," sobbed the servant. "She said as how she didn't want ta be disturbed."

"Indeed!" said Grandmother, and marched straight up the stairs to the door of the east room.

"Jacqueline!" she called in a tone of authority, but there was no answer.

"Jacqueline! Get up and open this door!"

Still no answer.

Outside in the kitchen garden Sheila was down on her knees beside the trash pile, the tears rolling down her face, kneeling in the ashes regardless of her new garments. Gathering up the bits of treasures, a wet, scorched nightgown of her mother's, and pressing it to her face, sobbing. Then throwing it down beside her to search wildly among the ashes for the old tarnished penholder. The paper! The paper! Was it lost forever?

10

GRANDMOTHER called a third time with no better result and then turning went swiftly and silently down the front stairs. To see her tripping down those stairs, a look of grim determination on her sweet old lips, one might have thought her sixteen and not at all weary from a shopping bout and a long journey.

She went straight to the telephone, and called up a well-known number.

"Mr. Crumb, is your son Jason around? Well, I wonder if he could jump on his bicycle and run down here with his bunch of master keys? Can he? Oh, thank you! As soon as possible please. And tell him to bring something along to break the lock in case the keys won't work."

Grandmother hung up the receiver, swung around to the kitchen, and went swiftly out to the ash-heap beside the excited Sheila.

"Is the paper there?" she asked anxiously.

"No," said Sheila lifting troubled eyes to her face. "And the sandalwood box isn't here either, nor any of the things that were in it! Oh! I ought not to have gone away and left them behind. Mother told me never to leave them!"

"There, now, child! Get calm!" said Grandmother in a low tone, "Don't give the enemy a chance to get in. Just remember that there's a God in heaven, and nothing really disastrous can ever come to God's children."

"Oh, do you really think so, Grandmother!"

"Why, surely, child. What is this Rainbow Cottage for if not to remind us that God always keeps His promises? He put His bow in the heavens to remind a fearful people that He had made a covenant with them, and it stands to-day as a sign that He always keeps His promises. There are plenty of promises in the old book for you and me to-day. When we have time we'll look them up. Now, get up off that ground. We'll bring everything in and clean it up. It's too bad dear but there must be some good coming out of this somehow. Your box won't be lost unless it's in God's plan for you and He sees it best. Janet," she turned to the tearful maid who was standing at a respectful distance, "bring out a basket with a clean newspaper inside."

Janet brought the basket and Sheila carefully picked up everything, poking the ashes all over to be sure nothing was left behind, but there was no sign of box or penholder, nor any of the other things that had been inside the box.

By the time everything was picked up and they had come into the house again they could see a man on a bicycle speeding down the beach hot haste.

Jacqueline Lammorelle attired in flaming orange and black silk pajamas, was standing by the window smoking a cigarette and looking out on the embers of the fire she had lighted in the kitchen garden.

There was a smile of amusement on her sharp little features and her red lips painted vividly to a cupid's bow showed her small gleaming white teeth in a wicked elfish grin. She was watching the stranger girl gathering up tenderly the old cotton rags which she had set on fire, even shaking the out the funny old-fashioned blue serge still smouldering, and carrying that in also. Grandmother and Janet had gone in now, and Jacqueline put her head back and opened her red lips in a hearty, soundless laugh that shook her slender young body with a noiseless mirth.

Then suddenly she heard footsteps on the stairs, and became alert. There was the sound of a rattling key in her door, and she turned sharp black eyes in that direction and saw her key slowly turn in its hole and descend with a sharp clatter to the floor. Then with catlike quickness she threw her cigarette out the window, and sprang toward the bed, flinging back the covers and diving in with a single noiseless motion that was so smooth and quick it was like the gliding of a beautiful snake.

When Jason Crumb flung back the door and Grandmother entered the room, Jacqueline lay fast asleep in the bed, the covers folded half way down about her, and one lovely sleeveless arm flung back engagingly on the pillow, the most innocent-looking smile upon her lips.

"Jacqueline!" Grandmother's voice promised swift retribution.

Jacqueline lay sweetly slumbering, not even disturbed by the menace to her rest.

Jason Crumb, after one keen glimpse of the rosy cheeks and lips of the sleeper about whom he had long held his opinion, faded swiftly down the stairs with a shake of his head. Grandmother walked determinedly across the room to the head of the bed, and reaching down took firm hold of one silk strapped shoulder and shook her grandniece with all her indignant might.

Jacqueline stirred prettily in her sleep and murmured sweetly without opening her eyes:

"Did someone call?" and then settled down into her pillow and went on slumbering as if nothing had happened.

Grandmother gazed at her an instant and then took hold of the covers of the bed and dragged them off to the floor, pulling the pillow out from under the sleek black head and flinging it on the floor also. Then she summarily walked to the bathroom and brought out a dripping wash rag which she dashed into the slumberer's face, covering her nose and mouth so completely that the girl gasped for breath.

"Get up, you hussy!" commanded Grandmother.

Jacqueline flung the wet cloth from her, opened her eyes sleepily, sat up, hugging her knees and looking sweetly dazed.

"Why Aunt Myra! What an original way to welcome one! So refreshing on a hot day! And I was having such a lovely sleep! How could you?"

"Get out of this bed!" commanded Grandmother, pulling at the under sheet.

"But Aunt Myra, I just got this bed made up so carefully!" complained the unbidden guest. "Please don't pull that sheet off. I got it out of the linen closet myself."

"Get out!" insisted Grandmother, pulling the sheet sideways.

Jacqueline sprang nimbly to the floor and reproachfully helped her great aunt to undrape the bed.

"But what's the idea, Aunt Myra?" she asked wistfully. "Didn't I get the right sheets? They seemed quite all right."

Grandmother gathered up the bedding in her arms and turned to face the interloper.

"You had no business to come into this room and you knew it. Janet told you that it was already occupied. You saw another guest's belongings in the room already."

"Oh, no, I didn't Aunt Myra. I truly didn't!" declared the miscreant, wide-eyed. "I was particular to open the bureau drawers and look, and I didn't find a thing except a pocket flash light with Angus Galbraith's card tied to it, and I knew he wasn't here yet because he told me himself up in the mountains that he wouldn't be here till to-morrow, and anyhow I knew he was going to be at his uncle's. So I looked in the closet and there was only an old dirty, smelly, woolly skirt and coat that I thought the cleaning woman must have left here because she was done with it, and a funny old leather bag with some coarse rags in it and a lot of trash, so I took it down and burned it in the back yard. I thought you would be pleased that I had been so helpful!"

Suddenly Sheila appeared in the doorway carrying the recovered property, her eyes wide and indignant, but a steady look about her white lips.

Sheila had been trained in the school of sorrow. She knew how to speak in a low controlled voice.

"They may have seemed like trash to you," she said with a quiver of her lips, "but they were very precious to me!"

Jacqueline stared for an instant, startled at the vision of a girl fully as good looking as herself, and dressed in what she knew to be a smart costume. Then she drew away toward the window and leaned against the wall, lifting her chin a trifle haughtily, yet smiling indulgently.

"Oh? *Really*?" she said sweetly. "I couldn't imagine it of course that anything as forlorn could be at all precious to anyone. I thought I was helping to clear up. I hope you'll excuse me."

"I'll excuse you," said Sheila gravely, still holding the armful of smoky garments, "if you'll tell me what you did with the rest of the things. Particularly the little carved box and the things that were in it."

"Box?" said Jacqueline drawing her slim, plucked eyebrows in puzzlement. "Why, really I don't remember seeing any box. You must have put it somewhere else. Or else perhaps it got burned up. I really didn't notice."

"It was not burned up," said Sheila firmly, "and I *must* have it please, right away. It had some very valuable papers in it. One quite important!"

"Now isn't that too bad," said Jacqueline sweetly. "I really didn't see any papers at all that I remember. Perhaps an old letter or two. But people never keep old letters nowadays. And as for valuable papers, those things are always registered aren't they? You probably won't have any trouble getting a duplicate. I have a lawyer friend and he told me that once.

By the way, nobody has introduced us. Who is she, anyway, Aunt Myra?"

"She is my granddaughter, Sheila Ainslee," snapped out Grandmother, "and I don't like the way you have treated her in the least."

The way she said "my granddaughter" made it plain that the relationship was just a little closer and a little finer in Grandmother's estimation, than it was between herself and Jacqueline.

"Oh, really!" said Jacqueline, facing about and appraising her rival with a wide, disagreeable stare. "Why, how thrilling! How is it I never heard of her before?"

Grandmother did not deign to answer. She swept the sheets into closer compass and waved her hand toward her grandniece.

"Just move over to the yellow room, Jacqueline, this room has been Sheila's since she came. Janet, take those dresses out of the closet and bring them to the other room."

"Oh, but really, Aunt Myra, you always put me in this room when I'm here. Don't you remember?" Then whirling on Janet. "Don't you dare touch my things, Janet! I'll move them myself when I get ready."

"They'll be moved at once!" said Grandmother. "What did you do with the sheets that were on this bed?"

"Oh, I threw them down the laundry chute," said Jacqueline as if she were greatly enjoying the scene.

"You took a great deal upon yourself!" said Grandmother irately. "However, it was almost time she had clean sheets anyway. Janet, get some of the linen sheets out from the top shelf and make up this bed again. But first move those clothes out of the closet! I am still mistress in my own house I hope. Now, Jacqueline, if you have anything in the bureau drawers you may get it out at once. Sheila's trunk will be here in a few minutes and she wants to unpack."

Jacqueline lolled in the window seat and laughed.

"I don't see why I should move my things. Let Janet move

them all if she is going to do any," she said perversely.

Sheila meantime had put down her bundle of things in the hall on a chair and came now and took the sheets from her grandmother.

"You are tired, Grandmother, let me make the other bed."

"No," said Grandmother decidedly, "Jacqueline will make it. She unmade your bed, and now she will make her own bed if it is made."

"But I made it once," laughed Jacqueline, giving a pretty little bored yawn, "why should I have to make it again? If I were at home I wouldn't have to make my bed at all."

"Then why aren't you at home?" asked the old lady, giving her a piercing look. "I was given to understand that you were spending the month in the mountains."

"So I was till I got bored silly, but you see my boyfriend left and came on here, so I came to be near him. That's plain, isn't it?"

"Perfectly!" said Grandmother. "Now tell me what you did with Angus Galbraith's flash light and the card attached?"

"Oh, was that Angus' flash light? I thought he had thrown it away on the beach somewhere. It didn't seem to be worth much. I'm sure I don't know what I did with it. Threw it away with the trash perhaps. How can I be expected to look after other people's keepsakes?" and she flashed a look of amused contempt at Sheila.

Sheilas stooped over Grandmother to hide the flush that came to her sensitive cheeks and took the bundle of sheets.

"I can at least carry these into the other room," she said.

"Very well," said Grandmother surrendering the sheets and pulling open a bureau drawer. "Then I'll move the rest of her things since she won't do it herself."

Grandmother drew the drawer entirely out of the bureau and marched out of the room, stopping on her way however to set the drawer down on a chair, pick up the key to the room which lay on the floor and put it in her pocket. Then she took up the drawer again and carried it briskly down the hall, though she was tired to weakness with all this excitement and anger, and her knees were fairly shaking under her. When she arrived in the yellow room she was puffing and panting like a steam engine, but she marched over to the unmade bed and dumped the contents of the drawer upon it.

"Now, Sheila, see if your box is here!" she commanded.

But Sheila only stood afar, and could see at a glance that her property was not there.

Janet carried the drawer back again, Grandmother following, and found Jacqueline calmly sitting in the window seat working at her nails with a little silver file, and humming a popular song, as if she had no interest whatever in what was going on about her.

Janet carried the rest of the drawers in and emptied them on the bed in the yellow room and Grandmother went back with them and looked over every article, but no sandalwood box appeared. Jacqueline remained indifferent.

But when they returned to the room the third time Jacqueline was not there, and a moment later they saw her out on the beach running along in her little pink bare feet and nothing on but her yellow and black pajamas.

"The hussy!" said Grandmother excitedly. "The *hussy!* I told her the last time she was here that I wouldn't be disgraced this way by her again, and neither I will. I'll send for her father. Janet, fetch me the telephone book, or call up the telegraph office for me."

It was Sheila who protested.

"Don't do it now, Grandmother. Go lie down for a little while and get rested. She'll surely be ashamed and come in pretty soon."

"Not she! Ashamed? She doesn't know the meaning of the word. She's a spoiled child and she knows it. Dotes on it! Just see her! The shameless hussy! Dancing all over the beach like a five-year-old! And who is that coming down to meet her? Hugh Galbraith's son Malcolm as I'm alive! Oh, I shall never be able to lift my head while she's here."

Sheila looked out of the window and there was Jacqueline dancing about on her pink feet about her sleek black head, her fingers interlaced, flinging up first one yellow and black clad leg and then the other, whirling, pirouetting, and then turning a series of somersaults right on the beach, and right herself on her pink toes again, like a mad sprite.

"Never mind, Grandmother, you can't help it now, and surely anybody who knows you will know you don't approve. Don't feel so badly. Please go lie down, dear. You look all worn out."

"I'm not worn out!" declared the belligerent old lady, "I've strength enough left in me to spank her, yet, and I'll do it when she comes in, see if I don't!"

"Now, Grandmother! You'll make yourself sick!" worried Sheila. "She's only a kid, anyway, isn't she?"

"No, she's no kid. She's twenty-four years old, nearly twenty-five. She's just a little devil, that's what she is! Look at her. Running to meet that young man! A married man too! She knows his wife is dreadfully jealous, and yet she runs and catches his hand. See, they are running now along the beach. Of, if my poor sister could have known that her daughter's child would perform that way she couldn't have died happy. That girl is just doing all this to torment me!"

"Well, then, Grandmother, why let her see that you are tormented? Why be tormented? Come on in the other room and let me help you into your loose kimono. Get your hat off and wash your face in cool water. Janet, can't you bring her a nice cold drink? Come. Grandmother, why bother about her? Just let—why—just let God manage her. Wouldn't that be best? She'll certainly get tired of acting after a while. And if she doesn't feel she has an audience it won't be half so much fun for her, will it?"

"Well, I suppose you're right, child," said the old lady suddenly sitting down as if her strength had given out and fanning herself with a magazine that lay on the hall table. "But it does make me furious to think she dared to touch your things! And that paper too! Sheila, we *must* find it."

"We'll find it," said Sheila calmly. "I'm sure we will. Or else, I've been thinking—perhaps there's some reason why God wouldn't want us to find it. I'm sure we'll find it unless there is."

"You're a dear child, Sheila!" She smiled and patted the girl's hair, as she knelt before her to unfasten her shoes.

Janet had hustled off for the cool drink and now came bringing it, the ice cubes clinking musically against the thin glass.

The old lady drank it slowly and then submitted to be led off to her room. At the door she paused.

"I'll lie down on one condition. You two are to look through everything and see if that box is about."

"I'd rather not, please, Grandmother!" said Sheila looking distressed. "I don't feel as if I should. She would never forgive me if she knew I had. If anything was missing of hers she would always think I had taken it."

The old lady looked at her thoughtfully.

"What about her having looked through your things?"

"That's it, Grandmother. It makes me very angry, and I'd just rather not think about it any more."

"You're a wise, good child!" said Grandmother.

"No, not good a bit," said Sheila with sudden tears in her eyes.

"Well, a wise child then, anyway. All right, I'll lie down provided you do the same as soon as your bed is made."

"That's a bargain," said Sheila. "Now, let me unfasten your dress and put your hat away, and your gloves. Here are your slippers. Now, Grandmother dear, don't think about anything. Just smile and sleep. Think where I'd be if you should get sick just now. I wouldn't know what to do."

"Well, run along. There comes the expressman with your trunk. Have him put it in your room, and here's the key of the door. Don't leave either the key of the door or the trunk around when you leave the room. There's no telling what that bad girl might take it into her head to do next."

When Sheila ran down to open the door for the trunk man she sighted two figures walking gaily along hand in hand, on the beach in the distance, and the smaller of the two wore bright black and orange garments. A great wave of dislike rolled hotly over Sheila, and she wondered that this moment of homecoming with a new trunk and a whole wardrobe of beautiful new garments had so quickly been spoiled for her. Somehow she felt as if she had no place here in this sweet bright cottage, no right in the family where this wanton girl belonged, no right nor place anywhere in the great world.

The expressman put the trunk down in the pretty room that three days ago had seemed to Sheila such a haven of peace for her storm-tossed soul, but she did not take out the key and open the trunk after he had gone. Instead she locked her door and dropped down on her knees beside the unmade bed and wept.

After a time she remembered her promise to her grandmother, got up and made her bed, washed her face and lay down to rest. But she did not sleep. Instead, she lay and fought the awful anger that surged over her when she remembered the poor scorched garments that used to belong to her precious mother. It just seemed as if she could not forgive that other pampered girl who had tossed her precious things into the fire so carelessly.

But meantime Janet was not idle. She had no scruples against looking through this haughty beauty's things, even if Miss Sheila had. She went through everything methodically, laying them in piles on two chairs, and discovered not one thread or scrap of paper that she thought looked like any of the things Miss Sheila had described. A little carved wooden box, some letters, some papers, a few bits of old fashioned jewelry, and an old tarnished silver penholder. Those were the things that Sheila had told her were missing. But there wasn't a sign of them.

Disappointed, at last she turned back to her task of hanging up the freakish garments Jacqueline had brought with her to the shore, and when that was completed she hurried downstairs to start the dinner preparations.

Sheila had been lying still for perhaps a half hour when she heard a gentle tap at the door. There stood Grandmother with her pretty white curls hanging down each side of her flushed old face, and a sweet smile on her lips.

"I just came in to talk with you a minute," she whispered, looking furtively behind her. "Has Jacqueline come in yet?"

"No," said Sheila, "I think she is still out there. They walked away up the beach and back again. See! They are standing out there now!"

Grandmother looked and there were the two, the man and woman, facing one another, the fingers of their hands linked in each other's, swinging their arms back and forth as children do, both talking animatedly, silhouetted against the evening sea and sky.

Grandmother looked for an instant and then determinedly turned around with her back to the window and sat down.

"I've just come in here to say that I think you were right, Sheila. I think we'll just not notice her antics. If she doesn't have a distressed audience perhaps she will stop sometime, get tired of it. Anyway if she doesn't I'll get her father on the telephone to-night and tell him to come down and manage her, for I can't. But I mustn't look out of the window and watch her carry on or I'll forget all my good intentions. It makes me so mad to see her. She thinks she's being so very modern and shocking me so much."

Sheila laughed in spite of her own anger.

"So now," went on Grandmother, "if you, child, think you can stand it to be your own sweet self and act as if nothing had happened, I'll try to do the same."

"I'll try," said Sheila smiling. "I've got no call to be disagreeable anyway. I'm really only an interloper here you know, and she knows it. She has more right here than I have. She probably thinks I have no right here at all. I've been thinking it out, and Grandmother, I've come to the conclusion that I ought to go away again. It would be a lot easier for you."

"Child!" said Grandmother getting up and walking the floor excitedly, two bright red spots springing into her cheeks. "If you talk like that I'll go right out there on the beach and spank that girl, big as she is. I can't stand it, dear, to have you talk that way!"

Sheila sprang up and went to her grandmother, putting her arms about her.

"Dear, I won't talk that way again if you don't want me to. If you'll just promise me up and down that you'll tell me if you ever feel it would be better for me to go. Will you, *please?*"

"I certainly will," said Grandmother with satisfaction in her voice, "if I ever feel that way! But I won't! I'm certain of that. I feel now as if you were more a part of me than any of my other grandchildren. Now that's the truth, child. I'm not just talking."

"Dear Grandmother!" said Sheila shyly, putting her face down in the old lady's neck and receiving a soft, trembling kiss on her troubled brow.

"And now," said Grandmother after a minute, "I've thought it all out. You are to put on one of your pretty dresses and look smiling and lovely at supper, and let this whole thing blow over. I don't know what she's here for, but I suspect some monkey shines with some young man. She has plenty of them. But we'll just try to be happy in spite of it, and perhaps to-morrow something else will turn up, and she'll decide to go somewhere else. How about the pink dress, the frilly one? Put that on. It's rather sophisticated and that is the only thing in the world that girl stands in awe of, sophistication! Let's give her some. I thought we'd have a call for that pink dress. Put it on and come down to the garden. I'll be down myself as quick as I can get this hair into order!"

So Sheila, her cheeks glowing for the fray, her eyes bright

with the tears she had been shedding, arose and unlocked her new trunk. She got herself into battle array in the soft, frilly pink dress that she had thought much too expensive and elaborate to buy, and when Jacqueline at last came pattering gaily in from the beach a new Sheila stood in the garden with a placid Grandmother, picking rosebuds for the table.

ANGUS Galbriath as he sailed through the silver sky, thought a great deal about the sweet, unspoiled girl he had seen that night.

He got to thinking about his mother, and a little girl picture of her that hung on the old gray castle wall at home in Scotland. There was something about that little Ainslee girl that reminded him of his mother's girlhood face. Sweet and unspoiled and clean and modest. Not wild and daring and bold like the girls he had been seeing in the mountains.

All the girls nowadays, especially those he had met the last two months, seemed sharp and hard, according to his standards. Of course times had changed since his mother was young, but he couldn't seem to think of marrying one of those sharp little giddy creatures that he was playing around with now. He couldn't think of a home with such a girl enshrined there as wife and mother. He sighed and wondered if such homes were out of fashion entirely. He didn't want to link his life with a girl who lived for herself. A girl who drank daringly, and boasted how many cigarettes she could smoke. Who wore clothes that would attract, and who considered every man, married or unmarried, her prey. That wasn't his ideal at all. He would rather never have a home than put such a girl at the head of his.

But probably that Ainslee girl would be like all the rest once one got to know her well. At least if she wasn't now it wouldn't take her long to get that way if she stayed east long and got acquainted with other girls of her generation and social standing. A pity! But probably he had over-estimated her.

However, he decided that he would see her again. In their brief talk she had greatly interested him. There was something deep and true in her eyes that held in his memory. He recalled her look when she had told about the humming-bird in the lily. He looked off into the silverness of the night and saw the starriness of her eyes. Then when the distant lights of New York began to be visible and garish against the dreaminess of the moonlight, he snapped himself out of it and prepared to get back to everyday living.

After a night's sleep he had so far recovered his normal attitude toward life and girls in general as to quite decide on waiting until the end of the week before returning to his uncle's summer house on the cliffs beside the sea.

He saw Maxwell Ainslee only for a moment when he stepped into his office to leave the papers Grandmother had signed, but they made an appointment to meet and take lunch together two days later.

By the time they came together for lunch Angus Galbraith had almost forgotten the slight girl who had charmed him for the moment. Not until Maxwell Ainslee began to thank him again for looking after the matter of the papers for him did she recur to him. Then he protested.

"You needn't be so grateful, Mr. Ainslee, the thanks are on the other side. I had a most delightful call and enjoyed both the ladies immensely. They certainly are a rest and change from the modern world. Your mother is like a picture of the old days. I didn't know there were mothers like that left. And the girl was charming."

"Girl?" said Maxwell, "I didn't know Mother had a girl visiting her. I wonder who it could have been."

"She introduced her as her granddaughter," said Galbraith. "Miss Ainslee, she said."

"Why, that's strange," said Ainslee, "I don't know which one it could have been. Jessica has just gone on her wedding trip. Rosalie and Annabelle are in Europe, and anyhow their name is Van Dyke, not Ainslee; and Damaris my sister Mary's daughter is named Deane. That's all the granddaughters except Jean and she's married and down in Mexico now."

"This girl did not have any of those names," said Galbraith, "she called her Sheila, Sheila Ainslee."

"You don't say!" said Maxwell Ainslee eyeing his friend with interest. "I wonder if that could be my brother Andrew's child. Seems to me it was a girl. She had a sort of Irish name I remember, but I thought it was Moira. Or—was that the mother? I'm not sure. It might have been Sheila. You see my brother Andrew was the youngest and a sort of a black sheep. He went away and married a very common person, we heard."

"It couldn't be the same one," said Galbraith shaking his head decidedly. "This girl was very unusual, and she must have had an extraordinary mother from the way she spoke of her."

"Indeed!" said Ainslee. "Now I wonder! You see we never could find out much about them. My brother didn't write often. He sort of disappeared from the family annals."

"Well, the girl is most extraordinary I should say, if one can judge from a few minutes' talk," said Galbraith and suddenly knew he was going back to The Cliffs as soon as he could get rid of a few engagements which he wished now he had not made. There was a girl who was insisting that he should come to dinner at her home on the Hudson. He had brought letters of introduction from across the sea to her family, and she was making the most of the acquaintance. He wasn't sure he cared for her type. There was a young widow whom he had met on shipboard who claimed a place in his attention. He had promised to take her for a spin in the air. She was sweet and sorrowful and a trifle pathetic, a clinging vine of the southern type. A man might easily yield to her sweet coaxings, and then be weary of them when it was too late.

There were a couple of men in New York besides Ainslee whom he knew and liked. He had made engagements with them, and they would be interesting, but he knew that as soon as he was free he was going back to see if that little girl was as sweet as he had thought.

Then he came back to the present and realized that Ainslee was still talking about his youngest brother.

"Queer how families get separated, isn't it? Take Andrew for instance, the baby, and naturally the longest at home, but somehow he always had the roving foot. Of course we all were off to school and college when he was growing up. I never felt as if I really knew him well. Queer dick, he was, always doing things he oughtn't to do. Never would settle down. Couldn't get through college because he got in with a bad set. I always thought he was the goat, and let himself be. Proud he was. If anybody suspected him of doing anything wrong he'd just let 'em think he'd done it. Often we never knew whether he had or not. We were afraid to defend him lest he had."

"How was he in business?" asked Galbraith more to seem interested than because he really cared.

"Well, there you are again. He wouldn't go into business. We couldn't seem to get him interested in anything. I offered him a chance in here with me, but no, he wouldn't look at it. Mother tried all sorts of things but his answer was to go off and leave her for months at a time, even a year or two without any word whatever. He got in with the wrong people of course, went with the down-and-outers, always taking up with the under dog. He was attractive, and older men made much of him. He got to drinking, too, and then he finished up with this marriage. We haven't seen him since."

"Did you know his wife?"

"No. Never even heard much about her except that she wasn't very high in the social order. She may have been as good as he was perhaps, but I'm afraid that wouldn't be saying much. He really was unexplainable and quite inexcusable. Mother of course was always hoping, even wanted to help him when he told her he was going to be married, but I put my foot down on that. The trouble with Andrew was, of course, that he was the baby, and he was spoiled. You couldn't really blame Mother for it. We were all gone. He was the last baby she had, and Father was gone too, died when Andrew was about eighteen. But it was very hard on Mother, and Andrew was old enough to know how he hurt her. When it came to marrying beneath him I thought the end had come, and we've never had anything to do with him or his wife."

"Well," said Galbraith thoughtfully, "either this girl isn't his child or else you've been misinformed about the mother, because from what that girl told me I'm sure she had a very superior mother!"

"H'm! Well, I'll have to run down and see what is going on at Rainbow. It's all right for Mother to do something for the child if she's really Andrew's daughter, but I shall insist that Mother shall not allow the wife to come down upon her. Mother is soft hearted and will let anybody do her if we don't protect her. But I draw the line at having Mother saddled with some common, low-down woman as a daughter-in-law, and that's what I've always expected she would try to do, come and live on Mother."

"I don't really think you need worry," said Galbraith slowly, watching Ainslee's fine, upright, almost self-righteous face as he talked, "because, you see, if it's this girl's mother, she's dead."

"Dead!" said Ainslee with a startled look, and then, with a relieved expression. "Well, perhaps that may make this situation a little less complicated. You see, Angus, you may think me a bit hard, but this girl, Andrew's wife, was a cabaret singer out in some wild western sort of place. You can readily see what kind of person she would have been, and how hard that would be for a lady like my mother."

"Well, I can only say that she made mighty fine job of bringing up her daughter, whatever she was," answered Galbraith. "But perhaps she's not the same one at all. You'd better run down and see for yourself. I'm going back in a few days, why not fly back with me? Leave your stocks and bonds to fend for themselves a few hours and come along."

"Maybe I will if I can get away. I'll think it over!" said the older man.

But Galbraith went out from that interview determined soon to see more of Sheila and find out what she really was. If this was the story of her father and mother that he had been hearing she must be all the more remarkable.

He went that evening to dine with the widow whom he had met on shipboard, and the next day to lunch with the girl with honey-colored hair, out on the banks of the Hudson, but neither of them could make him forget the girl with the great blue eyes under long black lashes, and the earnest, wistful young face. There was a haunting something about the memory of her. Where had he seen someone of whom she reminded him? Especially her eyes? It was someone abroad, he was sure.

The great brown eyes of the southern widow looked wistfully into his from time to time, her low, sweet, southern voice lingered softly on the vowels, her small hands looked fragile and lovely against the dull black of her mourning robes. He even made another engagement with her for Saturday, yet all the time he was wondering who else besides Sheila had those blue eyes under very long black lashes?

He went with his men friends to clubs and shows and dinners but he could not put his mind on what they were talking about because there was an undertone of thought running through everything. He felt that if he could only get by himself alone for a while and think connectedly, or if he could only see those black-fringed blue eyes again, he might be able to remember when he had seen them before, and why they interested him so.

As he sat under the gay striped umbrella on the smooth lawn of a lovely estate on the banks of the Hudson, and ate salad and sandwiches and iced drinks and fruits and talked of foreign travel with the girl with the honey-colored hair, he was thinking of the girl called Sheila, and of the name of her mother Moira. How was it those two names had always been linked together in some vague memory of his childhood?

It was somewhere around two o'clock in the morning of the third day after he had lunched with Maxwell Ainslee that he awoke with a feeling that he had run up a blind alley and found what he had been searching for. Sheila and Moira! Sheila and Moira McCleeve! That was it. He had heard his mother talk about Sheila and Moira McCleeve. They were sisters, and friends of his mother. Something had happened to them both, either they died or moved away. He did not know that part. He did not know that he ever had heard. But he knew where he had seen those eyes with the long black lashes. They were in an old painting on the gray walls of McCleeve Castle that he had visited years ago when he was a child, travelling with his mother, in Ireland.

When he closed his eyes he could see the picture yet, staring out of its dull gold frame on the stone wall of the castle, eyes of that peculiar blue on a dark haired lad of about sixteen. Some McCleeve ancestor it was, and of course had nothing whatever to do with that little girl in Rainbow Cottage who came from away out west in a small railroad crossing that wasn't even large enough to be called a town.

He thought it out for a time, and was annoyed and troubled that his long thinking had brought nothing but a vague old memory. He wished that he understood the laws that govern minds, so that he might know why his had insisted on following up this particular line of thought only to bring him to a dead idea. McCleeve's Castle was far away in Ireland, and the little girl with the wonderful eyes came from the west.

So at last he fell asleep.

About that time in a far western state a man of burly build and swarthy countenance was furtively stealing on a train and taking care that no one at the station should see him. He had little black beady eyes set too close together, and bushy hair that had recently been dyed a dark red. A heavy red mustache covered the selfish, cruel lips beneath. His clothes were worn and seedy looking, his shoes down at the heel, and under his ill-fitting coat his hip pocket bulged with something hard and uncompromising. He carried only a bundle wrapped in newspaper, and kept his face glued to the window, only turning his head slightly when the conductor came for his ticket, as if he were afraid he might miss something of the landscape.

Out across the desert the train wended its swift gliding way, like a serpent trailing along in the night, bearing a menace to those who were unaware. And the man with the newly-red hair and the cruel eyes hugged close to the window with his face in the shadow, and finally slept with the rest of the world.

12

JACQUELINE came fluttering down ten minutes after the dinner-bell rang, in a startling costume of silver and black velvet. More pajamas! Silver ones, and a black velvet jacket!

Her lips were painted more vividly than ever, so red they looked as if they were bleeding, her face was chalky white with powder and her eyelashes made so black and heavy with mascara that she looked a caricature of a human face.

Sheila gazed at her with horror. She had never seen such make-up before. Even at the Junction cabaret it was not practised to that extent.

Jacqueline wore very long jade earrings, reaching down on her shoulders and a necklace made like a green snake twining around her throat. She wore a jade ring two inches long on her little finger and another tiny serpent with jewelled eyes crept round her wrist. Her sleek hair was plastered out on her cheeks in sharp arrowheads, and fitted round her small head like a felon's cap.

Grandmother surveyed her in great disgust.

"Now, before you sit down, Jacqueline, you may as well go back upstairs and take off those snakes. You know what

I think about wearing such things, and I won't stand it. I haven't come to the point of eating in company with serpents—yet."

Jacqueline trilled a faint little ripple of laughter, her eyes twinkling wickedly.

"Oh, now, Aunt Myra, don't you like my sweet little pets yet? I thought you had got used to them. See, what pretty colors they have. The jewels are so cunningly arranged. The workmanship is choice!"

"Yes," said Grandmother shutting her lips thinly together. "I know. It speaks in the Bible about that! You probably never read it."

"In the Bible!" echoed Jacqueline surprised out of her impishness for the instant. "The Bible speaks about my serpents?"

"Yes," said Grandmother, "the serpent that yours are an imitation of. He was the anointed cherub, you know, Satan, that old serpent. It says 'every precious stone was thy covering, the sardius, the topaz, the diamond, the beryl, the onyx, and the jasper, the sapphire, the emerald, and the carbuncle and gold.' It talks about workmanship too."

"Oh, *precious!*" said Jacqueline squealing with wicked glee. "Now, what do you know about that! But really, Aunt Myra, you oughtn't to dislike them then if the Bible talks about them."

"Go take them off!" commanded the old lady, fairly bristling. "I won't sit here and eat with that thing creeping round your neck."

"Oh, well, I'll take it off just to please you then."

Jacqueline proceeded to unwind the slippery creature from her neck, and coiled it neatly on the tablecloth beside her plate.

"Take it away, I tell you. Out of my sight this minute!"

"Oh, all right!" said Jacqueline meekly, and swept her two little jeweled snakes off onto the floor as Janet was bringing in a platter of chicken.

Janet gave a little half suppressed scream and nearly dropped the platter.

Grandmother arose from her seat.

"Janet, put the platter down, and then you may bring the brush and dustpan and take up those two nasty beasts and carry them up to Miss Jacqueline's room. And the next time, Jacqueline, that you bring those things around they'll be flung in the trash heap and burned."

Jacqueline merely laughed and settled down into her seat. Then suddenly she caught sight of Sheila, and while Grandmother was saying grace she placed her two smooth round elbows on the table, her chin in her hands, and studied the other girl up and down.

Sheila was very angry to have this other girl treating Grandmother with such disrespect, for she had grown to love her already, but mindful of her promise she held her peace and tried to act as if nothing had happened. Ah! She had been well schooled in ignoring the unpleasant around her. How many days there had been hard, trying things going on at home that she had had to ignore, and stay serene for her mother's sake! Sheila found herself wondering if everywhere in life that had to be. Were there always things that one had to suffer and endure in silence? She thought of her father on his bad days. She thought of Buck. She thought of the people at the cabaret who had made it so hard for her mother. That new girl singer had been in a way much like this Jacqueline whom she had to look upon as a *cousin!* Why, even Aurelia in the cabaret had not been painted so grotesquely as this girl!

The meal was not a pleasant one. Grandmother served the chicken grimly. Janet served the vegetables indignantly. Sheila was utterly silent, wondering at herself sitting here in this strange atmosphere in this lovely pink dress, with a new grandmother and this terrible new cousin. But Jacqueline was entirely serene. She did most of the talking. She told some of her brother's outrageous pranks at school. Grandmother knew she was probably exaggerating them to shock her, and she neither smiled nor responded. But Jacqueline chattered on sweetly.

"I'm expecting a boy-friend to-night, Aunt Myra," she announced as they were rising from the table, "but you needn't bother getting out of the living room. I expect we'll sit out in the garden or under the rose trellis. Perhaps you'll have Janet take out a couple of chairs and put them over by the east wall beyond the rose bed just in case we find it cooler there."

"If you want any chairs carried out," said Grandmother grimly, "you'll take them yourself. But there's one thing I'll tell you. You're not going to greet any man in my house while you're wearing those tin pants. You can just go up and put on a decent dress, or, if you choose to ignore my request, you'll find the door locked when you do come in! I'm not going to have such goings on in my house!"

"Oh, Aunt Myra! Aren't you archaic!" laughed Jacqueline, dancing out the front door and swinging it wide behind her, skipping down the garden path in her silver trousers, the soft velvet jacket blowing about her as she went.

Down the garden to the wide centre path she went, and standing deliberately in full view of the window where she knew Grandmother could see her she took out a tiny gold case from her trouser pocket, opened it, took out a cigarette and lighted it.

Grandmother watched her grimly from the window for an instant as she moved to the side of the house. Then a big tear came out and rolled down her cheek.

Suddenly Sheila came up behind her, put her round young arms about her neck and kissed her.

"Grandmother, I hate her for making you cry!"

Grandmother turned about quickly, putting a frail arm around the girl.

"No, dear! Not hate. You can hate the evil but not the person."

"Oh, but Grandmother, I can't help hating her for the way she is treating you. I couldn't stand it the way you do."

"I'm not standing it," said Grandmother, "I'm falling down terribly on my job. But I just don't know what to say without actually driving her out. When she was little I spanked her. If she had had spankings enough she would have been a good girl perhaps, but I was the only one who ever spanked her, and I wasn't allowed to do that when her people were here. But I'm sorry, dear, that you should have this to see when you have just got home."

"Isn't it maybe because I'm here, Grandmother?" asked Sheila with a troubled look. "I'm not like her, and naturally she wouldn't like me."

"Thank God you're not!" said Grandmother fervently, but said no more, for as she turned about from the window she heard a step outside the front door, and looking up saw Angus Galbraith just lifting the door knocker, and behind him, a little way down the front walk, were his cousin Malcolm and his wife Betty. They were come to call, and there was Jacqueline in silver trousers out in the garden smoking a cigarette! Grandmother's face burned crimson with annoyance.

"May I come in?" asked the young man to the door. He was shaking hands with Grandmother, but his look went toward Sheila. Was she what he had been thinking, or had he idealized her?

Sheila stood just under the light in her fluffy pink dress. His eyes lighted up as he saw her, and something went from her eyes to his, some spark of friendliness and interest, and a thrill of pleasure quite unexpected. Their smiles flashed like sunshine and Grandmother caught a glimpse of it and was glad. She forgot for an instant the hussy out in the yard in tin pantaloons.

There came a cry from outside, Jacqueline hailing the Galbraiths gaily, flinging her cigarette to the feet of the lilies and rushing forward with a flash of silver.

The little party moved to the door again, Grandmother in the background wondering what to do—what *could* she do?

Angus and Sheila moved together, smiling, speaking quietly, drawing near the door because that was the thing to do, yet reluctantly.

"Did you find my card?"

"Indeed I did. You dropped it under the lily where the humming-bird flew. And the little light burned brightly all the way down and showed me where it was."

"Didn't the flash break?"

"No, it works beautifully."

Then she remembered that she did not know what had become of the flash light, and *suppose* he should want it back?

"I kept it for you—" she hesitated.

"Suppose you keep it in memory of our first meeting," he said, looking deep into her eyes and thinking how like they were to those of the boy in blue hanging high in McCleeve Castle.

Suddenly Sheila felt other eyes upon her, and unwillingly looking out the door saw Jacqueline's dark look smouldering upon her with fury in its depths. Saw Betty's eyes, too, with exactly the same smouldering look of fury in them as she looked at Jacqueline. It came to her that these two were struggling under the same feelings. Eyes could not have spoken plainer than Jacqueline's did to her, than Betty's eyes were speaking toward Jacqueline. And with a quick glance she saw Malcolm standing there beside Jacqueline, idly smoothing the velvet on Jacqueline's shoulder. Then looking up he caught Sheila's quick surprise and put out his hand to greet her, as ready to turn his attention to any other bit of cloth, or flesh.

But Jacqueline had been quick to seize an advantage. She turned to Angus eagerly.

"Oh, Angus, darling! Is it you? How simply precious! Do come out here and speak to me. Grandmother doesn't approve of my costume and won't let me come in."

She put her hand in and clasped Angus' hand and drew him laughingly outside. Then shamelessly she slid her arm within his and walked off down to the wicket gate.

"Good bye, folks," she called gaily, "me and my boy-friend are going walking on the beach. Better all come along. The evening's fine!"

Angus yielded to her compulsion reluctantly, but laughed back wistfully.

"Better come along, friends. I can't help myself you see!" he called.

Grandmother actually snorted, but nobody heard her. Each was too much engaged with his own feelings to notice the other. And Grandmother was very angry indeed. She was casting about in her mind to know just what she should do about Jacqueline. Would it be better to send for her father, or just to telephone Maxwell to come down and lay her out? Maxwell could do it if he would. He had a way with him that made people obey, and he never had liked Jacqueline.

But Malcolm Galbraith was not waiting for Grandmother to decide what to do. He seized Sheila's hand and drew it within his arm.

"Come!" he said gaily. "That's a challenge! Let's follow. You coming too, Betts?"

"I'm walking with Madam Ainslee!" said Betty coldly, casting a smouldering look upon Sheila that startled her again. But she was being walked away so fast she had much ado to keep her step for the first few rods. Looking back in deep distress Sheila saw Grandmother coming slowly down the path and out the wicket onto the sand with Betty Galbraith.

Where were they all going anyway, headed into the twilight along the alabaster beach beside an opal sea that was momentarily growing deeper azure, with here and there a star caught in its depths?

Sheila and her escort were well away from each of the other couples now, shut around by gathering shadows in a lovely misty intimacy. There was an exhilaration in walking in step with a strong man. Sheila had never done it before, but almost instantly her pleasure was at an end for the hand that had pulled hers within his arm now slid along the draperies of her delicate sleeve, slipping over the smoothness of her arm, down to her wrist, folded her hand warmly in a close intimate clasp, and held it, palm to palm.

Sheila drew back quickly, sharply, pulled at her hand with a sickening feeling of repulsion, and when he would not release her, said earnestly:

"Don't, please, I want to respect you and myself too."

"But what is there wrong about that, my dear? Why shouldn't you respect me and yourself too?"

"Would your wife like to see you holding my hand?" asked Sheila, and gave her hand a final wrench from his clasp.

"What? Betts? Oh, she's so used to that kind of thing that she wouldn't think a thing of it. Does it every day herself. Nobody thinks a thing of that nowadays, child. Where have you been hidden? You're delicious!" and he reached to capture her hand again.

But Sheila drew entirely away from him.

"There are men where I have been that do those things," she said gravely, "but I did not know that gentlemen did. I am sorry!" and she walked quite away from him.

"Oh, come now, if you feel that way about it I won't touch you. Don't go shy on me. Honestly I admire you a lot. Come, walk with me and tell me how you got this way. I never saw a girl like you before. You act as if I had insulted you."

"I am accustomed to thinking of things like that as insults," said Sheila sadly, "I did not expect to find them among nice people."

"I'm hit! Forgive me, won't you? I promise you I won't offend that way again."

"All right," said Sheila soberly, "I'll forgive you. But let us wait, please, for Grandmother and your wife. It is nicer to walk all together, don't you think?"

He laughed it off, and waited with good grace. When they came up, he gracefully took Grandmother, walking beside her, and left Sheila to walk with Betty.

Betty's smouldering eyes turned questioningly upon her as she fell into step with her, and studied her in the moonlight.

"You're not like other girls, are you?" she said suddenly, "I almost thought you were, but you're not."

"I don't know much about other girls," said Sheila sadly, "My mother was the only girl I knew well. Of course I went to school with other girls, but that was away out in the west near the desert. Some of them were nice enough, only we never saw much of each other except during school hours. We all lived very far apart and I—never went anywhere much."

"Weren't you bored to death?" asked Betty wonderingly.

"No," said Sheila gravely. "I had my work, and I had my mother. I'd gladly go back to it for the rest of my life if I could have my mother again."

"Where is she?" asked Betty. "Divorced?"

"Oh, no!" said Sheila in a shocked voice. "She's gone to Heaven."

"Oh! Heaven!" sneered Betty out of a great gloom. "What makes you think there is such a place?"

"Because the Bible says there is," answered Sheila with conviction.

"The Bible? I didn't know anybody believed in the Bible nowadays. It's just a collection of mythical literature, isn't it? That's what they taught us in college."

"I never went to college," said Sheila, "but if they teach that I wouldn't want to go, because I wouldn't give up the Bible for all the learning in the world. I never knew much about it till recently, but I know enough now to realize that I want to know a lot more."

"You're queerer that I thought you were," remarked the young woman of the world. "What makes you care so much for the Bible?"

"Because it has answered some of the questions of my heart. Because it has given me the truth about being saved."

"Saved?" echoed Betty, and laughed.

"Yes, saved. A chance to be at Home with God some day!"

"Mercy! I never thought God had a home!" remarked Betty bitterly. "I thought all God did was punish people for wanting to have good times."

"Oh, it isn't like that at all! He loves us and is getting ready a Home for us, a mansion. Didn't you ever learn about the many mansions. 'Let not your heart be troubled' and the rest of it?"

"Goodness no! I never even had a Bible!"

"My mother read it to me, and made me learn a lot of chapters when I was a child."

"Well, perhaps that's what makes you so different from everybody else. But I'm not sure I'd like to be like you. I'm terribly sick of being like myself. I'm coming to see you sometime when you are all alone and you can tell me more about it. Maybe I'll read the Bible too if it could only make me happy."

"I'd love to have you come. I've got a little book Grandmother gave to me to read that helps me understand things. We might read it together."

"Does that other girl, Miss Lammorelle—she's your cousin isn't she?—Does she read the Bible too?" There was a sneer in Betty's voice that brought quick sympathy from Sheila.

"I don't know," she answered. "I don't really know her very well. I never saw her till this afternoon. Yes, I guess she's a cousin, but very distant."

"Well, let me know if you find out. If she reads the Bible I don't want to. I've been watching her and I've been watching you. Here come the others. Now we can't talk any more. But I'm coming down to see you soon. I'll call up and see if you are free."

The others came up just then and there was no more opportunity for talk between them, but for the moment Sheila found herself free to think her own thoughts.

Were men all like that as Betty's husband had said? Did they think nothing of fondling any girl's hand? Was Angus Galbraith like that too?

Even with her little experience Sheila could see that Jacqueline would have no scruples against such things. Well, probably it was all true. Nobody thought anything of intimacies nowadays. But if that was true she would like to stay in a world where there was no social order. She would stay at home with Grandmother. She hated such things. Malcolm Galbraith had linked himself in her mind with Buck and his kind when he tried to caress her arm, and hold her hand. She was disappointed in him. She told herself she was disappointed in all men.

But really in her heart she was thinking of Angus. Did he do things of that sort? Very likely he did. He went off with Jacqueline, didn't he?

Well, she was glad she had found it out before she knew him very well. It wouldn't matter so much now that the little flash light with his card attached was gone. How foolish she had been to attach any special interest to a man whom she had met for only a very few minutes. He had done those few stunts in his plane just to be amusing and kindly. What a little silly she was to keep thinking of him continually. Well she would stop it at once!

And then Angus Galbraith deliberately turned away from

Jacqueline and came over to her. He was carrying a lovely shell in his hand and he brought it and laid it in her hand.

She caught a dart of anger from Jacqueline's hard black eyes as she turned to take the shell, but Galbraith was facing her so that he stood between them, and she promptly forgot Jacqueline, and her own resolves, and became absorbed in the story he had to tell about the shell. There was something in the way he came that seemed to try to say to her that it was not his wish to go away at all. But probably that was the way every man who tried to be a gentleman treated every girl with whom he spent a few minutes. It was perhaps just a way of flattering them.

Nevertheless her heart grew warm and pleasantly happy while she talked with him, and the rest of the evening sped away on charmed wings.

It was after they were all gone that the time of reckoning came.

Jacqueline had been gay with banter toward both men as they stood in the doorway for farewells, but when they were out of hearing she turned about with retribution in her eyes.

Grandmother had disappeared into the kitchen to give some directions for to-morrow to Janet, and for the moment the two girls were alone.

"So that's your game!" said Jacqueline with a hard line of her lips, and a hard glitter in her black eyes. "Well, you can just lay off, understand? Angus Galbraith is *mine,* and I'll take pains to make it too hot for you to stay here if you have anything more to do with him."

Sheila looked at the angry girl in amazement.

"I'm sure I don't know what you mean," she said coldly. "I'm not playing any game, and I have no desire to take Angus Galbraith or anybody else away from you. I met him before I went away to Boston and we naturally talked together, but not any more than I would talk with anyone who called."

"I don't care to discuss it with you," said Jacqueline, in the tone of a person in authority speaking to a menial. "I'm just telling you that you're to lay off Angus Galbraith. If you don't you'll be sorry, that's all."

"I don't like your expression," said Sheila with a steady look, "and since I haven't done anything that is wrong your warning doesn't seem to mean anything to me. If I happen to meet Mr. Galbraith again I shall probably treat him just as I have been doing. I don't see that my conduct was any different from yours. You walked down the beach with his cousin and he is *married*. Why should I not walk back with the other cousin? I didn't ask him to walk with me."

"Oh, shut up!" said Jacqueline angrily. "You needn't try to pretend to me that you're not hipped on him. I know the signs. Girls don't hide away calling cards with cheap flash lights tied to them if they haven't got some scheme up their sleeves. And I'm just telling you that it won't be very pleasant for you if you go poaching in my preserves. Try it and see!"

Sheila's cheeks flamed but she kept her steady look.

"So you know where the rest of my things are, do you?" she said quietly. "Very well. I know what to expect."

Jacqueline made an elfish grimace and suddenly turned and fled up the front stairs as lightly as a bird. Sheila could hear her close her door and lock it.

Sheila went over to a chair in a dark corner by the fireplace and sat down with her burning face in her hands. She felt as if she had been dragged lower in the last few minutes than she had ever been in her life before. And there wasn't a thing she could say unless she gave vent to her primitive feelings and challenged her hateful cousin to a fist fight. She was fairly frightened at the feelings that surged in her angry heart, and bright tears of fury stung in her eyes. How was she ever to get along here with this awful girl? She felt so degraded by what had been said to her that it seemed as if she just must run away and hide somewhere. Then she heard Grandmother calling to her from the head of the stairs, and she quickly brushed the tears away and went up.

13

SHEILA slept very little that night. She knelt for a long time at her bedside, weeping and trying to pray. It seemed to her that she had reached the depths.

When she finally got up and sat in her chair trying to reason herself out of this humiliation she told herself that she wished she had never met Angus Galbraith. To have had a pleasant thing like meeting a good young man for the first time in her life turned into this was ghastly! To be charged with having gone after a young man and tried to get him away from someone else!

If it had not been for Moira's careful training Sheila would probably have been able to laugh off the little incident as a trifle, and even perhaps been secretly proud that a desirable young man had chosen to talk to her instead of the other girl who was so much more sophisticated.

But Sheila, in spite of all her bravely dignified words to Jacqueline, felt as if she never wanted to see Angus Galbraith again.

If it had been possible without hurting Grandmother's feelings and requiting all her kindness with absolute rudeness, she would have crept out of the house that night and never returned.

When, because she knew it was late and she was afraid her light might attract her grandmother's attention, she crept into bed, it was to toss and lie awake, and resolve that she would never, never see Angus Galbraith again. Hour after hour she lay there and tried to tear from her memory the thought of him, and only succeeded in making some little word, or smile or look of him clearer in her mind. She was appalled, aghast.

Next morning when she came down to breakfast she was pale and grave. A new dignity seemed to have come upon her and, though she tried to smile at her grandmother, there was a trembly edge to it that made the old lady watch her furtively and wonder.

Not so Jacqueline. She was on hand with the lark, blithe and gay in the most feminine of orchid negligees. No one could possibly accuse her of not being demure this morning. She was like a merry lovely child. With her hair brushed plainly back from her forehead, no make-up whatever on her guileless face, no jewelry whatever, not even a ring upon her finger, with little trifles of slippers laced with cord up the front and around her ankles, she toyed with her breakfast and cast endearing glances at the old lady, called her "dear Aunt Myra" and told her "how quaint" she was.

The old lady eyed her with suspicion, but dropped no word to break the seeming harmony of the breakfast table.

Then, when Grandmother was suddenly called to the back door to inspect some fish that Janet was not sure ought to be bought, Jacqueline pushed back her plate, planted her charming elbows on the table in front of her, letting the ruffles of lace and orchid silk fall back further to reveal her lovely arms, and looked long and sweetly at Sheila who was gravely eating her strawberries with downcast eyes.

At last Jacqueline spoke:

"I've placed you at last," she said as if it were an achievement she had long sought, "I couldn't at all at first."

Her voice was like that of a pleased little child. Jacqueline was a real actress.

Sheila looked up wondering.

"Yes," said Jacqueline smiling. "You're the child of that scapegrace cousin of mine, Andrew! I used to just love to listen to stories of his escapades when I was a child. He did something terrible, didn't he? What was it? Did he murder somebody, or was it only embezzlement? I forget. Was he hung, or only imprisoned for life? I was trying to tell Angus about it last night but I couldn't remember which."

Sheila had arisen when Jacqueline first began to speak. She could not have turned any whiter than she was. Her eyes were wide and dark and ominous. She was almost regal in her bearing, like Nemesis, or a queen about to visit vengeance upon a vassal.

But Jacqueline maintained her sunny, naïve bearing and babbled on.

"And he married a barmaid or something didn't he? Or weren't your father and mother ever really married after all? I forget."

She lifted big dark eyes like pools of wonder to where Sheila had stood but the instant before, but Sheila was no longer there. With one catlike motion she rounded the end of the table and gave Jacqueline a stinging slap square on her pretty, enquiring mouth, followed by another, and another, so sharp and quick that the astonished tormentor had no time to recover, nor cry out, nor even move. Then like a wraith Sheila disappeared, dashing madly up the stairs to her room and locking her door behind her.

She tore off the pretty new dress of blue she was wearing, the dainty bits of lingerie that she had loved so when they were bought for her, even the shoes and stockings that were a part of her new outfit. She was breathless as she did it. Her heart was beating wildly.

She reached to her closet for the newspaper bundle of scorched things she had carefully salvaged from the trash heap, a sob gathering in her throat as she did so and escaping like a great gasp. She put on the things without stopping to look them over, her old clothes that she had worn when she came here. There were several burned places, but she did not heed them. Her fingers trembled as she fastened the blouse. It had a great scorched place across the breast, but she drew on the woollen coat over it and buttoned it firmly to her chin. She jammed on the little old felt hat that had been folded away to die, and then she gave one wild sorrowful look around the quiet room with all its sweet appointments, a great look of renunciation toward the closet and the trunk full of lovely clothes.

She caught at her little handbag that Grandmother had so carefully picked out for her and filled with all necessities. There was a pencil in it and a little note book.

She tore a leaf from the book and wrote:

> Dear Grandmother:
> I have done something that you can't forgive. I have slapped your other guest three times in the face and I hate her. I could not help it. She said awful things about my father and mother. But I know I must go. It won't ever be right for me to stay here now any more. Don't worry about me for I have taken five dollars of the money you gave me, and when I get work I will return it. But I love you, Grandmother, and I am sorry for your sake — not for her — that I did it. But I had to.
> Good bye, dear precious Grandmother,
> Sheila

She laid the little note beside the pencil on the bureau where it could not fail to be seen, took five dollars from the handbag and put it in her mother's worn old purse, then she tiptoed over to the door and opened it softly. She could hear Jacqueline down at the piano in the living room playing gay nothings and singing little trilly, silly words. She could hear Grandmother's voice in the kitchen talking to Janet. Now was the time.

She gave one more anguished look about the room and slipped softly out to the hall window which gave on to a gently sloping porch roof, ending in a wide rose-trellis with crimson roses nodding and smiling in full bloom about the edge of the roof.

Stealthily she climbed out of the window, a fugitive once more in a strange unfriendly world, slid softly down the roof, put a tentative foot upon the bar of the trellis and found that it held, and then went swiftly down past the roses, not minding the thorns that tore her face and arms, and clutched their best at her woollen garments. She hurried ruthlessly down from slat to slat, not daring to linger on the frail white wood lest it give way and let her down too soon and somebody might see her.

She was on the ground now, standing in a little pool of bright portulaccas at the garden end of the house. They smiled up at her confidingly, pleasedly, like a little dog of the family who might wag his tail at a guest. But she must not linger in this dear place. She must be gone at once before anyone saw her and made the way harder. She must not let that other girl see her in these disgraceful rags.

She dashed wildly across the flower bed, the garden walk, the little patch of lawn, down along behind the trellis, and stole quickly from the wicket gate, shutting it firmly behind her.

One last look back she gave, saw the beloved cottage, the door where she had been taken in, the vista of dining room beyond, the table where she had just eaten the last bounteous breakfast she would likely ever have, then heard her enemy singing a gay little wicked song and the fire burned hot in her heart. She vanished around the garden wall, keeping close behind its shelter, then dashed for a great sand dune and crouched down beyond it to reconnoitre.

The day was perfect, calm and blue with a lovely breeze. The waves were like the ruffles of white foamy lace on the negligee that Grandmother had bought for her. The sand was hard and white like marble, and off in the distance the rocks loomed black and clear against a summer sky. The little cottage lay smiling in the summer sun, tucked safely inside its sheltering wall, and not a soul in sight. They could not see her from here even if they were looking out the kitchen windows. It was too far. Besides they would not know her in these clothes.

Either way on the great wide beach there was not a soul in sight. Now was the time to go, and to go far and fast.

She arose, bent her head a little and started on blindly, walking as fast as she could, running sometimes between the sand dunes. When she dared to look back again the cottage was like a little picture on the horizon. But she must not stay her steps, not till she had rounded that curve in the beach and got entirely out of sight.

The last few rods she took in a run, and turned for one more glimpse before she said good bye forever. But the cottage now was only a tiny miniature far and vague and no one could possibly see her here.

She dropped down on the sand for a moment to rest and look around her. Up the beach a little way, towering almost above her head there loomed great rocks, and a lovely house of stone beyond on more rocks. It looked like the pictures Mother had drawn for her when she was a child, of the castle where she used to live.

Then a thought came to her. That must be The Cliffs where the Galbraiths lived, and they would see her perhaps from the windows. How terrible if Angus Galbraith should come down this way and meet her, see her in these soiled, scorched garments, these awful shoes! There was a hole burned clear through the toe of one where Jacqueline's fire had done its deadly work. Oh, she did not want him to see her! He would not know her perhaps looking like this, but she did not want to see him now. She must get away faster than ever.

Or suppose that cousin, the married one, Malcolm, should

see her! She shuddered. She had a feeling about him now that he was like Buck.

She rose swiftly and bounded away up the beach, faster and faster, scarcely raising her eyes to look ahead, not daring to look behind. Only she knew that she had passed the house. If they saw from its high, beautiful windows a shabby little figure flying along they would never think of her as Grandmother's guest. They would think of her as some poor fisher's child.

So she fled along the beach and tried to comfort and reassure herself.

Then she came upon a place where a great white motor boat was drawn up high on the sand, and beside it a lovely sail boat with its sails all neatly furled. It seemed to be a spot where the beach was sheltered, a sort of landing place where the water was quieter and deep enough to land a boat. Sheila knew little about boats and landing, but a sudden panic took her, for out on the bright water not so very far away there came another boat with sails unfurled and billowing beautifully in the breeze. It looked as if it were headed straight for her, and her heart stood still. She must get far past here before that boat could come in.

But the old shoes, down at the heel, began to hurt her feet, and her limbs were getting tired and weak with the fright, sorrow and anger that were mingled in her soul. It seemed as if every step dragged slower and slower.

And now she caught echoes of voices, a word now and then. There were people up above the cliff, perhaps belonging to that Galbraith house. They were laughing and talking. She passed a little jagged path that ran up the rocks a few steps at a time and then around them, with vines and short grasses fringing its edge. It sounded as if there were people coming down that path. She distinctly heard someone say: "I'm not going to stay in the water so long this morning." Then the dashing of the sea ahead against more rocks drowned the voices, and blindly she dashed on. There must be a shelter somewhere near where she could hide till all these people got down in the water, swimming, and then perhaps they would not notice her.

A rock jutted out ahead of her, and she darted around behind it. Ah! Sure enough there was shelter, a group of big rocks, huddled together like walls of different rooms and a great flat one in the centre, with a winding path around up to its top. The sea was just beyond that, and behind it there was a sort of hollow cave, rock-lined.

She slipped within, and hid behind a rock. She would wait here in the silence and quiet until those bathers were finished, or at least until they were out in the water where they would not notice. Then she would watch her chance and dart out and round the last rock, and so on farther up the coast away from all Galbraiths and their sort; away from this world that was not hers and did not want her.

So she lay hidden while Angus Galbraith and his cousins came down the rocky path and went into the sea.

From where she was she could just seet them as they stepped out into the water, the white of their bodies and the dark colors of their bathing suits flashing bright where the water touched them and the sun glanced off. She could easily identify the two young men, striding into the water with great bounds, flinging water at each other, dipping and shaking their heads like water spaniels. She had never seen people bathing in the ocean before, though she had of course seen many a picture of seashore resorts in the books she read. But the sight of it fascinated her even in her terrible predicament. What would it be to be doing things like this, having good times without a lot of worry and disgrace?

She watched the girls, plunging into the great waves and riding above them, the men swimming up and taking hold of their hands, laying them down on the swell of a wave, and holding them to float. The one in the red bathing suit must be Malcolm's wife. She thought she recognized the way she held herself. But who was the one with the gold hair in the blue bathing suit? Someone had called her Rose as they came down the cliff. The name had echoed to her ears and set her wondering. Was that perhaps a guest staying at the house? Her heart gave a queer little twist. Well, this Rose person belonged there among them. She was graceful and gay and her laugh rang out and echoed through the vaulted arch of the cavern where Sheila was hiding, giving her a lonely ache in her heart.

It was a long time they were out there in the water. Sheila slid farther down in her hiding place and heaped up sand to rest her head upon. She felt dreadly weary after her long race up the beach, and after her long night of wakefulness. She let her eyelids droop over her tired eyes and a few slow tears welled up from the depths of her misery and slid down her cheeks. It was cool and quiet here, and no one could see her old blue serge with its great burned hole in the front breadth, and its scorched blouse beneath. Little gay breezes played hide and seek among the rocks of the cove, and slyly kissed the tears from her cheeks. But Sheila was so tired she did not feel them. She only felt the gentleness and peace of the place, as she dropped off into deep sleep.

When she awoke everything seemed strange. She could not remember where she was. She did not know what had wakened her. Something cold and sinster was touching her hands, creeping up through her clothing, chilling her feet.

In sudden alarm she turned over and sat up and saw to her horror that there was water all about and below her, water creeping to her feet, water dashing up in a torrent at the sunny opening where she had come in. What could it mean? Where was she?

14

AT first she could not collect her thoughts, could not tell what kind of place she was in nor what had happened to her. Then slowly, bit by bit, it came back to her. She had slapped Jacqueline, had gone away from Rainbow Cottage, and had hidden in a cave. This was the cave but it was not like the place where she had laid down. It was dark and cold, and there was water all about her. Only the little heap of sand she had scooped up had kept her head out of the water. It was a chill, awful place, and what could have happened? Was this the strange thing they called the tide, that had come up and surrounded her? Was it possible that tides could sweep around and come so far from their bounds? She had no experience whatever to tell her the answer, and at first she was so dazed she did not know what to do. Must she wait here until it was gone? She tried to remember what they had said about tides and how long they took to turn.

But suddenly a great pounding wave greater than all that had preceded it, roared into the cavern rising like a frightful wall in front of her and breaking all about and over her.

She gasped for breath and struggled to her feet, losing one

worn old slipper in the attempt, and as the worst of the wave receded with a menace in its going that promised swift return she splashed wildly toward the opening where gray day still showed a hope.

She tried to remember how the land lay where she had slipped around from the beach behind the rock, but when she stepped to where she thought it was she found the water alarmingly deep and lost her footing. And when she drew back and tried again for a shallower place she stepped sharply on a jagged rock with the shoeless foot and drew back into her covert again with a cry of pain.

Then she heard another of those terrifying waves coming on with the roar of a locomotive, and shrank away, hiding her face against the rock and holding her breath till it was gone.

This one was worst than the last. She must do something quickly or make up her mind to drown.

Then with a mind sharpened by her peril she remembered a great flat rock that had loomed higher than the rest just ahead of her cove. There had been a path up its jagged sides as if people climbed there. Could she possible find her way up and would it be high enough to save her?

She opened her eyes and looked ahead. Was that it, the gray dim thing out there? Could she get there? The water seemed deep around it, but it was her only hope. For, looking around, now she saw that the entire cove was filled with water, and when she tried to cross it and get farther up the beach the water proved to be beyond her depth.

She waded out, to her knees, to her waist. The rock was just ahead of her now, and another breaker was coming. She plunged ahead and caught its sides and a sharp shell cut her foot. Ah! There was a cleft for her hand. She clung to it, and clutched for another jagged point, and strangely enough as she stood there waist deep in water clutching the granite wall, she heard her mother's voice singing as it used to sing to her where she was a child going to sleep.

Rock of ages, cleft for me,
Let me hide myself in Thee!

Ah! There came the breakers pounding like a great beast against the rock, roaring wildly into the cave behind her as if searching for her where she had been, and strangely enough not hurling her off her feet as she had expected. She seemed to be held in a little haven, where the worst force of the waves could not reach, a spot out of the path of the tide as it rushed in.

And as the water hastened madly away again out to sea, seeming to babble angrily that she had escaped its fury, she felt herself drawn slowly with it, closer, and yet closer to the rock, and lifted slightly till her feet suddenly found a little foothold in a crevice of the rock.

Her heart beat widly. Was this the beginning of the path up to the top of the rock?

She felt with the other foot, a little higher up, and, yes, surely there was a step, wide and low, and a place for her hand to hold. Could she get up before another awful volume of water overwhelmed her?

She sensed that on this side of the rock, a little farther to the left there was comparative calm, and here strangely she found the foothold led. She crept on like a little frightened bird, out of breath and drenched and cold, yet clinging. Whenever the water surged about her feet again she would just put her face close to the rock and cling, and always above the water's roar she could hear her mother's voice singing.

Once she almost lost her hold, and felt herself slipping back, for the water was still above her knees, but when the next wave receded she managed to draw herself on higher up. How high was that rock? High enough to stay above the highest wave?

Little by little she drew herself up, clinging with hands and arms and weary aching feet, sobbing as she crept along, and beginning to pray as she sobbed.

"O Rock! Hide me! Hide me! Hide me!"

After what seemed like ages she drew herself at last entirely out of the water, where she could see the little rocky steps up to the summit, and inch by inch she finished the way, and lay down upon that broad flat top. She remembered thinking as she dropped back and closed her tired eyes that it was about the size of a bed, and wondering if the water would get high enough to wash her away from it. There was nothing to cling to here, just broad flat rock, worn smooth by many suns and seas.

After she was rested a little she sat up and looked about her, but was almost too terrified to stand it. The sea was all about her everywhere and night was coming on. Was it night or only an awful storm? Her senses were too dazed to understand. Yes, a storm perhaps, for there were great dark clouds of purple and copper in the sky and a ship with gray sails closely reefed was scuttling off in fright against the horizon, masts tilted ahead like one running, and there was jagged lightning in the sky. It was awesomely beautiful out there, like doom and the judgment day, and she could not look at it. She bent her head, shut her eyes again, and prayed. When that storm broke, where would she be?

Somewhere down along that shore line, not so very far away was Rainbow Cottage, and peace and safety. What a fool she had been! What an awful fool! What did it matter what that silly Jacqueline had said? Even about her precious mother? Words could not hurt her any more. She was gone from this earth. Words of a girl like that meant nothing anyway. She had only been trying to anger her, trying to keep her from having anything to do with Angus Galbraith. Just words flung out like darts. Jacqueline had been battling for herself. She, Sheila, should not have minded. Even the infuriating insinuations could not have insulted either herself or her parents if she had not chosen to take them that way. What a silly fool she had been! She had condescended to fight, she who had taken Christ for her Saviour, fighting with a girl who obviously did not know Him.

She put her face down into her cold wet hands and sobbed. "Oh, forgive me, God, Forgive me, please!" she cried aloud into the seclusion of the howling storm.

It was very dark. The storm was rushing on, roaring terrifically. Lurid colors appeared in the sky, wild jaws of death in the sea, towering now and then even above her rock, rearing up like walls and threatening, then dropping and breaking with tempestuous noise just below where she was stranded.

All the little frightened ships on the horizon line had fled for safety. The storm had the sea to itself as far as she could see. It was dark. Frightfully dark. Off at her right, far away in the vague grayness and blackness a search light shot out its fitful glare, darted across the scene, clashed with the play of lightning, and shot in again. That must be the revolving light Grandmother had told her about.

Far down the beach a little light just like a speck of stardust appeared. That would be perhaps where Rainbow Cottage stood. It might be that Janet had a light in the kitchen. Or no, the wall around the kitchen garden would hide that. It must be a light upstairs. Maybe in the north window of the room that had been hers!

Oh, what a fool, what a fool! To have left that pleasant haven, that shelter that God had sent her to, just because she was angry and did that which was beneath a guest of the house—slapped another guest, a member of the family too! Just like a little beast she had been, snarling and fighting! Why had she let her hot temper get the better of her? How many times had her mother warned her that she had a hasty pride inherited from her father that would be her undoing, as it had been his, if she did not take control of it! Ah! But it was too late now! She had driven herself out of that lovely home, and the love of her Grandmother, and the place where God had meant her to be safe.

It took another hour of terror and slowly approaching death to bring Sheila to see that even after she had done that hasty deed that put her in the wrong, she should not have run away. That it was only pride and unwillingness to confess herself in the wrong and humbly ask pardon, that had sent her flying from that loving care. She should have gone straight to Grandmother and told her what had happened, should have gone straight to Jacqueline and asked her to forgive. It would have been humiliating, yes, but when one has lost control of one's self, and done wrong, one should be humiliated.

God showed her herself there upon that tiny islet in that great howling storm. God spoke to her little frightened soul. Earth things fell away. The crashing heaven opened brilliant gateways in the blackness of the clouds, and clashed them shut again. The other world seemed just above the rending of the skies. She gave a frightened look above. There were distinct layers of clouds of different colors each whirling in a separate course and horrid green and copper lights shivering in between them, with jagged lines of lightning flashing up and down the sky.

The water was rising now, she could sense that, even though it was too dark to see distinctly. Each time a great mountain of a wave rose between her and the horizon, it was higher than before. The spray was dashing in her face. Her clothing was soaked through. Her hair too. Her hat was gone, she did not know how long ago. She had no memory of where, or when it had fallen. She was freezing cold and shivering like a leaf in a gale, but she was scarcely aware of that, there was so much shivering, moving, noise about her. Her teeth were chattering, and her face was wet with tears and spray.

She sat up again and braced her arms out behind her, the flat of her hands upon the smooth rock, trying to find some place to cling, some way to make a suction between her hand

and the rock, but it was slippery and frightening. She felt dizzy and terrified.

Shuddering she lay down again and closed her eyes. It could not be so long now before that water would wash over her rock. There was no doubt about it any longer. Did it take long to die by drowning? Was it more than a gasp and a choking and then the end? She was not afraid to die, and she knew that it did not matter what became of the body after death, but somehow it seemed so terrifying to be swept off into that wide sea, to be tossed about by cruel waves, thrown against unknown rocks, floating down, down, and out among the strange, ferocious inhabitants of the ocean. She wouldn't know it of course. They wouldn't be able to frighten her then when she was dead, those terrible sharks and whales and other sea creatures about which she had read, but the thought of them now was petrifying. Oh, if the end would but hasten! Let it come quickly and be over!

She lay there trying to take her mind from such thoughts, trying to pray, trying to be calm. And then she felt the first wave really wash across her body and suck away back into the briny deep, holding her down for the moment, sucking her close to the rock. Just for the instant it comforted her, that the water was helping to anchor her to her rock.

It was some time before another wave reached so far, but when it came it destroyed her confidence, for it lifted her up for just an instant, and gave her that awful feeling of helplessness in the hands of the great cruel mighty ocean.

When it receded again she clutched at her rock and began to pray again.

"Oh God, please forgive me. Please make Grandmother know I am sorry. And please take me Home quick! I am so afraid!"

Was her mother out there in the storm calling to her to let her know she need not be afraid? She closed her eyes and tried to listen, and there came the old hymn just as she had sung it the night she died:

Other refuge have I none;
  Hangs my helpless soul on Thee;
Leave, ah! Leave me not alone,
  Still support and comfort me.
All my trust on Thee is stayed,
  All my help from Thee I bring;
Cover my defenceless head
  With the shadow of Thy wing.

It comforted her to listen. It helped her not to be so afraid when the next great wave lifted her higher than before, and almost washed her off the far edge of the rock into the sea. She was surprised when it ebbed away and left her still on the firm stone. She gathered strength to creep back as far to the inner edge as possible without rolling off. But she knew that only another wave or two and she would go.

She was deadly weary. If she could only go to sleep and not know when the next wave came. If she only needn't feel that choking sensation of drowning. She had never been around water very much. The little creek near the Junction House was the only body of water for miles around. A great body of water filled her with a fearful terror, now that the sun and the blue sky were gone.

It seemed very dark. The thunder was not so loud, and there was only a shiver of lightning now and then as if its strength had been nearly spent. The wildness of the clouds was passing over too, but it meant nothing to her any more. The cold and the terror and the weariness had her indomitable young spirit almost quenched.

It was nearly time for that last wave. She would be at Home forever. Christ had said it: "He that believeth" and she believed. "He that believeth *hath* everlasting life and *shall not* come into condemnation, but *is passed* from death unto life!" The little pink book that Grandmother had given her Sunday had explained all that. And she believed. Yes, she believed. It was all right.

There! There was the roar of the oncoming wave. This would end the agony. Was that a voice she heard high above? Was that an arm about her? What was that verse her mother used to say: "Underneath are the everlasting arms." Ah, God must have sent an angel to help her through this last wave. He wouldn't of course have come Himself, just to help a little lost girl all alone. But it was good to be held. Perhaps she was only dreaming or delirious, but there stood the wave towering up far above her. There seemed to be a light behind it. Perhaps that was the glory from Heaven's gate.

Now the wave was coming downward.

It fell with drenching drowning power, and the light went out as she went under gasping. This was the end!

15

WHEN Grandmother came up from the cellar where she had been inspecting a leaking water pipe she looked around for Sheila and could not find her. Then she called Jacqueline but was answered after long waiting and several calls, by a smothered:

"What is it?" from the yellow guest room.

"Do you know where Sheila is?" asked Grandmother.

By this time the door of the yellow room was open a crack and a petulant voice answered:

"Mercy no! How should I know where that little prodigy is? We don't inhabit the same atmosphere."

Grandmother went out into the garden and looked about everywhere, calling softly. There were not so many places in the garden to hide unless one stooped down behind the lilies, or crept between the hollyhocks and the garden wall, or under the rose trellis. Grandmother looked in all these places but found no trace of Sheila.

"That's queer," she said to herself, and went out the wicket gate and walked down beside the garden wall a few steps until she could look all up and down the beach, for she thought surely she must have gone to walk beside the sea.

But there was no one in sight up or down the beach. Grandmother peered each way, and then hurried back into the house and looked the first floor over thoroughly again, even calling to Janet who was still down cellar wiping up the floor and placing buckets to catch the drip till the plumber came.

"No ma'am, I ain't seen her," said Janet, "but I thought I heard her go up to her room when I come up that time ta get the mop."

Grandmother mounted the stairs and tapped at Sheila's closed door, but no answer came. Then she turned the knob and went in, but Sheila was not there. How strange! Where could the child be?

The closet door was open a crack and a blue morning dress hung on the hook of the door. Grandmother stopped startled. Wasn't that the dress Sheila had worn to breakfast?

She swung the closet door open. Yes, it surely was. Why had she changed her dress so soon? She wouldn't have put on her new bathing suit and gone into the water alone would she? Perhaps she wanted to get used to it when no one was about. But that was not safe. She oughtn't to have gone in the first time alone, when she was quite unused to an undertow and didn't know how to swim.

Grandmother cast a hasty glance from the window but saw no one down by the waves. Mercy! Suppose she had gone down where the quicksand was and got out beyond her depth before she realized!

Grandmother hurried downstairs again and out the door, though the wicket gate and out upon the sand again, walking briskly down toward the water, not an easy walk for an old lady when she was excited.

Suddenly she realized how futile it was for her to go out there. What could she do if Sheila was in trouble? She would call Jacqueline. She was a fine swimmer, a regular fish in the water.

She hurried back and called Jacqueline.

That young woman appeared with her face covered with cold cream.

"I'm taking a facial," she announced uncompromisingly. "I couldn't think of going into the water now. Besides I have a date later in the morning. I'm going horseback riding with Malcolm Galbraith."

"With *Malcolm!*" said Grandmother in dismay. "Isn't Betty going too?"

"Mercy no, I hope not," said Jacqueline, "she rides like a cow."

"But he is a married man, Jacqueline. You shouldn't go off riding with him."

Jacqueline laughed a merry little trill.

"Oh, Aunt Myra! You are too quaint for words! Did they really stop for things like that when you were a girl?"

"Well, you'll have to take your cousin Sheila with you, anyway," said Grandmother with her head high and a dangerous look in her yes. "I'll telephone to the stables at the village for a horse for her."

"Indeed you'll do nothing of the kind!" shouted Jacqueline. "I don't want that little spitfire along with me. If you try to send her I'll see that she has a mighty uncomfortable time of it."

"Jacqueline, what have you been doing to your cousin? Where is she?" asked Grandmother in sudden new alarm. "Have you been rude to her?"

"Dear me!" said Jacqueline, "how should I know what was counted rude a century ago? If you mean is Sheila sore at me, yes, I surmise she is. The trouble with her is she wants all the attention herself and she resents my being here. She as much as told me she had first rights in Angus Galbraith. She's a little cat, Aunt Myra, and you'll find it out pretty soon."

"Jacqueline, that is not true! Your cousin never said such a thing! What have you done with her?"

"I?" laughed Jacqueline slapping another gob of cream on her face. "Far be it from me to try to do anything with her.

If you mean where is she, I haven't the slightest idea, and I certainly am not going out to comb the sea and find her. If she hasn't enough sense to stay out of the water let her drown. It's not up to me!" and Jacqueline went into her room slamming the door and turning the key noisily in the lock.

Grandmother regarded the shut door sternly for a moment and then swung around and went to the telephone, calling long distance and shortly getting her eldest son on the wire.

"Maxwell, Jacqueline is up here and is making a lot of worry for me. I wish you would come up and do something about it. You always could manage her. If you don't want to do it yourself hunt up her father and make him do it. I've got my hands full, and something's got to be done."

"Jacqueline!" said the uncle, thoughtfully. "Why I thought she was up in Canada or the mountains or somewhere."

"She was but she came down here to cultivate your friend from London."

"Oh, so that's how the land lies. Well, look here Mother, what's this I hear about another granddaughter of yours being up there? Is that so?"

"Certainly," said Grandmother in her most imperial tone. "Your brother Andrew's daughter, Sheila, is here. She came in answer to my invitation."

"H'm! Well, that's probably the matter with Jacqueline. She's jealous, isn't she? And I don't know as I blame her, having to compete with a girl of that type!"

"What type did you say, Maxwell?" asked his mother severely.

"Well, you know better than I," hedged the son uncomfortably. "Certainly she can't be much, coming from stock like that, and brought up in the wilderness."

"Stock like what, Maxwell?"

"Why, really, Mother, you know yourself her mother was—"

"What *was* her mother, Maxwell? Did you ever take the trouble to find out?"

"All I know is what my renegade brother wrote about her. She sang in a saloon or something, didn't she?"

"I think you had better come and find out, Maxwell," said his mother in the tone in which she used to command him to come into the house when he had been swimming without permission. "All I have to say is that we have made a very grievous mistake in our judgment."

"But Mother are you sure she isn't putting something over on you?"

"That will be all that is necessary, Maxwell, along that line. Am I in the habit of having the wool pulled over my eyes?"

"But how do you know that this girl is my brother's child? Perhaps she's an impostor."

"Are you coming up, Maxwell, or will I have to send for Jacqueline's father?"

"Well, I'll try to get up within the course of the week if possible. This is a bad time for me, Mother."

"Yes, it's a bad time for me too, Maxwell. Good bye."

Grandmother hung up and looked at her wit's end. She stood a moment looking into space. There wasn't anybody on earth to whom she could turn for immediate help in the problem of the hour. She must look to heaven.

So Grandmother went into her own room, quietly locked the door on the world, and knelt down by her bedside, laying her troubles before the Lord.

A few minutes later she came forth from her interview with the Most High God with a less troubled brow, and in her eyes peace.

She walked straight to Sheila's room and began a thorough inspection. Carefully she went over every dress in Sheila's closet, trying to determine what the girl had on. The bathing suit was the first anxiety, but she found it at once hanging gaily, flying its bright colors on a hanger where the eye could not fail to see it at first glance. It was smooth and new, and had not yet been wet. That settled the worry about the ocean.

"My Father I thank Thee!" murmured Grandmother with a sigh of relief.

Then she went over the dresses, both those hanging up in the closet, and those that were still folded away in the trunk. As far as she could see there was not one missing. She sat down in the little rocking chair and tried to think over the things they had bought in Boston, but not one seemed to be missing of the lot. What could Sheila have on? How very strange it was! Of course it must be something that she had forgotten.

She got up and went toward the window to see if she was yet in sight, for the clock hands pointed to twelve now. It was very strange that she had not yet returned. Could it be that Jacqueline had played some joke and had her imprisoned in a closet somewhere? If that should turn out to be the case certainly something strenuous ought to be done about it. That girl was the limit.

Grandmother walked firmly over toward the window almost confident that she was going to see Sheila coming down the beach. Probably she had been off exploring by herself. Probably Jacqueline had hurt her feelings and she had gone away awhile to get calm, but she would know by the height of the sun that it was almost lunch time. Surely she would soon be back.

But the sea glowed brightly in the summer sunshine and no Sheila nor anybody else came walking down the beach.

Grandmother wondered about the horseback ride. More time had elapsed than she had realized while she looked over the new dresses and folded them back in their places. Had Jacqueline gone in spite of what she had said? Oh, how mistaken her poor sister had been to bring up the naughty beauty to have her own way so completely! She must go and look her up at once. And perhaps Sheila had come in by this time, quietly, and would be downstairs reading. How the child loved books! How wonderful that she should have had that taste, out there in the wilds! It had of course made all the difference in the world in her culture.

But as Grandmother passed the bureau on her way back to the door her eye was caught by a written paper standing up against the pincushion, and her heart contracted anxiously. What was this?

She took the paper in fingers that began to tremble, for she really was getting old and there had been a great deal of unusual excitement the last few days. It seemed almost more than she could bear if there was to be more of it.

She sat down weakly in the rocking chair, and with the tears coursing down her cheeks, read the letter twice over, and then she put her face down into the scribbled note and cried outright.

With the letter still in her hand she knelt again presently and brought her trouble to God. Then after a few minutes she arose and went down to the telephone in the living room.

Nobody was about. Janet could be heard ironing in the kitchen, singing in nasal twang at the top of her lungs:

> *To the old rugged cross,*
> *I will ever be true.*

There were no sounds of footsteps up in the yellow room. Probably Jacqueline had gone out horseback riding in spite of what she had said. The coast was clear with no listeners. She did not want even Janet listening to her conversation, so she took the telephone into its tiny booth and began.

She first called up the station in the village, and got the station agent. There was one morning train at half past ten. Sheila would have had time to catch that if she had walked fast.

"Is that Mr. Cather? Well, this is Mrs. Ainslee, Mr. Cather. I am calling up to know whether my granddaugther reached there in time to catch the morning train? Yes, she was walking. You say she did not? You are *sure?* Well, thank you. No, she probably will have turned back if she discovered how late she was. No, I don't suppose she will wait for the afternoon train, it would be so late, but of course if you see her, will you kindly tell her to call me up before she gets on the train? Thank you."

Grandmother was trembling from head to foot when she hung up the receiver and tried to steady her lips and her hands.

She pressed her cold fingers on her closed eyes and took a deep breath before she began again. She tried to keep the tremble out of her voice as she called up The Cliffs.

It was old Mrs. Galbraith who answered her call.

"Oh, is it you, Marget," she said, trying to sound entirely natural, "How are you this morning? Yes, isn't it a lovely day? But it seemed to me when I looked out just now that it was clouding up. Yes, we have had lovely weather. Wonderful for so early in the season. But Marget, I was calling to speak to young Mr. Angus, your nephew. Is he about, I wonder?"

The voice at the other end of the wire was pleasant and reassuring. Grandmother felt reasonably sure she had not revealed her excitement in her voice.

"Why, no, Myra, not just now. He went off in his plane a little while ago. He had an errand somewhere. But he said he would probably be back about two o'clock if he wasn't detained. He got started good and early. I'm sure he'll be back soon. The young people went down to take a swim this morning early, and then he came right back and flew away. Aren't the rest of them down at your house? They went riding. Malcolm and Betty, and Rose Galway, a girl that's visiting Betty. I believe they took an extra horse down for some girl at your house. Your niece was it? Was that your sister Annie's child? How I'd love to see her. I suppose she's just as sweet and unspoiled as Annie was? What's that? Your *Grand-*

niece? Now Myra, don't tell me Annie's child has been married long enough to have a grown up daughter! Why — was she older than you? Oh, yes, I remember. Well we *are* growing old, aren't we Myra? And now about Angus. I'm sure he'll be home soon. Shall I tell him to call you up as soon as he gets in? All right, Myra. I'll tell him. No, no trouble at all. Come up pretty soon and bring your niece. I mean your grand-niece. Good bye."

Grandmother turned from the telephone with a stricken face and went to the window. She was looking out toward the sea but she was not seeing anything. Her eyes were full of anxious tears, and her heart was talking with God.

"Father, take care of my little girl. I don't know anyone to ask but Angus. If he is the one to help won't you please send him soon before she gets too far away to find?"

She wiped the tears away and stook looking out to sea.

Suddenly she became aware of dark clouds on the horizon, crowding up together and hastening in to shore. Why! The day had been so bright just now. Could it be that a storm was coming up?

And what would become of Sheila if there was a storm? Surely with five dollars she would be able to take shelter somewhere, but if she was in a house it would be impossible to locate her. She had so hoped that Angus would be willing to fly a few miles up the coast and see if he could see any trace of her. She could not have wandered far by this time if she went on foot. And surely she would not dare spend much for carfare if she had but five dollars.

Her heart sank as she watched the clouds gathering, and she began to pray again. It seemed somehow that she was anguishing for her lost baby Andrew as she prayed. Sheila was all she had left of Andrew now. And Sheila was gone!

"Oh, God, my Father. I can't do a thing to find her. Won't you do something please?"

Then the telephone rang sharply close beside her and she rushed to take down the receiver.

"This is Angus Galbraith, Mrs. Ainslee," said a clear strong voice. "Is there anything I can do for you?"

"Oh," said Grandmother in that pleading wistful tone with which she had been talking to God. "Oh, I wonder if you could? I'm afraid not, now a storm is coming up, and it wouldn't be safe for you."

"I'm at your service, Mrs. Ainslee, whether it's safe or not. What can I do?"

"Perhaps you'll think it silly, what I was going to ask," said the old lady quite trembling now, and afraid to suggest her idea, "but I didn't know who else to ask to help me. You see my granddaughter, Sheila, has gone away, and I don't know where to find her. I thought perhaps she might have gone up the beach, and you would be willing to fly along and see if you see anything of her. But I'm afraid now this storm will make it dangerous for you, and besides she may have taken shelter somewhere."

There was a sob in Grandmother's voice now; and there was something alarmed and electric in the voice that answered her sharply.

"You mean Sheila?" he said. "Little Sheila? Where was she going?"

"Oh, that's what I don't know!" The Grandmother's voice was choked with trouble. "I telephoned the station but she didn't take either train."

"When did she leave?" The tone was crisp and business-like.

"A little while after breakfast," said Grandmother. "I didn't miss her until after ten o'clock, and then I thought nothing of it at first. But later I found a note saying—well—saying something had happened, between her and my grand-niece I think, and she seemed to think she ought not to stay here."

"There! Mother!" the young man's voice was tender. "You needn't stop to tell me anything more now. We won't waste time on that. I think I understand. You just rest and I'll go out and find her. Of course I'll find her. And I'll bring her back to you without fail. You needn't worry!"

"Oh, you are good—!"

"No, don't waste time on that. Just don't you worry. I'll bring her straight back to you, no matter where she is. And I'll try to keep you posted if I don't find her immediately. What color of dress was she wearing?"

"That's it," said Grandmother, "I can't find anything missing except an old worn dress she had on when she came. Dark blue, and a little old felt hat. But I'm not sure. I thought those had been thrown away."

"I see. Never mind, I'll know her anywhere. She is lovely! Now, go and rest. I'll get back as soon as I can."

"But—the storm—!" said Grandmother timorously.

Did she hear a sound of thunder?

"The storm has nothing to do with it. I'll ride ahead of the storm. I'll ride above it if necessary. My machine is all ready to leave at once. I just got back. Good bye. Keep good cheer!"

He had hung up, and Grandmother in a daze of hope hung up too.

16

THERE was a distinct sound of thunder in the sky. There was a lurid look about the atmosphere. There was the sound of pounding horses' feet outside on the beach, coming up to the wicket gate. A chime of laughing voices.

Grandmother looked out and saw Malcolm Galbraith and Jacqueline riding up to the gate, and far down the beach, galloping fast, came the other two women, Betty and Rose, at a breakneck speed. That had probably been the way they had been riding all the morning one couple far ahead of the other two! The hussy!

Grandmother watched from the cover of the curtain, for the instant angry enough to forget her pain and anxiety.

She saw Malcolm spring from his steed and help Jacqueline to dismount, saw their hands linger together longer than was necessary. The hussy!

Then as the other two horses came nearer with pounding feet, she saw Malcolm and Jacqueline rush laughing to the gay red car that stood outside the wall, and begin to pull up the top and fasten on its curtains.

Then the first raindrops began to fall and Malcolm mounted hurriedly, joined his wife and her guest and they went clattering off up the beach in a great hurry. Jacqueline ran into the house, her head bent to the gale that had begun to blow.

Grandmother suddenly slipped upstairs on feet as silent and fleet as if she had been several decades younger, and was lying peacefully on her bed taking a nap when Janet tapped at the door, to say that lunch was ready.

"I think if you'll just bring up a cup of tea and a bit of toast, Janet, I'll not come down just now. I've a bit of a headache and I'll be better for a rest. You can ask Miss Lammorelle how soon she will be ready for her lunch, but Miss Sheila is away. She may be back in time for dinner to-night, I'm not sure. I'll let you know later about setting the table."

In great dismay and trepidation Janet went downstairs.

Janet was too sharp a maiden to think for a minute that Grandmother's calm statement comprised the whole of the situation, and her prejudices told her that Miss Lammorelle was somehow at the bottom of all the trouble. But she went obediently downstairs and prepared a tray of the nicest things she could get together to tempt the appetite of the adored old lady.

Then she tapped at the door of her sworn enemy and asked her in alien tones when she would be ready to eat her lunch.

"Why, you can just bring me something up here, Janet," said Jacqueline, "I'm feeling a little tired and I want to lie down after my bath. Make me half a dozen of those rolled caviar sandwiches, a nice fruit cup, some aspic jelly and some black coffee. Is there any of that blueberry pie left from last night? And some of the jelly roll too. I think that will do. Don't forget to put plenty of butter on the sandwiches."

Janet went down stairs and cut some thick slices of bread, warmed up a saucer of kidney stew, made a cup of tea, found some dry sponge cake left over from last week, cut a small helping of butter, and put an orange on the tray whole. She carried it up and set it down on the floor at Jacqueline's door, tapped on the door, said "Here's yer lunch," and fled.

When Jacqueline finally got up out of her silken luxury and opened the door, calling in indignation for the handmaid to obey her commands, Janet was down cellar picking up the laundry and couldn't hear.

Meantime the storm was well under way, tearing up the coast at many miles an hour, and Grandmother, having swallowed her scalding hot tea, was lying down with closed eyes praying and trying to trust and keep from trembling.

Out into the teeth of the gale rode Angus Galbraith, silver wings flashing against leaden sky, copper lights threatening on every side, wild wind and clouds in a tumult together.

Angus Galbraith had ridden into many skies as threatening, under circumstances demanding endurance and courage, and involving sometimes great sums of money, but never had he ridden with sterner face, and heart more anxious. Something in Grandmother's tone had gripped his heart. Something in the vision of a frail little girl wandering alone upon a wind swept beach where he knew there were sinking sands and treacherous tides that shut off alluring points of land and often engulfed them completely, spurred him anxiously on. He wondered if the dear old lady knew all these possibilities.

Just that morning at the breakfast table they had talked about the time three children got caught off Loman's Point and nearly drowned before they were rescued; how a mother and baby asleep in the cove had floated out to sea before they were rescued; men brought their dead bodies back to their desolated home. There had been mention of other cases and Angus urged his plane low in the teeth of the wind and watched every inch of the beach as he flew. His heart was beating wildly as if he were down there on the beach running, instead of up in the sky flying.

He kept thinking of the lovely girl with the big blue eyes and the way she had looked last night in the fluffy pink dress. Little things she had said, little lights in her face, the quaint turn of a phrase. Such clean, clear eyes, such strong sweet lips.

What did the horrible fear that clutched at his heart mean? Suppose she were gone, utterly, dropped out of their sight and knowledge forever, either in the sea, or in the great wide world, what was it going to be to him, more than if any other girl he had met casually once or twice had been lost? Oh, common humanity would demand a decent interest in anyone whose fate was unknown, but why did he have this ghastly feeling of personal loss and personal fright? Did it mean that he, whom everyone supposed to be thoroughly hardened to all womankind had at last found a face that could move him?

On up the coast he went, farther and farther, until he knew he was far beyond any point she could have reached in a day's journey on foot.

Sometimes the storm was so heavy, the sky so black that it was impossible to see the earth. Sometimes he had to rise far above it, but he combed the coast desperately whenever the weather conditions made it possible.

The storm had increased so rapidly as he went that he began to see he was accomplishing nothing at present, and might better get back and see what could be done from the earth.

All the terrible things that might have happened to her began to come in vision to him, and he forgot that he was going through dangers himself in thinking of the frail girl, perhaps exposed to this awful storm.

As he neared the cliffs the storm seemed somewhat to have abated, as far as the sky was concerned, and he could better see the coast.

He began to identify the landmarks with which he had become more or less familiar during his few days stay, and his various flying trips. He wondered if it might be well to go on down the coast. Why had he taken it for granted that she would have walked north? Of course her grandmother had telephoned the station, and it was likely she would have been seen by someone and reported if she took the way south. Yet perhaps he had better go a few miles down and see.

Then he swept in sight of the cliffs upon which the Galbraith house was built, standing out against the wild sky like a castle on the crags of Scotland.

And there, just below it, was the cove, and the tall rocks standing like sentinels in front of it. He thought of the cove. Could she have taken refuge there and got caught? But no, she would long ago have been swept out to sea if that were the case, and no girl in her senses need get caught there in broad daylight, for when the water first began to come in she could surely wade out and get past the little depression in the land that always filled up first when the tide turned.

Then he noticed that all the tall sentinel rocks were out of sight under water except one, the farthest out to sea, and the tallest. He remembered hearing them say that it was only when the sea was tossed by a most terrific storm that that rock was under water. Yet as he came closer he saw that only the dark top was barely showing. This must have been a storm of more than usual violence, for as he was looking a great wave engulfed and completely hid the top of the rock for a moment. And then he saw a dark object. Was that somebody on the rock or only a peculiar formation? He could not be sure but as he got nearer he looked closely, yet he could not see it move. Perhaps it was just the rock. But his impression had been that that tallest rock was one smooth surface on the top. He had climbed up there this very morning when in bathing, just to look off at the majesty of the water.

But now as he swept over the rock he saw a human face, white and still, lying there almost as if it floated on the sea. What could he do? The tide was high. There was little beach to land on and if he waited to take the plane to the landing field above the cliff by the house and climb down the rocky steps he might be too late. On a little farther down around the curve of the rocks there was still a stretch of beach visible. He did not hesitate. He swept down with a terrific roar of his engine that could be heard even above the roar of the sea, and made a hurried landing in a most unfavorable spot. Struggling against all odds, his mind on that white face out there in the sea, he did not think of peril to himself or his plane. He only knew that he had landed somehow, and struggled out into the sand, which was deep and hard to run in. But he ran, his heart pumping like a great engine. Flinging his helmet and as many other garments as he could tear from himself as he ran, he plunged down the beach toward the rocks.

The noise of his landing had brought out the Galbraiths from The Cliffs, and had brought Grandmother to her window, and Jacqueline to hers.

His people shouted to know what was the matter, but he could not stop to answer. He tore on up the beach to the cove, and the family on the cliff turned their eyes toward the rock and saw the girl lying there in peril.

For once Malcolm came out of his merry self and rushed to help. He called to his mother to telephone for the life guard up the coast toward the village. He brought out life preservers and ropes and even pushed the lifeboat down the sand.

His mother went in to answer the telephone which was wildly ringing, and found Grandmother wanting to know if something had happened to Angus' plane, and if he was hurt.

"There is someone out on the big rock, Myra," answered Mrs. Galbraith. "Hang up please. I'm phoning for the life guards."

Mrs. Galbraith knew nothing of Sheila's being lost. Angus had gone out quietly to his plane when Grandmother telephone him. The people at The Cliffs had no idea that anyone they knew might be out there drowning. They were simply interested for common humanity's sake.

Jacqueline had been listening at the door when she heard Grandmother telephoning, and now she appeared in gay pajamas.

"What is it, Grandmother? Is someone hurt? I think I'll get in the car and run down the beach. I know the tide is high but there is room enough to get around the garden wall, and a hard road beyond that. I'm going!" Jacqueline danced excitedly toward the stairs.

"Go back and get on a bath robe or waterproof or something," ordered Grandmother severely. "If you haven't a raincoat of your own you'll find one of Jessica's in the hall closet under the stairs. *Don't go without it!* And *I'm* going with you. Get your car turned around and I'll be down at once. It's Sheila, I'm sure, out on the rocks. Maybe dead. I don't know. Take some blankets from the linen closet. Janet," she called in the same breath, "fill a hot-water bag quick and wrap it in a blanket."

Jacqueline paused for an instant with blanching cheeks as Grandmother spoke those awful words "Maybe dead," then she adjusted a demure little mask over her giddy face and danced on down to the hall closet. In view of the seriousness of the affair perhaps it would be as well not to rouse Aunt Myra too much by refusing to wear the raincoat. One could always drop it off opportunely and it looked as though one had sprung into action from an afternoon nap, to go this way. Jacqueline knew how to assume gravity when it suited her plans.

Janet filled two hot-water bottles and brought them in an incredibly short space of time, and as soon as Jacqueline had turned her car Grandmother was at the gate with blankets and restoratives, and they whirled away down the beach.

Janet watched them away thoughtfully, cannily. Then she hastened to the kitchen and put on plenty of hot water, prepared a tray, put a saucepan with a bit of soup left over from dinner last night on the back of the stove to heat, got out the coffee and tea, both, in case of sudden demand for either, and then with a quick, wild glance out the window to where the airplane and car were parked, she stole briskly up the stairs to the yellow guest-room now occupied by Jacqueline.

Once inside the room she gave a quick, comprehensive glance about, that took in every item in sight, and then went, with the agility and stealth of a cat, across the room and flung open the closet door.

A waft of strong perfume from Jacqueline's many colored garments met her nostrils, and she turned up a discriminating nose and said aloud, "Pah!" Then she drew a chair to the open doorway, and mounting it, carefully inspected the closet shelf in its farthest recesses.

"I thought so!" she told herself aloud, putting a triumphant hand back to the right hand corner, and pulling out two of Grandmother's best linen sheets crumpled into a tight little wad away back out of sight. They were rammed in tight and she had to pull to get them out, for whoever had placed them there had carefully put a heavy bag, weighted with shoes, in front of them.

As she gave the final pull, something small and hard fell down on the closet floor, and a still smaller object followed it, striking the door frame and dropping in two parts, one of which rolled out into the room and spun across the floor and under the bed.

In great astonishment Janet got down from her chair and crept under the bed after it, her heart beating wildly. Suppose it was something belonging to Miss Jacqueline. She would be very angry. Suppose they should suddenly return and find her, Janet, under the bed!

She clutched for the tiny yellow object and brought it out wonderingly. It was an old-fashioned wedding ring, worn thin, but with the marking still inside. Janet carried it to the window to read what it said. That ought to tell whose it was.

"Moira from Andrew."

There it was in fine little script, still clearly discernible with a date that seemed too long ago to Janet to bother with.

Wasn't Andrew the name of Mrs. Ainslee's son, the name of Miss Sheila's father? And Moira must have been Miss Sheila's mother, since it was a wedding ring. A dawning comprehension came into Janet's eyes. Then this was something belonging to Miss Sheila! She had come up in this interval of the absence of the guest to hunt the sheets that had been missing from the laundry, and which Jacqueline had said in her presence that she had put down the laundry chute. Here they were. And here perhaps was where the fantastic Jacqueline had hidden Sheila's missing things. What were they? Didn't she say something about a carved box? And letter? Well, if they were here she would get them before Jacqueline could return.

She gave a quick glance from the window and saw the red car still parked beside the airplane. She put the ring in her apron pocket under her clean handkerchief and dived into the closet again. There was a tiny cube of a white box, worn on the edges but lined with white velvet. That would be the ring box. But something else had fallen. She poked around on the floor under the trails of Jacqueline's evening dresses and her hand came upon a small object about the size of a pencil, made of tarnished metal. Was that the penholder that Sheila had spoken about?

She studied it curiously a moment and then new panic came upon her. She must find all the things before they got back! She ought to get more blankets hot too. There was no telling what had been happening out there. And they might be back any minute now.

She put the penholder in her pocket with the ring and climbed the chair again, pulling out the pillowcase now. Yes, there were more things behind there, and they evidently had been stuffed in a hurry, perhaps while they were being examined. Likely somebody came to the door and she had to get them out of sight quickly.

There was a package of letters tied with a faded blue ribbon. They looked as she brought them out to the light as if some of them had been pulled out and hastily stuffed back again. Back of the letters there was a wooden box. She could feel the carving on it before she pulled it out where she could see it. There were more papers in it. One on the top that looked like some kind of legal paper, with a border around it and two hands clasped under a wreath of orange blossoms. That was like her sister Allie's marriage certificate. And there under it was a yellowed envelope with a long curl of yellow baby hair showing under the flap. It had been carelessly handled for the hairs were loose and flying. Oh, Janet was sure she had found Miss Sheila's things all right enough. Her only care now was to be sure to get everything before Miss Jacqueline got back.

She got down and spread out the pillow-case carefully on the floor, and then bestowed everything she had found in it, adding those from her pocket to the collection. Then she went swiftly into Grandmother's room and got the flash light that always lay on her little bedside table. She climbed the chair once more and turned the light full on the closet shelf, and into every corner, making sure there was not another thing hidden there. Then she got down and turned the light on the closet floor again.

When she was satisfied that she had everything, she gathered the corners of the pillow-case carefully and carried it into Sheila's room, laid it in the bottom bureau drawer just as it was, and locked the drawer, carrying the key downstairs with her and hiding it inside the kitchen clock.

Janet gave a glance out the kitchen window and beheld a little group around the red car, and a body being carried in a tall man's arms. That probably meant that someone was drowned or hurt and might be brought home soon. She hurried to Grandmother's ample store closet for more blankets and set them heating before the open oven door. Three clean ammonia bottles she carefully filled with hot water, slowly, so they should not break, and wrapped them in pieces of old flannel that Grandmother always kept on hand in the linen closet. These she carried upstairs, and after another look out the window toward the cliffs she threw back the covers of Sheila's bed, laid the hot blankets within, put the hot bottles inside them, and covered them in. She wasn't sure of course that it was Miss Sheila they were bringing back, but it seemed to her it was mighty likely to be, so she was prepared.

Then she went downstairs and made a big pot of hot coffee and a big pot of tea. Janet always liked to be ready for emergencies.

17

WHEN Jacqueline drew up her car as near to the scene of action as she could get, though the sea had come roaring into the inlet and shut off the approach to the cove, there was a little knot of frantic people watching, while Angus battled with the angry waves.

Grandmother had brought her binoculars, and was standing up in the car looking off toward the rocks, a stern little gray figure with her cloak blowing about her and her white hair pulled loose from the felt hat she wore, floating off behind her.

Jacqueline sprang from the car and prepared to get busy. She dashed up to the group standing on the highest dune and began to chatter in a light high key, but found it didn't carry to the strained ears attuned to howling winds and roaring seas. One of their own family was out there fighting with storm and tide for a human life, and another one was coming down to help, to go out into the angry waves themselves, if need be. Jacqueline found that the limelight was not turned on herself just then.

Then down the hill, picking his way from crag to crag, not taking the winding steps, but choosing a quicker, more perilous path, came Malcolm Galbraith. He was attired only in the trunks of his bathing suit and his white flesh gleamed against the dark threatening of the sky behind him. Yet in his bearing was something Jacqueline had never seen there before. A high fine courage, born of the moment perhaps, and the necessity, yet a heritage from generations of noble braves behind him. Something of this Betty his wife must have seen in him when he wooed her perhaps. He was not in the least like the handsome idler, the careless playmate, that Jacqueline knew. Sheila, could she have seen him now would not have known him. This was not the gay trifler who had tried to toy with her hand and look deep into her eyes. The spirit and courage of all the brave Galbraiths through the centuries were in his look as he plunged down the cliff and took a hazardous dive from a frail promontory.

Even as he took that perilous drop into an angry sea, his cousin had reached the rock, had lifted the inert girl, and was slowly, painfully battling his way to shore with her against fearful odds, and Malcolm set himself to reach him with the life preserver whose rope was held by a man servant from The Cliffs.

For an instant Betty, his wife, felt a thrill to watch him. The next instant Jacqueline arrived and began to clap her hands prettily and cry "Bravo! Bravo! Wasn't that simply precious!" and Betty turned and looked at her with a bitter sneer on her lips, and walked back to the car where Grandmother stood.

Malcolm was still doing a brave thing, though no longer necessary, for it soon became evident that he could not reach Angus. He was having his own struggle to save himself, for the waves and the undertow were mighty. But Betty had lost her thrill and was no longer watching. Jacqueline might enjoy the exhibition to her heart's content.

All eyes were now on Angus as he struggled toward the shore. Again and again a rope was thrown to him, and again and again he almost made it, only to have it snatched from his grasp by an angry sea, like a strong man playing with a tiny human kitten.

Grandmother remained standing in the big red car, with the glasses to her eyes, and that set look on her face. Grandmother was still praying.

"Oh, God don't take her away from me now. I didn't know I was doing wrong. Forgive me. Give me a chance to make it up to her. Father! Oh, don't let her die now!"

Softly her lips moved in prayer, while her trembling hands continued to hold the binoculars to her eyes.

And up on the cliffs her old friend Marget Galbraith was praying too as she watched her dear gay, wayward son, and her beloved nephew in the raging sea. She was coming hurriedly, uncertainly down the steep rocky path from her house, following the others, bareheaded, her gray hair flying in the wind, the driving rain drenching her white anxious face. She drew a little gray knit shawl closer about her shoulders and tried to hurry faster as she came on, praying.

The sea had carried Angus and his burden farther down the shore line toward the car, which would have been a help, only that it also carried him farther out to sea, and the beach here was steeper for a landing place. Yet he was holding his own though the waves caught him and his burden and threw them about, pommelling them till it seemed to the little group of watchers that there was scarcely a shred of hope for them. They stood with blanched faces and bated breath, waiting for the outcome. Oh, would the coast guards never come? Could they do anything in such a sea even if they got here in time?

Malcolm was still trying to reach his cousin but it looked from shore as if the sea itself had determined to keep them apart. At every stroke he was caught and whirled about.

And Betty saw with quick surprise that Malcolm was not trying to save himself. The ancestral Galbraith courage was still working. Jacqueline saw and wondered. Jacqueline was white and frightened. Death seemed so near, so inevitable for all three. She hated thoughts of death. She began to wish she had never left her gay house party in the mountains and come questing after a man who wasn't in the least interested in her, a man who was out in the sea making a hero of himself to save another girl.

Then just as Grandmother was beginning to feel that her knees were going to crumple under her, Angus caught the rope flung out, and slowly, steadily, they pulled him toward the shore. While Malcolm battled his way shoreward alone till at last, almost as if the sea were tired of trifling, it flung them all angrily forth, where they reached a solid footing.

Angus staggered up to safety, and stood for an instant holding his burden and gasping for breath.

Sheila lay in his arms, limp and inert, her long dark hair streaming down like a wet garment, her sodden clothes clinging to her quiet form. Grandmother's heart gave a great shudder as she looked at her. Was she gone already? Had it been too late?

Then Angus started slowly toward them, staggering with weakness, and just an instant later Malcolm gained the shore and sprang forward to help.

Angus reached the car just as Betty arrived with blankets. She folded one about the unconscious girl, gathered up her dripping hair and wrung it out capably, tucking it out of the way inside the blanket.

Malcolm just behind seized another blanket with a great red border and threw it around his scantily attired cousin. Then he tried to take Sheila, but Angus would not give her up.

"Get into the car quick," said Grandmother, "You can't work over her here, and The Cliffs is too hard a climb. Somebody send the doctor down."

"I've already sent Rose up to tell him," said Betty quietly. "He'll likely be there as soon as you are."

"There are two hot-water bags," said Grandmother, "Betty, put one under her hands and the other at her feet.

Angus pull that blanket over your chest. We must drive fast. Now, Jacqueline, get us there as quick as possible."

Jacqueline, white lipped and silent, drove like Jehu across the sand, even down into the edge of the waves in one or two places where the dunes were impassable. Malcolm, looking stern and anxious, his white flesh gleaming in the rain, stood on the running-board, holding lightly to the top of the car, and Betty, whom no one had remembered, came running, panting far behind in the rain, getting her feet wet, stumbling and even falling, crying out with a sobbing breath. They were all sure that Sheila was dead.

Back at the cliff half way up the rocky climb, old Marget Galbraith halted to get her breath and mop the wet gray hair out of her eyes. She turned her sad eyes out to sea, looked at the cruel rocks and shuddered. Then she said aloud:

"Oh, my God I thank Thee!"

After that she climbed on up to her home to wait for news.

As soon as the car stopped Grandmother clambered down on her trembling limbs and hurried into the house.

"Get a fire on the hearth as soon as possible, Janet," she ordered as Janet threw open the door.

"I already done it, M's Ainslee," said Janet.

For Janet had taken up her stand at a second story back window and had seen the two men come up out of the sea, one bearing a limp burden. Her eyes were red with anticipatory tears, and wide with question, but she would not ask.

"The doctor will be here soon," said the mistress.

"He's on the upper road now, drivin' hard," said Janet, "I seen him from the window. I got hot blankets in her bed, and a flannelette ni'gown heatin'. I got hot coffee an' tea both, ef anybody wants it."

Grandmother swept her a grateful look and turned to hold open the door for they were bringing Sheila in, and the doctor's car was just driving up beside the wicket.

Jacqueline lingered a long time outside with her car, getting it parked just to suit her. She hoped that either Angus or Malcolm would come out to help her. Not that she needed help, but she was really afraid to go in. She was fearfully, desperately afraid of death. Was Sheila dead?

She didn't understand why one of the men didn't come out to see what had become of her. Men usually did that when she absented herself even briefly. But no one came, so she slowly, reluctantly, walked into the house.

They had taken Sheila upstairs. She couldn't tell whether she was alive or not. She was afraid to listen to find out. She could hear grave voices, and now and then Grandmother asking questions.

Janet came down pretty soon with something dark and wet in her hand. She dropped it into a big enamel pan and hurried back upstairs with trays of cups and the coffee pot. Janet didn't turn her head nor look at Jacqueline standing there at the window with her back to the room, gazing at that tearing, tossing sea, and shuddering at the thought of one having to die in the sea.

Jacqueline would sooner have cut her tongue out than ask Janet how Sheila was. She hoped that Janet had not seen her.

She began to wonder what had become of the rest of the Galbraith party? She went softly into the kitchen to look out the back window down the beach, and saw Betty coming, her head out to the gale. What had Betty come for? What a fool Betty was! Did she think she could hold her husband by standing around glowering?

Jacqueline turned away from the window and saw the wet thing that Janet had brought down and put in the pan. She shuddered and tried to turn away her gaze as if it had been a casket or something connected with death, but her eyes were held irresistibly upon it. Was that a hole—several holes—right in the front breadth of what looked like a skirt?

She stepped closer. It was blue serge and those were burned places in the goods!

Then slowly the color stole up into Jacqueline's selfish little face, and she turned sharply away.

Was that the dress she had put in the fire the day Sheila arrived? Was that what Sheila had worn away when she left? Was it all perhaps that she had of her own?

Jacqueline could scarcely conceive of such a state of things, but somehow she sensed the truth, and an unaccustomed surprising shame filled her. She did not know what to make of it. A feeling that she, Jacqueline Lammorelle, the favored one, the annointed cherub of her world, had been unworthy. It had never entered her head before that such a thing could be, and she would not accept the thought, but it stayed with her even against her will and made her more uncomfortable than even the thought of death could do.

She hurried away from the offensive sight of the pathetic little worn-out dress with the holes that she had put into it. But as she passed through the dining room she heard Betty's footsteps going up the stairs.

Not to be outdone, and to lose no chance of making Betty jealous, Jacqueline prodded herself to follow.

The two men, wrapped in togas of blankets were standing barefoot in the hall outside Sheila's door drinking cups of coffee that Janet was serving them, and conversing in grave tones. They seemed to Jacqueline ages removed from her, suddenly. They did not look up when she came, nor seem to notice her. She was almost upon them before she realized that this would be so. She looked blankly about her and there was nowhere for her to go but to follow Betty into Sheila's room, and she did not want to go to Sheila. Yet she had to.

Sheila was lying softly in the blankets, tucked to the chin, her long hair with seaweed twined among it was spread upon the pillow, getting itself into little wet rings on the ends, and about her brow.

The doctor was standing by her side feeling her pulse, and Grandmother was leaning over, administering a spoonful of something. Sheila's eyes were closed. But she could not be dead or they would not be feeding her, would they?

If she was dying perhaps she would have to stand there and see her die! Oh, that would be awful!

Yet somehow she couldn't go out there in the hall and stand with two men who did not see her. She had never experienced men before who did not see her.

Betty had gone over to the bedside and was already making herself useful, holding the medicine glass for Grandmother. But there was nothing for Jacqueline to do. Jacqueline was ornamental, not usually very useful.

Then, just as she stood there uncertainly in the doorway, trying to think what to do, Sheila opened her eyes and looked straight at her.

There was bewilderment at first in Sheila's eyes, and then a dawning eagerness. Startlingly she spoke:

"I'm sorry Jacqueline, that I slapped you!" she said in a weak little voice; yet every word was clear, "I—was afraid—God was—going to take me—before—I got a chance—to tell—you—how ashamed I am—that I got—so angry! Please—forgive—me!"

The voice was very sweet, though exceedingly weak. Jacqueline was quite sure that it could be heard out in the hall. She was quite conscious that the two grave voices had ceased speaking when Sheila uttered the first word. Jacqueline's face grew crimson up into the sheeny black of her hair. She stood dumb before the girl on the bed, unable to stir or speak, or even to show anything in her usually well controlled face except consternation. She was aware that two pairs of bare feet had moved in the hall and were standing in front of the door. She felt in her heart that two pairs of grave eyes were looking straight at her.

And now, for almost the first time in her remembrance, Jacqueline had nothing to say, and could not think of anything smart or funny wherewith to reply to this simple apology.

"Better not talk any more," said the doctor gently.

"Tell her you forgive her, Jacqueline," commanded Grandmother without turning her head, and Betty stepped back and gave her a significant questioning look, and a place to stand next the bed.

Jacqueline found herself stepping forward and stooping down over Sheila, then she said in a queer, strange voice that didn't seem to be hers at all:

"Oh, that's quite all right, dear, don't think of it again!"

She put in the "dear" as if it were a dose of medicine that had to be swallowed. She didn't know why she said that dear, she was sure it wasn't in her heart, not any feeling of dearness. Only just a desire to get this awful ordeal over, and to stand in well with the audience.

She had tried to put a gay little trill to her tone, to get back her perfect assurance that had always stood by her everywhere, but somehow something was wrong. It seemed as if some terrible Presence was in the room. She wondered if it could be that Death stood near, waiting for that ceremony to be over.

She looked apprehensively toward the doctor, standing there with his fingers on that little white wrist. Did he know? If she thought Sheila was about to die she would certainly scream and rush from the room. She couldn't stand it much longer.

She tried to think of something more to add to a gracious acceptance of an apology as between the dearest of friends, but words had failed her for once. Even thoughts had failed her. She felt as if she were standing before a judgement bar, and was more frightened than she had ever been in her life.

But she found to her amazement that nobody was thinking about her. Only that unseen Presence which might be Death, standing over there in the corner behind the doctor in the shadow, seemed to be aware of her, and it was with the utmost effort that she kept herself from shuddering.

She who had delighted to flaunt herself in startlingly brief array, to uncover her flesh to the world in the merest scrap of a bathing suit, or bare her back and breast to the public gaze with costly evening attire, felt suddenly that her little naked soul looked very small and mean and vulgar as she stood here in this quiet room with her one-time enemy lying there in a blanket forgiving her and trying to come alive again. And all because of a mean, untrue thing that she had said. She knew it was not true when she had said it. If she had not seen Moira Ainslee's marriage certificate she never would have thought of it.

If her own jealousy and selfishness could have but been visible and tangible she would have seen them lying then at her feet, slimy creatures of the earth, coiled low, and looking up at her with slithering, evil eyes of green.

She found presently that she could fade away out of the room without causing any notice at all.

The two blanketed men had finished their coffee and stood aloof, conversing again in serious tones. What were they waiting for? She dared not ask them. She slipped past them with downcast eyes, appropriate to a state of sorrow on account of a near relative's critical condition, and went back to her own room, closing and softly locking her door. No one noticed her going in the least. She had a strange feeling that she wanted to cry. And she never cried. Even when she was a small girl she had scorned to cry. She had always preferred to make somebody else do the crying.

She went and stood by her window, looking out toward the sea, tossing blackly, the window crossed and recrossed with wild, dashing rain. She reflected on what she had just done, just said, and was angry. Very angry to have been placed in such a situation.

The presence of Death was not in this room. She could take out her own natural feelings here and look them over, and she found herself furious.

What right had that girl, digged from whatever pit she was—as witness the dress she had worn to go away—to apologize to *her?* Apologies were out of date. They belonged to the Victorian age. No one apologized any more unless he wanted to make others feel that he was better than they. And that was the way that Sheila had taken to bring her into disrepute, to put her down and spit on her! To bring out the difference between them in the eyes of the household, and the neighbors.

Ah! Sheila was perhaps no Victorian after all. Perhaps she was wiser in her day and generation than anyone suspected. Perhaps she wasn't sick and weak at all. Perhaps she was just a fine actress, making them all believe that. Perhaps even that thing in the shadows that had so terrified her was not the presence of Death. Perhaps it was just the devil in Sheila laughing in his sleeve that she, Jacqueline, had had sweetly to accept an apology! If Sheila's mother had been a singer or an actress perhaps Sheila was just acting with a consummate skill.

She let her anger boil in thoughts like these, seething round till it resembled the far fury of the sea she was watching. And then her quick ear caught voices in the hall, a sound as of someone taking farewell. Was it the doctor?

She opened the door a crack.

Angus stood at the head of the stairs, wrapped well in his blanket.

"No, Malcolm," he was saying. "Don't bother to go after the car. I'll just run along this way. There'll be nobody to frighten with the sight of me but the fishes, and I doubt if they are out this afternoon. Yes, I'm perfectly fit for a run up the beach. Nonsense!"

Jacqueline preened herself and assumed her sweetest smile. She came upon the scene at once.

"Why, I'm taking you at once in my car of course," she said smiling into his eyes. "You wouldn't deprive me of driving the hero of the occasion back to his home would you?"

She saw with quick anger that Angus had stiffened as she approached, and now he answered her with cold formality.

"That's awfully kind, Miss Lammorelle, but it isn't in the least necessary for you to take your car out in the rain again.

It sounds to me as if it were raining harder than ever. I'll just run up the beach with my cousin."

"Oh, it's no trouble whatever," carolled Jacqueline, ignoring the cool tone. "I'm going out anyway. I just love this wild weather. And I have an errand at the station. Malcolm can go with us."

Suddenly Betty appeared in the doorway with lynx eyes on Jacqueline.

"We're all going," she said. "I'm not needed here so I'll go back with you, Malcolm."

"Oh, there's room for you all of course," said Jacqueline sweetly. "Angus and I'll sit in front and you and your husband can sit in back."

With what dignity he could summon in his present attire, Angus reluctantly consented to ride, but Jacqueline had scant satisfaction from his company. He let her do the talking, responding in monosyllables.

Jacqueline studied him furtively and wondered what he was thinking about. Then she started along another line.

"Do you know, I'm just thrilled to death to know you, Angus Galbraith! I think you're simply the greatest hero I ever knew. I think what you did this afternoon was wonderful, simply *wonderful!*"

"You're mistaken," said Angus with annoyance in his tone, "there was nothing wonderful about it. I've been out in worse storms simply for amusement."

"And to think you did all that for one who was practically a *stranger!*" carolled on Jacqueline, ignoring his protest.

"You're mistaken," said Angus, growing more annoyed every minute. "Your cousin and I are very good friends indeed!"

"Oh, *real*ly," said Jacqueline with a lifting of her slender brows. "How lovely for poor little Sheila! Really, it's too sweet of you to be so nice to her. Just now especially, when you know she has practically no friends at all, and when she's so frightfully distressed about her poor renegade father."

"I was not aware of her friendlessness," said Galbraith in a cold tone, "but that of course had nothing to do with it."

"Oh, no, of course, not with a man like you," Jacqueline gave him a sweet glance intended to be impressive, and quite aware that Betty was watching her, though she knew her voice could not be heard on the back seat in all this wind.

"But you know," went on Jacqueline, when Galbraith made no comment whatever, "just now is when she's so worried and so sort of alone, it certainly must be a great comfort to her."

"Why just now?" asked Galbraith almost haughtily. "Has she been passing through some sorrow?"

"Well, I don't know that you'd exactly call it sorrow. Of course her mother has just died I understand. But that can't have ever been such a loss from all I've been told. Of course you know we Ainslees have never really had anything to do with her. She's simply here because Aunt Myra felt sorry for her I suppose. I don't imagine she'll stay long."

"And why shouldn't the loss of her mother be a sorrow?" Galbraith's voice was stern.

"Well, you know she wasn't just of our class. I never did know just what she was, but something like a barmaid I think. It's really commendable of course what Sheila has made of herself in spite of such handicaps. It's so unfortunate when people of good blood get mixed up with the lower classes, don't you think? But you know her father was always doing wild things. I can remember when I was just a little girl hearing of his terrible escapades. And now it's so unfortunate, Sheila not knowing just where he is. At least I gathered that from some things she said to Aunt Myra."

"Do you think that Miss Ainslee would like to have us discussing her private affairs?" asked Galbraith.

"Oh, she'll never know. I just thought I ought to warn you not to say anything about her father. You might ask after him or something, and that might make her feel badly. I don't exactly know what he's been doing. Perhaps he's in hiding. Or he might even be serving time in prison. I'm not sure that Sheila even suspects that of course, but I know from the few words I overheard that there is some tragedy. I know they always told me Aunt Myra felt perfectly terrible about him. It's dreadful, don't you think, when a man born into a good family simply drags them down like that? I'm not sure but it was embezzlement. The family didn't talk much about it, you know."

"I see," said Galbraith. "Well, perhaps it would be better if we didn't talk about it either. Now, Miss Lammorrelle, if you'll just let me out here, I'd like to run down the beach there and see if I can locate some of my wardrobe that I broadcasted, before the tide carries it to China."

Jacqueline stopped her car sharply. She was not thin-skinned but there was that in the young man's tone that made her feel as if she had been slapped in the face again.

She watched him get out of the car and was about to start on again, vexed with herself and him, and already planning how she could get Malcolm into the front seat with herself, when Malcolm called out:

"Wait a minute, Jac, I'll go down with him and help. I remember where some of his things are I think: just you go on up with Betty and don't wait for us. We'll climb up the crags when we find his things." He swung open the back door and sprang out, casting his blanket from him, and running down the dunes toward the beach.

Jacqueline put her foot on the gas and sent her car shooting forward on the upper road, and scarcely spoke a word to her single remaining passenger on the way.

When Betty got out she asked her to come in, but Jacqueline declined brusquely.

"I've got to get my errand done and get back," she explained coldly, "I might be needed you know."

"Yes," said Betty almost sympathetically for once, "that was a close call, wasn't it? But you think she's all right now, don't you? She such a darling girl!"

"I'm sure I don't know," Jacqueline shrugged her shoulders indifferently. "What did she crawl out on that rock for anyway? That's what I'd like to know. She knew a storm was coming up. If you ask me I think it was merely a stage setting for a fine gesture, and she just didn't calculate the power of the tide and the storm."

"Oh, Jacqueline! What a terrible thing to say!" exclaimed Betty. "I'm sure she's not that kind of a girl at all!"

"Well, who can say?" shrugged Jacqueline, "I'm sure I hope not. One doesn't want one's family to do questionable things of course, no matter how much reason they have for it. But I must be hurrying back. I don't want dear Aunt Myra to be left there alone. Good bye. So kind of you to come down. I'm sure I hope you won't take cold from being wet. And just forget what I said, of course. It's all between you and me."

Having planted another seed of suspicion in the Galbraith family Jacqueline sped on her way, noting angrily the two manly figures already climbing the cliff. They had wasted little time in searching for the lost garments.

18

JACQUELINE'S car had no sooner started from the cottage to take the Galbraiths home than Janet came softly, breathlessly up the stairs and waited on tiptoe at Sheila's door, peeping softly in.

"M's Ainslee, could I speak ta ya a minit?" she asked in a whisper.

Sheila opened her eyes and smiled.

"Come in, Janet," she said in a weak little voice, "I'm all right now. I'm sorry I made so much trouble for you."

"Oh, Miss Sheila!" said Janet ecstatically, "I didn't know you was awake. Oh it wasn't no trouble at all. I just loved to fix your bed for ya."

"It was lovely and warm, Janet. Thank you. You were wonderful."

Janet grew crimson with pleasure.

"What was it you wanted, Janet?" asked Grandmother from her rocking chair, looking tired but happy, and just a bit trembly round her lips.

"It was just something I thought I'd tell ya, M's Ainslee," said Janet hesitating. "Somepin' I thought perhaps ya oughtta know before Miss Jacqueline comes back. I thought mebbe ya'd come out in the hall a minit so we wouldn't bother Miss Sheila."

"Yes?" said Grandmother putting her hands on the arms of the rocker to try and rise.

"Don't mind me, Janet," said Sheila earnestly. "Just tell Grandmother here. She's tired. She ought to sit still."

"Oh,—" said Janet in dismay. "Well, then mebbe it can wait a spell."

"No, Janet, just tell whatever it is. Miss Sheila is really feeling much better. Has anybody been here or anything gone wrong?"

"Oh, no, M's Ainslee, it's just about the laundry. Them sheets that Miss Jacqueline said she put in the wash you know?"

"Yes?" said Grandmother, on the alert at once.

"Well, it's only that she didn't done it."

"What?"

"She didn't put 'em in. When I looked over the laundry they wan't there. I looked all over but I couldn't find 'em."

"That's strange," said Grandmother puckering her brows together. "I'll have to ask her again what she did with them. She surely didn't burn them up, did she? My best linen sheets?"

"No ma'am, she didn't. I was watching her all the time. I knowed she couldn't have did that. But I knowed they must be somewhere, so when you all went down to the beach, after I got the water hot and the bed fixed, and the coffee doing, I went an' I found 'em."

"You found them? Where?"

"In her closet away back, stuffed in the corner of the shelf!"

"How strange!" said Grandmother. "What could have possessed her?"

"Yes," said Janet and turned as if she would go away. Then pausing at the door. "There was some other things there too."

"What other things?"

"Oh, some other things. They fell down, leastways some

of them fell down and then I went and got your flash light and I found some more. I got 'em all out, I'm sure. They didn't look like they belonged to her, and some of 'em was what Miss Sheila had said she missed, so I wrapped 'em all up in the pillar-case an' snuck 'em inta the bottom drawer of Miss Sheila's bureau, an' here's the key. I wanted you ta know afore she come back."

"Oh!" said Sheila, suddenly sitting up in bed, her eyes bright and the color coming into her pale cheeks. "What were they, Janet?"

"Oh, just a box, an' some old letters tied up, an' a little ole penholder, an' a ring. There was a ring in a little box, an' it fell out on the floor, that's how I knowed the rest was there. The penholder fell out too, and rolled under the door. But I got 'em all out. They're down there in that drawer in the pillar-case now, and I wanted you should know it, fer fear she'd come back an' find out an' make some kinda fuss about it."

"Oh, let me see them!" said Sheila eagerly.

"I'm afraid I hadn't oughtta told ya now so soon, Miss Sheila," said Janet anxiously.

"Oh, yes, it'll do her good!" said Grandmother cheerily, getting up with alacrity and going over to the bureau. "Get them out, Janet, and put the whole thing on the bed and we'll look them over. Then you can run down and start supper, and when you get things going bring up a cup of that broth we had for lunch that nobody ate because we were so worried about this child, — at least I mean nobody but Jacqueline!"

Janet, with fervent relief in her face, pulled out the bureau drawer where she had stowed the bulging pillow-case and brought it carefully to the bedside, spreading it out before Sheila.

"Oh, Grandmother! There it is!" she said eagerly, reaching for the old penholder, "and there is Mother's wedding ring!" she slipped it on her finger. "And there is Mother's dear

little concert dress!" She lifted a frail fragment of white tarla-
tan covered with silver spangles.

"My dear! Do you mean that is the case that contains the
valuable paper?"

"Oh, yes, at least Mother said it did. I never opened it. I
was somehow afraid."

Janet stole down to the kitchen, joy in her heart, a light
shining in her faithful eyes. Her heart beat high with happiness. She had found Miss Sheila's things, and she had foiled
that snake of a Jacqueline. She set about preparing the evening meal, triumph in her eyes. Maybe Miss Jacqueline
would never know what became of the things she had
purloined. Maybe she had only put them away for mean-
ness and would never even think of them again. But Janet
knew they were back with their owner again who loved
them, and she Janet had been smart enough to find them and
restore them. She walked as on winged feet and almost felt
a crown upon her head she was so happy to have served in
this way.

Meantime, upstairs, Grandmother suddenly became aware
of the bright excited eyes of the girl who had been through
so much to-day.

"Child, you must lie right down! I ought not to have let
Janet tell me about this before you. You shouldn't have had
this excitement to-night. It could have waited until to-
morrow."

"No, Grandmother, please don't take them away," said
Sheila earnestly, "I'll lie down. I truly will. And I'm so glad
to have my dear things back again! You can't think how glad
I am. Just leave them a few minutes till I count them over and
be sure they are all here."

"Well, just a minute then. Now, let me fold this dress
smoothly and put it away in the drawer. And these letters.
Are they yours or your mother's?"

"Oh, they are Mother's. From her sister in Ireland I think
most of them. A few from Father. There is a picture in one

of them of the castle in Ireland where my mother used to live when she was a little girl. I'll show it to you."

"Not to-night, child. We'll go over them all one at a time and you shall tell me all you will about them, but that will have to wait until another time. I've too recently got you back to run any risks with your health. Now, this pretty box. It is sandalwood, isn't it? I used to have a fan of sandalwood that I loved. See, I'll put the letters in the box. And the ring? Or do you want to wear it?"

Sheila took the ring off.

"I'll put it in its box to-night," she said. "Perhaps Jacqueline might notice it and ask questions. I wonder if she saw it? I wonder if the things were all in the box or pulled out?"

"Well, never mind now. We'll ask Janet all about that, later. We'll just put them away now out of sight and probably Jacqueline won't even know we have found them. Not right away anyway."

"But the penholder, Grandmother. Let us open that, please!"

Grandmother's hand was trembling as she held the little tarnished silver rod in her hand. She wanted terribly to open it at once, but Sheila should not be excited.

"Yes, please, Grandmother! I shall think about it all night if I can't find out what is in it. I've been wondering a great deal about it. I've been fancying all sorts of dreadful things; and out there on the rock I thought of it and worried a great deal that I had not opened it before. I don't want to run any more risks, Grandmother, I want to know what is in it!"

"Will you promise to put it right out of your head, no matter if it is really disturbing?"

"Yes, Grandmother, I have *you* now, and nothing can be quite so bad as it was when I was all alone."

"Well, then we'll open it," said Grandmother, her voice as eager as Sheila's.

They had quite a time unscrewing the case which had been closed so long that it had formed vertegris about the edges and grown fast. Grandmother tried, then Sheila tried and at last they pulled together. Then the top came off and a small yellowed paper fell out on the bed.

Sheila reached for it, unfolded it carefully with trembling fingers, and spread it out. Grandmother put on her spectacles and bent over to read.

It bore a date a little over four years before, and the ink was poor and fading, turned a bit brown. Neither was the paper of good quality. It was written in a bold, scrawling hand, and not easy to read but they made it out, their two heads close together.

> I, Bucknell Hasbrouck, do hereby swear and declare that Andrew Ainslee had nothing to do with the robbery of the Hazen Bank. He did not know of it until afterwards, and has never profited one cent by it, either at the time or afterwards. I write this statement in consideration of a favor he is about to do me, but not to be used until I give him permission when his service to me is ended.
>
> Signed,
> Bucknell W. Hasbrouck

Sheila read the paper over twice, puzzling to know what it could mean, but Grandmother was softly crying. She had caught but the one idea and that was enough for her. Her Andrew was not guilty!

"Why Grandmother, dear! You are crying!" said Sheila, suddenly looking up. "Isn't it good news? Why should you cry?"

"Yes, dear child, it is good news," said Grandmother, "but I'm just such an old fool that I can't help it."

"But what does it mean, Grandmother?"

"I'll have to think it out, child. I can't understand it all yet, nor why he did it. There must be something crooked behind it yet. But it means, if it is proved to be Buck's handwriting, that my Andrew can safely come home sometime I hope, if so be that he is still living to come. But even if he is dead, it means that his name can be cleared of a great crime. For it was not just robbery, Sheila, it was the killing of two good men who were guarding the bank. Oh, Sheila, my dear. I am so glad."

She stopped and kissed Sheila and with their arms about one another they seemed to come closer than ever before.

"And now, dear," said Grandmother, "this paper is very important. It should be guarded carefully. Would you like me to take it into my room and put it in my little safe? Your grandfather made me have a safe built in when we first built this cottage. It is in my room. Do you want me to put it away for you, or do you think you would rather keep it yourself? It is yours you know."

"You take it Grandmother. I know you will guard it better than I could possibly do. You are his mother!"

So Grandmother carried the precious paper away with her, after having put Sheila's things carefully under lock and key in her new trunk, and Sheila lay back and fell into a sweet sleep.

Rainbow Cottage was very quiet that night. The evening meal was eaten in detachments. Sheila was fed first, delicately, with strong nourishing food, and put to sleep again, though she declared she was fully able to get up.

Grandmother ate simply, and sparingly, at her table alone, hovered over by Janet, lovingly.

Jacqueline came in late after Janet had gone out for a little while to a small cottage up above the road where lived her sister, married to an officer of the state police. Grandmother called down to her that her supper was keeping hot on the back of the stove and she would have to serve herself as Grandmother was getting ready for bed.

Jacqueline sulkily ate her supper, banged out some popular modern music on the piano for a while, smoked numerous cigarettes, exulting in the fact that she was doing it in Aunt

Myra's sacred living room without rebuke, and finally went unhappily to bed. Things had not gone at all to please Jacqueline that day, and she was glad to have it over, hoping for better results on the morrow. It went terribly against the grain with Jacqueline to have a young man rebuke her, and that was what she knew Angus Galbraith had done. She tried to be very angry with him, to plan a fine revenge upon him, but somehow his attitude had only intrigued her, and she felt that she *must* find some way to conquer him. She lay awake scheming a campaign that would have done credit to one Lucifer, had he been sufficiently interested, and arose blithely in the morning to start a new line entirely.

Grandmother had not slept a great deal during the night and had spent the time laying plans for a new order of things.

The storm was still raging. A gray, forbidding ocean was lashing madly at a shrunken shore and dashing its futile fury against the rocks. Not a ship was in sight off shore. It seemed as one looked forth from Sheila's window that morning that the world was all water, awful green and brown and gray water. She shuddered and turned her eyes away from the sight. Perhaps some day she would be able to face a storm like that at sea again and call it majestic and beautiful. But she was not yet far enough from her awful experience upon the rock to even think of it calmly.

The only thing that kept her from losing her self-control when she remembered it all was the thought of that strong arm that had reached her, and lifted her, and held her during that last terrible wave.

She knew now that it had been Angus Galbraith's arm, but she had thought in her delirium of fright that it was the arm of the Lord God. And somehow now as she thought of it the two were blended in one, and she was glad it was so. For Angus Galbraith did not belong to her, except as a rescuer. He would probably never be in her life even as a friend, although she felt sure he would always be friendly. For had not Jacqueline made it plain that he belonged to her? And

Jacqueline would never share even the simplest kind of friendship with her, she was sure of that. She would make even bare acquaintance impossible.

But it was nice to think there was a strong, fine, courageous man in the world who was willing to brave and dare what he had done for her. So it was better that she should think of him as having been sent to her by the Lord God, and that there was nothing personal whatever about his act of courage.

But that first morning after her rescue she lay quietly thanking God for her safety, and trying to think of all the wonderful things she had to be glad for this morning.

The rain was still beating biasly across her window panes, and the storm might be dashing just as madly over that rock where she had lain a few short hours before; but she was here, safe and warm like a bird in her nest, with Grandmother's love about her, and the sure knowledge that Grandmother wanted her, and that her Lord God loved her and had sent Angus Galbraith to rescue her.

She hadn't told about what had driven her away. Grandmother hadn't asked her yet. She had said they would talk about all that later when Sheila was up and stronger, and they had time alone. But the touch of Grandmother's lips on hers, and the feel of Grandmother's little, warm, soft, rose-leaf hands as she took her face in them, the hug of her frail little arms about her, had all made her know that Grandmother loved her and wanted her, and that she must never, *never* run away again. Not even if she did a thousand things that she knew Grandmother wouldn't like. She belonged there. Grandmother would forgive her always. Ah, that made it so very sweet to try not to do things that Grandmother wouldn't like. So very happy a thing to try and do what would please Grandmother.

Why! That was like being saved, wasn't it? Once you were born again, you were in God's family and would never be turned out even if you sinned many times!

Look at Grandmother with her father! Her Andrew was always to her her baby, her dear son, though he had sinned many times, and wandered very far away from home.

And that was the way God did with His children. She was God's and Grandmother's and need not be afraid anymore anywhere.

Jacqueline slept late that morning and then happily took herself away in her red car to The Cliffs, seeking a more congenial atmosphere.

As soon as she was gone Grandmother went softly to the telephone and called up The Cliffs, asking for Angus.

She enquired most solicitously for his health after his Herculean struggle in the water yesterday, and then when he said he felt no ill effects, she asked him if he would do her the favor to come down and see her a few minutes alone; that she would like to ask his advice about a matter, and would he please not tell anyone where he was coming.

Angus came promptly and was closeted with Grandmother for a couple of hours in the little room off the living room.

Janet was sent up to Sheila to request her to remain in bed till lunch time and try to sleep, and there was no one to interrupt.

At noon Janet came up to tell Sheila that Grandmother would like her to dress and come downstairs for lunch if she felt able, and when Sheila came down, lovely in one of her little new knitted frocks of a soft blue with white trimming, she found Angus sitting by the fire in the living room and rising to draw up another chair for herself. It all seemed so pleasant and cosy. It was like the home her mother had told her about where Mother had lived when she was a girl.

While they talked for a few minutes and waited to be summoned to lunch Grandmother slipped away to the telephone and when she came back she wore a look of relief.

"It's all right," she nodded to the young man. "He'll be at home this afternoon and is very eager to see you."

"By the way," said Angus Galbraith to Sheila as they rose to go into the dining room. "I'm probably going west on a business trip. I wonder if there is anything that I can do for you? I may go quite near your former home."

He watched the girl as he spoke. She seemed to shrink into herself and to lose her brightness.

"Oh, no," she said sadly, "there's nothing there now any more but a grave. But thank you for thinking of it."

Grandmother looked at her thoughtfully as they sat down and said:

"That reminds me, Sheila, is your mother's grave marked? Had you put up a stone with her name, yet?"

"No, Grandmother, I couldn't—yet."

"Well, perhaps Mr. Galbraith would attend to that for us while he is out there. When it's so far away it's rather nice to have the stone placed at once. Don't you think so dear? You want just something very simple for the present, I should think?"

"That would be wonderful, Grandmother, but—"

"That's all right, child. No buts. You would do that for us, wouldn't you, Mr. Galbraith?"

"I should be most happy to serve in any way whatever," said the young man.

"Then that's settled. After lunch you can write out directions and whatever inscription you want put on it, and tell just how to find it. Now, Mr. Galbraith, will you ask the blessing?"

Sheila listened in wonder to the quiet words of reverent grace from the lips of the young man. To have a woman pray was nothing strange, but the men she had known did not speak to God except in curses. It gave her almost a feeling of awe toward him, and made her have a shy kinship with him also, that he knew her God well enough to speak to Him.

It was a beautiful hour they had together with no inharmonious element at all, for Jacqueline had not come back, having elected to stay at The Cliffs for lunch, hoping that Angus would return.

It was pleasant and cosy, Grandmother and the guest did most of the talking, Sheila quietly enjoying it all. They purposely did not mention the terrors of yesterday. All were glad just to enjoy the security and warmth and cosiness of the hearth and the nice luncheon and the feeling of home. The falling rain gave them a pleasant shut-in feeling.

But when they rose from the table and went into the other room by the fire Sheila looked up to Galbraith and said:

"I can't ever thank you for saving my life. I can't find words to tell you how wonderful it was to be lifted up out of that awfulness. It was so good that I just floated off into nothingness."

He looked down at her with the sweetest smile.

"Don't try to tell me now," he said gently. "Sometime a long time off when we have got beyond the terror of finding you there almost beyond aid, I would like to know all about it. But now just let's be very thankful to God that He let me come in time. And you don't know how glad I was that I was there!"

He reached down, took her hand and pressed it for just an instant, smiled, then put her in the nicest chair by the fire and went and sat down opposite her. Presently Grandmother came back and they talked again. Such a nice, pleasant time. Sheila felt so happy, happier than she had felt since her mother left her.

By and by they spoke again of the mother's grave. Sheila drew a rough diagram of it, and told how she had outlined it with stones that she had herself brought. She located it for him between two other graves with wooden crosses, so that he could not mistake it. And then she wrote her mother's name and the date of her birth and death.

Galbraith took the paper and read it and looked startled.

"Why, my mother knew a Moira McCleeve," he said wonderingly. "There were two sisters, Moira and Sheila. They lived in a beautiful castle over in Ireland. I wonder if they could be related to your family."

"How wonderful!" said Sheila with shing eyes, "My mother had a sister Sheila who died after they came to America. And they lived in a castle once. McCleeve Castle. I have a picture of it upstairs."

"Run and get it child," said Grandmother eagerly. "I haven't seen that yet."

So Sheila went up and brought down several little old photographs, faded and yellow with age, and an old daguerreotype of her mother's father and mother.

"Yes, that's the castle," said Galbraith looking at the picture. "I've been there myself. It's a beautiful place."

They looked a long time quietly at the sweet picture of the mother, Grandmother and her guest each secretly thinking how much Sheila resembled her. Then suddenly, while Angus still held the picture in his hand the sun shot out unexpectedly. It shone through the window by the fireplace, laid a bright ray upon the little old photograph and glorified it. It was almost startling the way it brought the picture out and made it seem real, and so much like Sheila!

Then they looked up in astonishment, realizing that it had been raining all the morning, raining but just a moment before.

"Why the storm is over!" said Galbraith. "Rejoice!"

"The sun is out!" said Grandmother, "and there'll be a rainbow! Look! There it is!"

They hurried to the window, Galbraith and Sheila side by side, and there it was, the great bow in the garden, as if its colors were sucked up from the drenched flowers at its foot. And it reached up and up in a majestic span till it arched the heaven, its other foot in the sea, the wild turbulent sea, which nevertheless had taken on new colors of gold and green and rose, colors that seemed to be drawn over the rainbow arch from the garden just behind the gray sea wall.

It was a wonderful sight and they stood silently and watched it for a moment. Then Galbraith quoted:

" 'And I saw a new heaven and a new earth.' I wonder! Will it be anything like that Mrs. Ainslee?"

" 'Eye hath not seen, nor ear heard, neither have entered into the heart of man, the things which God hath prepared for them that love Him,' " softly answered the old lady. "Nevertheless, I think sometimes He opens the window of heaven a crack and lets us get a glimpse of what it might be." Janet opened the door just then to ask Grandmother a question and Grandmother trotted away and left the two alone.

"It looks as if you could go out and touch it," breathed Sheila.

"Let's try it," said Galbraith catching her hand and leading her out.

They stood at the head of the garden walk, and there it was among the drenched lilies and roses, just a few rods away from them, yet so evanescent.

"I think this is your rainbow," said the man looking down at Sheila tenderly. "God is showing you that His bow of promise is always over you. He brought you out of the tempest into this."

He looked down at her and found her face quivering with emotion.

"I knew about this," she said slowly. "Grandmother had told me. And I thought about it when I first lay on that rock. I thought I would never see it. But here it is. I ought to have remembered that even if I had been drowned the Bible says there is a rainbow up around the throne."

"And here are you," said the young man gravely. "Oh, I'm glad God let me save you. I'm glad it is this rainbow you can be looking at for awhile, and not the other one yet, not till by and by. We—*wanted* you here."

His voice was very earnest, and it almost took Sheila's breath away.

"It is good of you to care," she said gravely. "I—think I'd

like you to know, now, before you go away, because I might not have another chance to tell you, how wonderful it was to have your arm come under me just before that last wave. I thought that I was drowning, and that it was God's arm, and yet it seemed like you too, as if God and you were all one."

His face took on a very tender look.

"May that always be true," he said reverently, "may myself always be put out so that God and I shall be as one, and that One *God!*"

Grandmother came down the garden path just then and they said no more, and very soon Galbraith took his leave, but Sheila went up to her room and knelt by her bed to pray, to give thanks for the beautiful day and the beautiful friend — even if she never saw him again on earth, still he would be a beautiful friend — and the beautiful rainbow of promise!

19

JACQUELINE came home late in the afternoon cross and disagreeable. She had spent the morning playing endless games of bridge with Betty's husband, while Betty sulked beside the fire reading a book, with eyes that held smouldering fires, and did not see the words she was reading.

Though Betty's invitation to lunch was most ungracious, Jacqueline had stayed because she hoped that Angus would return. No one seemed to know just where he was gone, nor when he would come back. She had turned on the victrola and danced for a long time with Betty's husband, Betty declining to dance. She said she was tired. Then when the storm had somewhat abated Jacqueline invited them out for a spin to watch the ocean, but Betty said she was afraid she was taking cold and didn't want to go out; so Jacqueline went out to ride with Betty's husband.

But now at last Betty's husband had palled somewhat upon her, and she upon him perhaps, and she dropped him at The Cliffs and came on to the cottage, thinking to call up later and beg Angus to come down and spend the evening. Then she would have him all to herself. She was planning to let Grandmother and Sheila understand that she wanted the living room for her own private use.

She put away her car and came in, finding Sheila alone in the living room curled up in a big chair by the reading lamp engrossed in a book.

"Oh, it's you, is it?" she greeted her cousin with a tone both indifferent and insolent.

Sheila looked up and smiled pleasantly.

"What kind of heroics are you staging for this evening?" Jacqueline asked disagreeably. "If you have any more tragedies up your sleeve I wish you'd give us warning. It's awfully upsetting to have a thing like that sprung on one all at once."

Sheila gave her a puzzled look, tried to smile. Was this a new style of kidding? Probably it was.

Jacqueline went upstairs to her room but presently came down again, dressed in a daring red evening frock with long jet earrings dangling down to her shoulders. And her lips matching her dress.

She walked straight over to Sheila and stuck out her hand under the light.

"How's that for a ring?" she said triumphantly.

Sheila with a hope that this was an overture of peace looked up from her book again and saw a magnificent diamond on the third finger of Jacqueline's left hand.

"Angus is a good picker of diamonds, don't you think?" asked Jacqueline. "I thought he came across in great shape. I just thought I'd mention it, since you didn't seem to pay attention to my claim on him."

Something in Sheila's heart seemed to click and go down way into the pit of her stomach, and then rise up and choke her.

She tried to summon a faint smile.

"Oh," she managed to say weakly, "I'm sorry you feel that way about me. I'm not trying to get any one's property away."

"I didn't say you were. I only gave you warning, see? And I don't want any more rescues at sea staged or anything else to attract his attention, understand? Now that we're really engaged perhaps you'll understand that you can't get away with any of that tragic stuff again."

Sheila's eyes grew wide and her indignation began to rise.

"I — don't know what you — mean!" she said with dignity.

"Oh, yes, you jolly well know what I mean. Just lay off my property that's all. We've been out all the afternoon together, and had a gorgeous time. Been miles up the coast looking at the sea." Jacqueline tossed her head triumphantly. "And this is the result!" she held the hand out and the great stone sparkled wickedly at Sheila.

But suddenly Sheila leaned back her head and laughed, a long, low, silvery laugh, without a bit of rancor in it.

Jacqueline whirled around angrily and watched her, and Sheila sobered at once.

"I shouldn't have done that," she said gravely, "excuse me please."

"I hate apologies!" said Jacqueline. "Nobody makes them except to try to make you think they are better than you are!" and she whirled out into the kitchen where Janet was preparing the evening meal.

"Janet, I'm starved," she declared. "Where are those little tarts you were making this morning?"

"Why they were all et up at lunch, Miss Jacqueline," said Janet with satisfaction in her tone.

"All of them? Why how could they be? You must be a perfect pig yourself if that's true. There was one apiece, for I counted them, and they were immense. I don't see how you could possibly eat more than one yourself unless you eat between meals."

"We had comp'ny ta lunch!" said Janet offendedly.

"Company?" said Jacqueline whirling around as if Janet were answerable to her for having had company without her permission. "What company did you have?"

"Mr. Angus Galbraith was here most all day. He jus' left," said Janet bitingly. "He et yours."

Jacqueline whirled around angrily and stormed back to visit her wrath on Sheila, but Sheila had quietly taken her book and fled to her own room to smother her laughter in her pillow, for she meant, when she should go down to dinner, to allow no vestige of amusement or triumph to show in her face.

Somehow she felt as if she wanted to kneel down and thank God that He had let her know the truth about the man who had been so kind to her. If he hadn't been here with her and Grandmother she might never have known that Jacqueline's tales were false. And she had to own that she wouldn't have liked that ring story to be true, because if he were engaged to Jacqueline she wouldn't have felt like even letting him fix Mother a little white stone in the wilderness to mark her grave. Was it wrong to want to keep a friend, just a friend and nothing more, for just a little while? She didn't want to take him away from anyone, nor to hold him utterly for herself, but she did want to know that the kind things he had said and the way his arm had held her had really been hers to remember.

When Jacqueline retired to the telephone booth a little later and called up The Cliffs, Betty answered the call. She asked for Angus.

"He has just gone away in his plane!" announced Betty bitingly. "I don't know when he is coming back. He said he had some business that might even take him to the west coast. In which case I don't suppose he'll be back before the end of summer."

Jacqueline tried to get some information about where he had gone, but Betty was adept in saying a great deal without telling anything, and Jacqueline finally retired baffled from the field.

The next morning she brought down her suitcase when she answered the call to breakfast.

"I'm leaving, Aunt Myra," she announced. "I had a Long Distance last night from the mountains and they want me to come back for a week-end. I may return here afterwards and I may not. It depends."

After breakfast Jacqueline slung her baggage into her car and with little ceremony of farewell drove away.

"Thank the Lord she's gone!" said Grandmother feverently and reverently.

And Betty Galbraith when she heard it echoed the same thought, if less reverently, still fully as fervently.

Betty came down that very afternoon to see Sheila.

Grandmother and Sheila were sitting in the garden, reading. Grandmother had several lovely comfortable garden chairs that were easily transported to a shady nook, and a little marble table that stayed out in the rain all summer, so it was easy to live in the garden on pleasant days.

Sheila had been reading aloud to Grandmother, in a little gray book, and stopping now and then to answer questions about her past and her mother and father. But she was deeply interested in the book they were reading. Its subject was the life of victory that is the right of every believer in Christ. Sheila had never heard anything like that. She gathered it all in hungrily.

"This is written so clearly," she said, "I do wish I had had some books like this to read to mother, she would have loved them."

"You have a very good mind, my dear," said Grandmother. "The man who wrote that book is a great scholar, as well as a deeply spiritual preacher. Angus Galbraith tells me he is a personal friend of his, in London."

"Wouldn't it be wonderful to know men like that!" said Sheila. "How I would like to ask him some questions."

"Perhaps you may some day, who knows?" said Grandmother.

And just then Betty Galbraith walked in at the wicket gate.

"You two look as if you were having the best time together!" sighed Betty jealously, almost hungrily.

"We are!" said Sheila. "We're reading about wonderful

things and talking them over. I'm just enjoying Grandmother so much!"

"Will I spoil it?" asked Betty sharply, looking from one to the other.

"Why no, of course not," said Grandmother.

"But you won't go on talking about the same things you were," said Betty, eyeing the little pamphlet in Sheila's lap, "You'll get up topics you think I'll enjoy."

"Why, no, we won't, child," said Grandmother, looking at her with kind eyes. "We'll go on talking the same as we were if you really think you'd enjoy it."

"That's it," said Betty. "Nobody seems to think I'd enjoy what they do. And mostly I don't. But I'm sure I'd like to learn to enjoy what's making you so happy!" she ended wistfully.

"Tell her, Sheila," said Grandmother. "It's new to you. Let's hear what you got out of it."

"Why," said Sheila smiling shyly, "I never realized before that all we can possibly need or want is in Jesus Christ. If we are restless He is our peace; if we are tempted, He is our strength; if we are unhappy, He is our joy — so that if we keep utterly depending on Him in every circumstance, life gets to be a glorious march of victory every day. Not that we'd ever get to be perfect on this earth, but in so far as we let Jesus Christ live our lives for us, victory would be the habitual thing, instead of defeat, as it is in most of us. And that kind of joyous life is what He meant us to have. It's one thing that His death and resurrection accomplished."

Betty stared.

"I didn't know anybody to-day believed that it accomplished anything," she said.

Sheila looked troubled.

"Oh, I do," she said. "And Grandmother does. My mother believed it. You can't even start to understand any of this unless you believe that Jesus Christ is your own personal Saviour. Grandmother, isn't that the place to start?"

"It surely is," said Grandmother. " 'Except a man be born again he cannot perceive the kingdom of God.' And you are born again if you believe that 'God so loved the world that He gave His only begotten Son, that whosoever believeth on Him should not perish but have everlasting life.' "

"I've heard that of course," said Betty, "but I didn't suppose anybody really took it for anything but a saying. Oh, maybe a few fanatics. But not people who lived normal lives. What is being born again, anyway? Why do we have to be born again? And how could one believe in something that didn't seem reasonable?"

"That's a lot of questions," said Grandmother. "I'm not sure that I can remember them all. But you see it's this way. The whole world were sinners. 'Dead in trespasses and sins' God says. That means spiritual death, which is separation from God. So you see, in order to have life, we must be born again from the dead, not of flesh and blood this time, as we came into our earthly families, but born of God's Spirit, by accepting the life He offers in His word. In that we are born into the family of God. That is simple enough. And as for believing, it isn't being intellectually convinced, you know. It is an act of the will. It is saying 'I will trust myself to this thing and let God prove it to me afterward!' For instance that night you were all here to supper I remember I offered you some shrimps and you said you had never tasted them. I told you they were delicious, and you tasted them and found it was true, didn't you? You believed what I said enough to trust me and taste. The Bible says 'O taste and see that the Lord is good. Happy is the man that trusteth in Him.' You can't be intellectually convinced till you have tasted of course. But belief is just accepting and tasting."

"You'd really have to accept Him, wouldn't you," asked Sheila shyly, "before you could have Him live in you?"

"I can see that of course," said Betty, "but how could His living in you, as you call it, make you happy? It wouldn't make you forget any of your disappointments, would it? It wouldn't give you all the things you wanted and haven't got, nor get you rid of all the things you didn't want, would it?"

"It would do a greater thing than that," said Grandmother thoughtfully. "It would change all your wants. I think if we once got to *know* the Lord Jesus Christ, even just a little bit, we would fall so in love with Him, that we would want just what would please Him. For instance, I am quite sure that when you first fell in love with Malcolm many of your own tastes changed automatically. You wanted certain things because he liked them. Isn't that so?"

Betty flushed and nodded, but at the same time looked so wistful and despairing that Grandmother's heart went out to her.

"I know," she went on, "human loves disappoint us sometimes, but Jesus Christ is never a disappointment in any way."

"It seems unbelievable to me now that I was ever willing to give up my own life to somebody else," said Betty miserably. "And it seems just as awful when you talk about letting God do what he wants to with you. It would be terrible to have to think of pleasing *Him* all the time. It would be slavery. Why, you couldn't do *anything!* Life is bad enough now for me."

"No, child, it isn't slavery to try to please someone you *love*. It's the greatest joy. Besides, you know we aren't going to stay on this earth so very long. Even if we live to be really old the time goes very quickly. As I look back to the time when I was your age it seems only a few months ago. Are you at all happy about leaving this earth, Betty?"

Betty shuddered.

"Oh, no!" she said. "If I could just convince myself that when I died that was the end of everything, I'd go out there and climb on the rock where Sheila was day before yesterday and let the water take me off. I would really. I'm sick of living. Yes, I am! Nothing is the way it ought to be. People disappoint you and things don't satisfy. I've found that out long ago. But I'm afraid. I was afraid when we were watching Sheila out there in the water, and the boys struggling to save her and themselves. I was terribly afraid. I'm always afraid when I think about death, or when anybody dies! I'm terribly, terribly unhappy. I don't see why we ever have to die."

"We wouldn't if it weren't for sin," said Grandmother. "But Betty, Jesus Christ can change all that for you. He can make you happy and unafraid."

"Well, I wish He would then," said Betty great tears suddenly filling her eyes. "Sometimes I feel just desperate. I never saw anybody that seemed really happy till Angus came. He's like you, too, I guess. I saw his Bible lying open on his bedside stand the other morning. I guess he reads it. And then when Sheila spoke about the flowers the other day, wondering what God had made them for, it seemed as if she had something that I didn't have. Anyway I wanted to find out. Of course I've always know you were that way, Mrs. Ainslee, and Mother and Father Galbraith are just wonderful, and they say grace at the table and go to church a lot. But they aren't young. Their time of having fun is almost over. Maybe I'll feel that way too when I get old. I suppose it's the only thing left when people get past the place where they can have gay times forgetting what comes after."

Betty looked thoughtfully off toward the sea, her brow troubled.

"What would I have to do after I accepted Him—if I did?"

"Whatever He told you to do."

Betty looked mystified.

"But I mean what would I have to give up? Don't you have to renounce the world and a lot of things when you do that? I don't know what my husband would say to that. He thinks I'm terrible already."

"This little book says," said Sheila eagerly, "that it isn't a question of giving up anything. You just hand over your-*self,* and then it is His responsibility to tell you how to walk with Him."

"It sounds strange and hard," said Betty, "awfully queer too. It doesn't sound attractive."

"But it's wonderful," said Grandmother with an other-worldliness in her face. "It makes even the hard things beautiful. And then you've always got some One to go to when you are troubled and perplexed. Child, believe me, I've been through a lot of hard things in my time, and if it hadn't been for the Lord Jesus I couldn't have borne them. If you get so you are willing to take God's promises of salvation and really take the Lord Jesus into your life you'll find a joy you never even knew existed. But you can't understand it as long as you are deliberately living for the flesh—for the things of this world that pass away."

"I wish I could feel that way," said Betty looking wistfully from the old face to the young one.

Just then Janet came wheeling the teacart out with glasses of iced tea and little delicious sandwiches and cinnamon toast and for the moment the conversation was broken up.

Grandmother ran into the house to answer the telephone, a long distance call that kept her several minutes, and it was then that Betty said suddenly, looking around with quick alarm:

"Why where is Jacqueline? Why isn't she out drinking tea? She isn't up at The Cliffs vamping my husband again is she?" Her voice was very bitter as she said it.

"Oh, Jacqueline went to the mountains this morning. Didn't you know it?" said Sheila, and in spite of her there was a lilt in her voice.

It was then that Betty looked really glad for a minute, and expressed her mind about Jacqueline, and then after a thoughtful pause she added:

"I hope I haven't hurt you. She's your cousin I know. But somehow she's so different from you."

"She doesn't know the Lord," said Sheila gravely. "I've been thinking about that. I've been wondering if she wouldn't be very different if she did."

"I doubt it," said Betty sharply. "She'd be one person who would never give up self and go according to some other will, I'm sure. Not even God's."

Then after a moment she said thoughtfully.

"Well, if she's really gone, and not coming back again next week to worry me, I might even look into this thing myself, I don't know. I'm sure if I could get what you've got I'd be glad."

"Oh," said Sheila, "I'm afraid I haven't got very much yet. I'm just beginning to learn. I wish you'd start too. It would be nice if we could study together."

"Perhaps I will," said Betty. "I'll think about it. I have days on end when I'm bored silly. I'm not sure I would be interested and I might be only an incubus, but maybe I'll try it out. I may as well confess that it was you who made me willing to listen to it. I certainly was impressed with you, coming right out of death's jaws the other day, and then being willing right off the bat that way to ask Jacqueline's pardon for slapping her. I'm just sure whatever she did that you were in the right. Anyone would know she had given you just cause. And you asked her pardon! I couldn't forget that!"

"I guess there is no just cause for yielding to one's natural self," said Sheila thoughtfully. "She made me awfully angry. But if Christ had really been living in me He wouldn't have slapped her. When He was reviled He reviled not again. 'He was led as a lamb to the slaughter yet He opened not His mouth.'"

"But don't you think we can ever punish people for what they have done?" said Betty aghast.

Sheila looked perplexed.

"I suppose so, when we are given the rule over them, but this wasn't a case like that. I was reading this morning 'Vengeance is mine, I will repay, saith the Lord; therefore if thine enemy hunger, feed him, if he thirst give him drink — ' I guess I knew all the time that it wasn't my business to show her where she was wrong."

"Well," said Betty wistfully, "I can't see it that way, but maybe you're right. At least it's worth looking into. I'm coming down again, if you'll let me."

"Come down every morning you can," said Sheila. "I know Grandmother would love to have you and I'm sure I would."

So it came about that there were few mornings thereafter when Betty Galbraith did not come and sit in the garden with them studying God's Word.

Day after day her interest grew, and her face sweetened and softened.

One morning Malcolm Galbraith walked into the garden right in the middle of the lesson, and took a seat.

"I've come to find out what it is Betty is doing down here that's made such a difference in her," he said, and though there was a hint of the old twinkle in his eye, his voice was almost grave. "No, don't stop, please. I mean it. I want to understand this thing that has got hold of Betty and made her so sweet."

Betty flushed up to her forehead and had a half frightened look. She thought he was making fun of her. She was almost ready to cry. But Malcolm sat gravely down beside her and reached out for a side of her Bible.

"Now, please go on, just where you were and don't mind me. I really want to see what you are doing. I'm not here to criticise."

Quite simply Grandmother went on reading.

Malcolm listened attentively and with apparent interest.

When it was over, Janet, wise beyond her generation, came wheeling the teacart down with cups of bouillon and sandwiches, raspberries and cake and coffee.

"Oh, boy!" said the uninvited guest, "I'm coming every day after this! I always used to go to the Sunday School picnics for the ice cream."

He was courtesy itself, waiting upon them all, quite his old gay self, yet with an undertone of seriousness about him that was not habitual.

Betty watched him in wonder. This was more like the man who had won her to marry him. She watched him as he approached Sheila, but there was nothing in his manner that made her feel the old jealousy. Had she changed or was he changing?

"I'm coming again," he said gaily when they started home. "May I, Grandmother?"

"You are always welcome," said Grandmother. "If you are really in earnest. If it's only to make fun we don't want you."

"I couldn't make fun," said Malcolm with an unwonted look in his eyes. "This seems to be real. I must know more about it. Betty's got hold of something. It's beginning to hit me tremendously. If she's going religious on my hands I'll have to do it too, or leave her. I never saw such a change in any human being in three weeks in my life. I want to get at the Source."

"Jesus Christ is the Source, Malcolm Galbraith," said Grandmother. "He is 'the way, the truth, and the life.'"

So Malcolm came down with Betty almost every morning, and somehow Betty began to have a happier look on her face. They were almost like two lovers, always sitting near to one another, watching out that each had the right place. And one day they drove down instead of coming by the beach, and brought Marget Galbraith with them.

"I had to come, Myra," explained Grandmother's old friend. "I had to see what it is these children are so interested in. It's made a big difference in our house. Even Hugh is noticing it. I guess I'll have to get in on it too."

"That's nice," said Grandmother. "I've just heard of a wonderful young man from one of the big Bible Schools who is speaking at a Conference place not far from here. He's coming over to-morrow to show us how to go about this study better. The more we have the better I'll like it."

20

THE young Bible teacher proved to be a great find in every way.

The original group had grown by several additions now, a few summer friends who dropped in one at a time.

But one morning quite out of the blue, Jacqueline arrived, utterly unexpected and unheralded, according to her usual custom.

The group was just filing into their usual places in the garden, where Grandmother had placed more chairs now, and added a table or two for the convenience of the class. The teacher had just alighted from his roadster and was coming into the gate as the red car drove up. He gave its driver a keen appraising glance and wondered. Jacqueline give him a keen appraising glance and decided she had come just in time. Only she didn't understand the leather case he held in his hand. Was he a doctor? Was someone sick?

Jacqueline alighted and followed the young man up the walk and around to where she heard voices in the garden, and stood a moment in amazement looking over the mixed company gathered there, wondering what it was all about.

"What in Pete's name!" she called as she spied Malcolm Galbraith. "What the heck is going on here? A party?"

Betty looked up and her heart sank. Then she turned a quick look at her husband.

But Malcolm stood gravely regarding the newcomer.

"Here's a chair, Jac," he said, just as if she had always been attending the class. "You got here just in time. The teacher has just arrived."

"Teacher?" said Jacqueline looking wildly around. "For cat's sake what is this? A bridge party?"

"No, it's a Bible study class!" said Malcolm, his face quite serious. "Sit down, Jac. It's wonderful."

"For heaven's sake, Malcolm! Let's get out of this quick. Come on Betty, you come too." She leaned over and motioned to Betty.

Betty came reluctantly toward her, struggling with a new found grace and an old temptation.

"Come on Betty, help me get a bathing suit," whispered Jacqueline. "I'm dying for a swim. Can't you and Malcolm sneak out? Who is that young chap over there by the table? Can't you give him the high sign and sneak him along too? Let's get out of this saint's rest. I shall expire!"

Betty looked frightened again and turned a sorrowful glance at her husband, but Malcolm came to the front in a new character.

"Sorry, Jac," he said pleasantly, yet a trifle formally, "Betty and I are committed to this, and really you couldn't tempt us away. The young man over there by the table is our teacher. He's a cracker-jack. Better sit down, Jac, it's worth it, it really is! No kidding!"

Jacqueline looked at Malcolm with a face in which amazement and incredulity were struggling for the uppermost. Then she gazed at Betty curiously.

"Is that so, or is he kidding me?" she asked sharply.

"Oh, it is so!" said Betty radiantly.

"Good night!" said Jacqueline turning away in disgust.

"This is no place for a child of sin like myself. I'd better pass out of the picture."

"I wish you would stay," said Betty with a gentle note of pleading in her voice that caused Jacqueline to turn and look at her again, curiously.

"Well you are changed, if that is really true," she said bitterly. "Thanks, no, I prefer the world, the flesh and the devil!" and she swept on down the walk to the wicket gate and out to her car. In a moment more they could hear her motor throbbing as she flashed along the beach toward a more congenial world.

It was that very night that Sheila saw a face against the dark window, looking in. A face that strangely reminded her of terror and her flight. It couldn't be of course, but it looked a little like Buck's face pressed against the screening, looking in.

Sheila had been studying down in the living room by the big table where her study books were scattered, and it had grown late without her realizing it.

Grandmother was a little tired that evening, and confessed to it for a wonder, and Sheila had sent her early to bed.

Janet also had gone to bed right after supper with a toothache, and Sheila had had a long uninterrupted evening. She had always enjoyed study, and this new opening up of scripture was to her an ever increasing wonder.

But there was something else beside the study that made her glad to-night to have this evening to herself. She had inside her Bible a letter that afternoon received from the far west, and when she finished the study she had prescribed for her evening's work she meant to read it over again, slowly, and enjoy every word of it.

It was not the first time that Angus Galbraith had written to her since he had taken his first flight westward. He had written to Grandmother a good many times, and often sent her messages, and several times he had written her concerning her mother's grave and the progress he was making about the stone, and the fixing of the cemetery lot, if lot it could be called on that bleak prairie.

But this letter was more like a pleasant chat than business. He told her it is true about the placing of the stone and the arrangement he had made for the perpetual care of the lot but he entered more into detail about his journey, with descriptions of this and that. He had been to see Ma Higgins and her insignificant husband and he gave her messages that brought the tears to Sheila's eyes. She had never realized how Ma Higgins really had loved her, and had missed her after she left.

He told of visiting the place where she had lived, and how he had looked around and tried to think of her there getting ready for life, with that wonderful mother of hers. How he dignified her home in the shack with her mother. How he honored her beloved mother!

It seemed he had even been to the cabaret and seen where her mother sang. People had told him of her last wonderful song, of her clean fine life, and the strength of her character. He had been for miles around there meeting people she used to know. She wondered as she read on how he came to meet all those people? Yet she rejoiced that he had. It seemed so wonderful to have this new friend linked to her life with her mother in this way. And she did not any more shrink from having him know her poverty and the squalor of her early home. He looked beyond the outside shell. He understood something deeper than appearances. He had seen the beauty with which her mother had surrounded her life, a beauty which could not be purchased with money nor gained by education or travel. A beauty of the heart life.

She had read the letter over for the third time before suddenly she felt that there was someone in the room and a cold chill of fear, a terrible premonition of evil, seemed to possess her.

She looked up to dispel this sense of an enemy at hand, and there stood Buck!

Her strength seemed running from the ends of her fingers and seeping out from the toes of her slippers as she sat and looked at him in horror.

Yet even as this great fright seized her something whispered "God kept you on the rock in that terrible storm, and can He not keep you through this also? Remember the Rainbow!"

Then something cool and quieting seemed to come to her, a strength not her own. Quite calmly she folded her letter with her cold fingers, and laid it smoothly in her Bible, looking all the time into the evil eyes of the man who stood amusedly, contemptuously, looking at her.

Then she rose and reached out to the table where the telephone extension always stood.

He did not move but continued to watch her with that smile of amusement on his hateful face, while she took down the receiver and tried to call the operator. She was trying to think whether she had better call The Cliffs or the private officer who had charge of watching this section of the shore cottages, when Buck's voice broke harshly on her senses with a laugh.

"That won't do any good," he said. "You don't suppose I'm a fool, do you? You can call as much as you like and no one will answer."

Instantly there came to her the thought, "Ah, but the wires *up* are not cut. My God will hear when I call."

She hung up the receiver quietly and put the instrument back on the table.

"I see," she said quietly. "Well, won't you be seated?"

He laughed.

"No thanks," he said, "and you won't sit there long either. I've chased you good and far, and now you're going to do what I told you you had to do before you sneaked away on me. You're going to listen to me."

"Excuse me a moment until I call my Grandmother," said Sheila, thinking to get away where she could call someone, and then realizing how futile it was to suggest that. She saw by the man's eyes that he knew he had her in his power.

"Not much I won't. Your Grandmother's good and fast asleep and she's going to stay there till I get ready to wake her up. I made sure of that before I came in. The kitchen girl is asleep too. I heard both their snores before I made a move. Now, you stand right still where you are till I tell you what I want of you. If you do just as I say you won't be harmed a hair, though I ought to pay you good for the trick you played on me running away, and I would anyway, if it weren't a matter of time with me. But if you don't do what I say I'll pay you back good and pretty and that's a fact! See that gun? Well, maybe you don't know I'm considered the neatest shot in the state of Idaho."

Something seemed suddenly to come up into Sheila's throat and choke her. Something like a veil kept dropping down before her eyes. A great dizziness swept over, but she shut her lips firmly and kept her feet, steadying herself by the tips of the fingers of one hand resting on the table.

She had seen guns out in her western life, and they had not seemed so awful to her as this one, here in Grandmother's sweet, safe living room. It looked so large, so crude, so horrible!

Was this a dream perhaps? Maybe she had fallen asleep in her chair. Maybe she had a nightmare. But she must be very careful not to make an outcry whether it were real of fancied, for Grandmother must not be wakened.

"What is it you want of me?"

She felt her stiff lips forming the words, her strange voice speaking them.

"All right. That's sensible. You're going to be reasonable and do what you're told, are you? That's right. Well, then, we won't waste time. You just keep your eye on my gun and do as I say and I'll be through with you in a short time. You've got a paper I want, and you're going to get it for me. That's all!"

He saw by the startled look in her face that she knew what paper he meant, but in a moment she was able to answer him steadily again.

"I haven't any paper that you could want, I am sure," she said, looking at him with a clear eye.

"Oh, so you've learned to lie!" he sneered. "I thought they told me you was such an honest person!"

She did not answer that. She waited to be guided. Her throat seemed powerless to utter anything more, her words would not come.

"Now, we'll begin again," said the man. "You've got a paper that I want, and I mean to have it. In just three minutes you're going to get it and bring it to me or I'm going to shoot your ankles so you can't walk any more."

"I couldn't do anything for you certainly if you did that," said Sheila, and wondered why those words had come from her lips, they were so futile.

"Yes, you could. You could crawl, and I'd find a way to make you do it, don't you forget it! Now, that paper. You go get it right now. Get me?"

"What kind of paper is it you want?" asked Sheila to make time, though she wondered how that would do any good. She would have to make a whole night of time if she would hope to escape. She began to think she was so frightened that her good sense was leaving her.

"You know what paper it is that I want. Your dad gave it to your mother and told her never to part with it, or words to that effect. Your mother must have told you the same thing. Your dad had it put away good and safe. He told me he had it in a pencilholder. Yes I see you know. I'm used to watching the pupils of eyes. I can read 'em. Now, you go get that paper and make it snappy. I gotta get a train."

Sheila had been considering. There was no point in trying to deceive a man like this. She would tell the truth.

"Yes," she said calmly, "I have heard of such a paper. My

mother told me about it but she did not tell me what was in it. She gave me directions about it and I have carried them out. I had that penholder, but I do not have it any more."

"That may be a lie too, but anyhow you know where it is and that amounts to the same thing."

"No, I do not know where it is," said Sheila. "I was to give it to someone else and I did so. I do not know what they have done with it."

"Well, I do. I can figure out pretty darn well who you were to give it to, and that's your blooming grandmother, and I have had it all figured out clear across the continent what she did with it and that is, put it in her safe in her room. I know that safe. I was here when it was built in when I was a kid. That was where she always kept her money, and where your father always could find it. We knew the combination, or we could figure it out. So, that's where it is. If I hadn't known that I wouldn't have risked my skin coming here where there's a price on my head. But I've got to have that paper, and I'm so desperate. Now, do you want me to truss you up and tie you in a chair with a wad in yer mouth, or will you go up and help me get that paper out of the safe? Your job will be to get the paper while I keep the old lady asleep, see? If you won't do that, I'll tie you in that chair and make short work of the old lady, for I mean to have that paper, come what will. I only gave it to your father once when he got the upper hand of me for a little while, and I mean to have it back. If you go along nicely and do what I tell you you'll have your dad back again soon. He's in the can now serving time fer me. That's the price he paid, or thought he paid for that paper, but if you don't do as I say your dad can rot in prison for all I care. See!"

Sheila felt things getting dark before her vision. Was she going to faint before she could decide what to do? In that case he would have his way and what might not happen to Grandmother? Oh, it was just like being on the rock with the last wave coming! She tried to reach out and remember the strong arm of God and the rainbow and get her thoughts steady.

"Oh, God, I can't hold out much longer. Show me what to do! Send help! Oh, send me help!"

21

JANET'S toothache had been soothed to quiet by the hot water bag she took to bed with her and she had fallen early to sleep. But the hot water bag had grown cold and the tooth had started to ache again, and Janet had wakened up to misery once more. The obvious thing was to go down to the kitchen and heat more water, for if she tried to fill the hot water bag in the bathroom she would be sure to waken the old lady, and she would come trotting out to see what was the matter. She had the ears of a detective even in her sleep.

It seemed to Janet that it must be long past midnight and that all the house would be in bed.

So Janet arose and donned her dressing gown and heelless slippers and stepped cautiously forth into the back hall. Every step must be guarded, and she must wait between the steps to be sure she was not heard. It was not far from her door to the top of the back stairs. Once down the top step she would be safe from sound. The top step always creaked a bit.

But as Janet reached the doorway that led into the front hall she saw a light coming from downstairs. Had Miss Sheila forgotten to turn out the living room light, or were there burglars in the house? Janet was always thinking of burglars because her brother-in-law belonged to the state constabulary.

She paused and held her breath and heard a man's voice. If Miss Jacqueline Lammorrelle had been here it would not have been strange for she sat up all hours of the night with callers, and made the old lady very angry. But surely Miss Sheila would never do that. Yet in a moment more she heard Sheila's voice and was filled with consternation. What man could be down there with her? She came a little nearer to the stair head to peer down, with the idea of clearing Miss Sheila of anything wrong she might think about her, and to her horror she saw a man with a gun pointed straight at Miss Sheila and, Miss Sheila standing white and calm there before him. She glanced backward down the hall where Grandmother's door stood open, and she could see the dim outline of Grandmother's form under the white counterpane, lying there. Miss Sheila was down there in the living room all alone with a burglar and something must be done.

Janet was terribly weak and frightened but she managed to be cautious, and swing herself back to the stair head and down each step of the back stairs without a sound. She crossed the pantry and opened the swing door into the kitchen, thankful that only that day she had oiled the hinges where they squeaked. Could she get the back door open without a noise? Yes, the key turned quietly, and she held the knob like a vise, so that her fingers ached when she let it go after she had closed it behind her.

Then like a wraith she flew through the night, holding her kimono close about her, flying through the deep sand by miracle, wallowing up the bank to the road, and across more sand to her sister's cottage, dark in every window now, and still as the dead.

When she reached the door and began to pound on it her hands were trembling so that she could scarcely knock, and then it was a long time before she could rouse her sister. And after she was roused, she couldn't seem to get her to hurry.

Her brother-in-law was out on his beat, it seemed. There was nothing to do but try to reach him by telephone, though it was almost time for him to come in. Janet telephoned wildly and managed to tell a coherent story, but when it was finished and she hung up she sat down suddenly in a chair and began to cry. Then she sprang from her chair and ran to the door.

"I must go back!" she cried. "Miss Sheila's all alone with a burglar!" and with that she ran out into the night again.

Grandmother had dropped early into a pleasant sleep, and was dreaming of Andrew when he was a little boy in a white dress, with his hair curled in a lovely golden curl on the top of his head, bright blue shoes on his tiny feet, dimples in his laughing cheeks, and stars in his happy eyes.

But Grandmother was attuned to every feature of Rainbow Cottage. She knew every creak and groan of every bit of lumber in a storm, and she could always tell when anybody went up and down the back stairs, even if they went like cats.

When Janet stepped her softly slippered foot on the top step of that back stairs, although she couldn't hear a bit of a creak, Grandmother was wide awake, and sitting up. Grandmother was that way.

She sat still for an instant and listened, and then she became aware of low voices in the living room. What had happened? Had somebody come in to call, and wasn't it as late as it seemed?

Softly she stole to the head of the stairs and listened. Grandmother could walk like a feather, and she knew the creaking boards in her floor as well as Janet.

She heard a word or two that Buck said, and she knew his voice at once. She did not need the second glance she took, leaning down cautiously at the side of the rail to get a good look, and to see her precious Sheila facing that awful gun.

Like a feather she stole back to her pillow and took from

beneath it her trusty weapon, a great flash torch light. It was the biggest and brightest torch she had been able to find in the city of Boston, and its light would travel far. She had seldom used it for there had not been need, but she had put it to test once or twice and it worked well.

Like a feather she floated over to her window and sent her torch flashing far up the beach to where she knew a state policeman lived. Several times she flashed it into the windows of the little house, and it traveled like a great yellow pencil across the beach and lighted up the windows of that little cottage by the road. She flashed till she saw a light appear in the cottage and someone at the window moving around. Someone was looking out the window, and then she flashed it on and waved it round in circles. Would they know that that was a cry for help?

"Oh God, make them understand!" her heart cried out as she tiptoed lightly across the hall to the yellow room and flashed her signals again toward the north, straight into window after window up at The Cliffs. Yes, a light appeared there, to her joy. She knew that in one window at least it must have traveled into the face of some sleeper, for the bed in that room was directly opposite the window. She waved her silent signals violently again and then floated back to her own room and going to her closet took out a great pair of Indian clubs that had belonged to Andrew in his college days. She had kept them there ever since he left, hidden way back behind her garments, and these she now grasped in her left hand. But it took all her courage to open her bedside table drawer and take therefrom her last resort, a tiny revolver that her son Maxwell had insisted upon her possessing if she was going to stay alone in the cottage by the sea.

Grandmother was terribly, terribly afraid of that gun, even though it contained only blank cartridges, and there wasn't a single bullet in the house. But she now stealthily tiptoed to a spot of the bare floor by the window, that was directly over where Buck Hasbrouck stood. She raised her left arm high, letting the clubs fall and roll about with tremendous uproar. At the same instant she shot off the revolver out the window, all six cartridges. She slid her feet into shoes and with the heaviest tread she could muster, she marched toward the stairs.

The Israelites conquered Jericho with lamps, pitchers and trumpets, marching around the city seven days. Grandmother fought for her dear girl with flash light, revolver and Indian clubs, tramping her hardwood floor valiantly. Just as she felt her strength was at an end and she was going to fall all the way down the stairs, she heard the sound of motor cycles coming like great comets through the night, and up from the road there came the sound of horses' hoofs, beating on the asphalt—the state constabulary!—and behind them a car shot down the road from The Cliffs.

Grandmother's barrage had lasted no more than ten seconds, and then she descended in all the glory of her pink flannelette nightgown, her lovely white curls floating out behind her, her gun in one hand, her big torch burning before her, and Indian club bumping down the stairs ahead of her. Buck Hasbrouck, hardened criminal though he was, turned white at the strange unwonted sounds. With his gun ready for action he was stealthily, rapidly backing toward the door as Grandmother spoke:

"Bucknell Hasbrouck, put down that gun. There is a man waiting at the back door and two more at the front, and it's too late for you to try to get away."

Grandmother wasn't ever quite sure whether she said that before she saw the handcuffs snapped around Buck's wrists or not. But when it was all over, and he was led away between two state police, she branded him once more with his true identity, by crying out his name, and then dropped down suddenly and weakly on the stairs, the torch and the other Indian club rolling together down into the living room, recalling a policeman to see if another burglar had turned up.

After things had quieted down and Malcolm Galbraith

and Betty who had dashed down to see what Grandmother's light-signals meant, had gone home again, Janet brought up a tray with milk toast and a bit of chicken breast and coffee, and then they had to tell the whole story over again. They were all so excited it was no use to try and go to sleep again right away, and besides the east was already showing a streak of pink.

"But you know," said Grandmother thoughtfully, after everything they could think of was told, and Janet had gone back to bed again, "he couldn't have found the paper anyway, for it wasn't in my safe."

"It wasn't?" said Sheila. "How wonderful! How did that happen?"

"Why, I sent it the very next day by Angus Galbraith down to the Hazen Bank, and they have it in their vault. That was what I was talking on the telephone so long about. I had the president on the long distance wire. That paper will convict Buck Hasbrouck, and clear the name of my boy, Sheila. Oh, how good God has been to us!"

Sheila was still a minute, and then she said:

"How I wish that my mother could know."

"Perhaps she does," said Grandmother thoughtfully.

"Oh, do you think so?" said Sheila softly, her eyes starry bright. And then she added sorrowfully, "But where is my father?"

"Perhaps we'll find that out some day," said Grandmother hopefully.

22

ANGUS Galbraith had been a long journey and had passed through many strange experiences, trying to carry out his mission to that far western spot. He had passed as a prospector, cattle owner, investor, anything that happened to fit the necessity, and he had hung around strange people and strange places listening to men talk.

He had luncheoned at the counter where Sheila used to serve, eaten apple pie and drank coffee such as Buck had ordered from her; and fitted the tales Ma Higgins had to tell to the shy sweet girl he had met by the sea. And she had come to be enshrined in his heart.

He had even been to the cabaret where Moira used to sing, and found those who had heard her, and who often recalled her singing. "Like the angels" some of them said, and sighed, knowing there would be very few angels in the rest of their way.

And at last he had found out the tale. In a shanty where old settlers sometimes recalled stories when they felt it was safe, he heard the tale of how Buck Hasbrouck had been at the bottom of crime after crime, and escaped justice, and how at last when justice seemed inevitable he had managed to fasten it upon one, Andrew Ainslee, Handsome Andy, they called him.

He dared not ask questions. He was a disinterested stranger and so he must remain if he would hear the whole story, and he lingered as long as he dared. But one day he heard a word that gave him a clue as to where his man might be found, and at last he came to the prison.

But when he finally was led to the man whom he had sought so far, he saw at a glance that he was not long for this world, yet Angus could not explain that look of something alive in the haggard face that gave it vividness. Also he saw in spite of the different coloring a startling likeness to Sheila. A way he had of raising his hand, the lifting of his chin, a trick he had of smiling faintly with one corner of his mouth. They all gripped the young man's heart. He knew at once that it was with more than pity that he regarded this man. There was something really lovable about him, even in his disgrace, and he could understand why he had been popular and spoiled in his youth.

It was only a plain hospital ward of the prison, and he lay on a crude cot, with few comforts about him, yet there was something princely about him in spite of his surroundings. It was easy to see, even now, how high born Moira McCleeve had believed in him and loved him, and been willing to risk joining her life to his.

He had something about him too of his mother's proud features and Angus Galbraith was glad that at last his search was ended.

He sat down beside the man and they began to talk.

At first he did not tell him who he was nor where he came from, just talked as any visitor might to a prisoner, a sick man.

"Yes," said Andrew Ainslee, in a voice that sounded much like his elder brother Maxwell's, only not quite so firm and opinioned, "I'm not long here now, and I'm glad. In any case my time would be out in another nine months, but I can't wait for that. I've got a call to another country, and I think I'm going soon."

Angus tried to say something about being sorry he had to go from such a place as this, but a surprising smile lit up the man's face as he answered.

"Oh, I'm not minding that," he said "This place has been the gate of heaven to me, and I'm glad I was sent here. You see sir, I've always been a failure in life, made a mess of things for all I loved, you know, just by wanting my own way. But when I came here I found the Lord, and I am saved. Probably if I had never come I might not have listened. But here there wasn't anything to do and I was going wild. When a man came and told me the Lord Jesus still loved me, I had to listen. It was my only hope. Do you know the Lord, sir? If you don't you wouldn't understand."

"Oh, yes, indeed I do!" said Angus with a genuine ring to his voice, and a thrill in his heart that he should come to seek a lost soul and find in him a brother in the Lord.

After that it was easy to get close to the other life and find out bit by bit the way that had ended in a prison cell.

Andrew Ainslee told it briefly and simply.

"I was just a fool and thought I knew best about my life. I broke my mother's heart. My brothers turned against me, after my father died. Later I got mixed up in a crime that I hadn't committed,—didn't even know about it till after I went away. I didn't write home for a long time. I was bitter at them all for not believing me. But I was wrong. I got to drinking of course, and that led to worse things, till I really got my conscience blunted and let things get by me that I wouldn't have thought of in younger days."

Angus Ainslee laid a friendly hand on the coarse sleeve the man was wearing, and the sick man flashed a grateful look at him. He had had little sympathy, hadn't deserved it either of course, but it touched him deeply from this stranger.

"Then I found a girl," went on Andrew in a husky tone, struggling with emotion. "I kept straight for her sake for a long time. Then when our little girl was born I got hard up and went to gambling again, and drinking."

The man's voice broke.

"She was a wonderful girl, not like the girls such a man as I was usually meets or cares for. She was up against it too, and I married her. Fool! I thought I was good enough to do that! She was a wonderful girl, a Christian girl, high born. I wish I could tell you what she was!"

"Yes, I know," said Angus quietly, "my mother knew her mother and sister. I have been to Castle McCleeve myself."

"What? You know who I am? And you knew Moira? And you came here to see me, a dying convict?"

"No, I didn't know Moira, but I've heard much about her, and I know your daughter Sheila."

The man was still for an instant, a gray look coming over his face.

"Then they know where I am," he said. "I hoped I could spare them that. Moira died. You knew Moira died, didn't you? The man who made a lot of trouble for me told me that. I hoped sometimes that perhaps he did not tell me true, but I did not dare to write. I wanted to spare her knowing where I am. I do not think she knew. I hope she did not know."

"No, she did not know. As long as she lived she kept hoping you would come back. She died a little over six months ago."

The man lay still breathing hard.

"But Mother, and Sheila? They know where I am? Perhaps I oughtn't to care. But it was to save Mother this that I came away from home, to save her from having a son in prison. If I had stayed at home I would have been sent to prison for another man's sin, and it would have been prison for life. Yet she had to have the shame after all. And my little girl has to grow up and think she is a convict's daughter!" He sighed deeply and turned his face away for a moment. Then he looked up again with a ray of light in his sunken features.

"But there's something you can tell them when I'm gone. I'm not serving time for my own crime now. I'm taking the place of another man. No one around here knows it. I did it voluntarily. It was a bargain I made with him in a time when he was in a tight place. Maybe I was wrong, but I did it so that Mother could have some evidence, when I was gone, that I didn't do the deed for which I know people back home have blamed me. I got a paper signed by the criminal himself, exonerating me, and I paid for it with my life. I didn't think that would be the price when I did it. I thought the five years would go fast, and then I could go back with my paper and live among my people. I thought with that evidence I could take my wonderful wife and child back and really live out the rest of my days. But God saw things differently, and I am content to go. Only I wish Mother could have had that paper! But now that Moira is dead I don't suppose it's in existence any more. Or perhaps Buck has made Sheila give it to him. He threatened to if I didn't keep my bargain."

"Well, friend," said Angus with a joyous ring to his voice, "you can set your mind at rest on that point. Your mother has seen the paper and it is now in possession of the president of the Hazen Bank, and your family and friends all know that you had nothing to do with that robbery nor the two murders that resulted from it."

"Thank the Lord!" said the sick man in a weak voice in which there was a sound of tears. "I don't deserve it, but thank the Lord! And now I can die at peace. I've done plenty of things I shouldn't have done, and I've sinned against all my dear ones, but I'm glad to be free of that terrible crime in the eyes of the world before I die."

"I've something more to tell you, too," said Angus taking the thin hand in his and holding it warmly.

"I've just had a telegram this morning saying that Buck was arrested last night, when he entered your mother's cottage by the sea and tried to force your daughter to tell him where that paper was. And besides the evidence which the paper had already furnished, and the perfect set of finger prints which they had been able to get after the robbery and murder, which identified Buck as the criminal without any doubt, there was found in his pocket another paper, rolled tightly inside an old tin pencilholder. It was a memoranda that had been made out by the bank clerk concerning some of the stolen property. It had evidently been lying with the rest and they grabbed everything. It's going to be important evidence in the case against him."

"He found it then!" said the sick man excitedly. "It was a paper he dropped the night I helped to get him away, though I never knew there was a reason like that for his wanting to get away quickly. He dropped the slip in the car I drove for him and I found it after he had gone. I didn't know at the time whether it was important or not. I made out that it was written on bank paper by the lower edges of the letters where it had been torn off. It had the Hazen Bank name on it, and of course, afterwards, when I read the newspapers, and knew what had happened I kept the paper to use as evidence if there ever was a chance. But I couldn't go back any more. I had helped him to get away and they probably knew I had. There was no hope for me!"

"They didn't all believe you had had any part in it. Your mother never believed it. She told me so!"

"She didn't! Oh, my precious mother, how she must have suffered! I shall never see her again on this earth, but I've written her a letter to be sent her at my death."

"You're not going to have to wait till you die," said Galbraith deeply moved. "You're going back to see her and tell her all about it!"

The prisoner looked at him bewildered, and then smiled sadly.

"I wish that might be," he said, "but I know it can't. I asked the doctor the other day if there was any chance I could live till my term was out and he told me I had only a few weeks left at most. And I know myself that I am growing weaker every day now."

"But your pardon is on the way here," said Angus, with a light in his eyes. "I've been to the Governor and made all the arrangements. I think it will be here in the next mail. And I have an airplane here to take you home as soon as it comes. Your mother is expecting you. Do you think you can stand the trip if we take it by easy stages?"

"Can I stand it?" said the sick man rising up on one elbow. "Oh, Lord! You are too good to me! I shall see my mother before I die. I shall feel her kiss of forgiveness. I know she has forgiven me or she would not let me come home! And I shall perhaps see my little girl again before I go to see her mother and my Lord! Oh, sir, you are a stranger but you have brought me the best thing that life could bring. I don't know why you have done it but I know I never can thank you enough. I'll just have to ask God to do it for me."

They started two days later, as soon as they could get the prodigal son arrayed in the fine raiment befitting his station, and the silver wings flew fast and carefully, to make it as easy as could be for the invalid. By slow stages they reached the east, and one bright morning landed safely on the broad white beach beside the Rainbow Cottage garden wall, and the son was at home at last with his mother, the father with his child.

Those were wonderful days while the death angel lingered and left Andrew Ainslee with his mother and child a little before he went to heaven.

That first night, after the invalid had been put to bed in his own home Sheila and Angus went out together into the garden, where the silver moonbeans were glorifying the drowsy flowers. Angus led her far down to the end of the garden where the old sea wall rose grayly in the moonlight, making sharp deep shadows over the rose beds, and then he opened his arms and Sheila walked into them.

"My darling!" he said softly as he folded her close. "I've loved you since the first minute I saw you, and known you were the one girl in the world for me if you would have me, but you've been so sweet and shy I wasn't sure whether you cared at all. I was even afraid when I put out my arms just now that you would turn and walk away from them. It seemed almost presumption to expect you to care so soon."

She lifted her sweet eyes to his face in the moonlight and looked at him adoringly.

"Why, Angus, I've loved you longer than you have me, for I saw you first. Out there on the step when I was sitting at the dinner table, and before you knew I was here, I saw you and my heart gave a great leap up for joy. I didn't know there was such a man as you, and I loved you at once, only I was afraid to let myself know it."

They had much to say those long moonlight evenings when they sat in the garden or walked together on the sand.

Daytimes they spent most of their time with Sheila's father, holding sweet converse, and speaking much about the Lord, and heaven, and Moira who would be waiting for him.

The fresh air and good food and most of all the presence of his dear ones, and the relief from the terrible thing that had hung over him so long, gave the invalid a short reprieve.

He told them the simple story of his conversion in the prison cell. It seemed almost unbelievable that he had been saved in this quiet way and was so changed.

His brothers came to see him and marvelled, and spoke gently to him where they had meant to blame. His sisters hurried home from Europe to see him once more before he left the earth forever. And his sweet daughter sat at his feet and loved him, while his mother trotted her dear old feet almost off waiting on him.

And then one day, quite quietly, he slipped away at sunset, into the beyond.

The young Bible teacher had the service, and spoke of

Christ's coming again for His own, and bringing with him all those who sleep in Jesus, and Grandmother looked up and wiped her brave old eyes and smiled.

"That didn't seem like a funeral at all," said Betty happily to her husband as they walked back along the beach after the service.

23

SOME people in the summer colony by the sea thought it was a little queer that Grandmother allowed a wedding so soon after a funeral at her cottage, but that didn't make any difference with Grandmother. The happy preparations went on just the same. In fact the dear one who had gone had wished it to be so. It was only because he failed so quickly and unexpectedly at the last that he was not present to be lifted to the couch in the garden which it had been hoped he might occupy at the wedding.

A few days before he left them, there was a joyous gathering of the clans. For when they heard their brother who had been lost was found, and that there was to be a wedding in the family the children and grandchildren trooped home, all but Jessica who was half way round the world with her bridegroom.

Mary and Damaris Deane had been home several weeks; the Van Dykes cut short their outing; the family in Mexico rushed up at once to see their long lost uncle Andrew before it was too late, and Max with his boy came up from New York several times before his brother died.

So they were all there the day of the wedding, a subdued

happiness upon each. There was no sadness to think that the poor storm-tossed life of Andrew Ainslee was gathered home to God.

During the few days he had been with them they had seen the very light of heaven in his face, and he had talked with each one of them about the change that had come to him, until his going to a real heaven had become to them a fact. They had known him before as a reckless scapegrace but he left a testimony behind him that would never be forgotten by his family.

So Grandmother went about her happy preparations for the simple wedding with a light in her eyes. Her son Andrew would not return to her, but he was safe, and she would go to him some day not too far away, or meet him in the air with her Lord. Grandmother was content.

The wedding was planned for the garden, but the day before it was to take place, the cousins looked anxiously at the clouds. Yet the bride Sheila was going about with such a shining countenance that one could only wonder and not complain.

When they woke up the day of the wedding it was raining and the twins were most outspoken against the weather, but it did not seem to trouble either Grandmother or Sheila, and Angus was too happy to be troubled by anything. He had that morning extracted a promise from Grandmother to go across the water with them in a couple of weeks when they should return from a little trip together, and spend the winter with them. So he was well content.

The wedding plans were quietly transferred from the garden to the house. The ceremony was to be at two o'clock with the Bible teacher minister officiating. The young people were terribly disappointed, all except the bride and groom who didn't seem to mind whether the ceremony was in the kitchen or the air, they were so quietly happy in each other.

But then, at the last minute, the sun suddenly shot out, the blue sky burst through, and a great rainbow flung its span across the sky! The sun was going to shine on the bride after all. The bridal train were in ecstasies, for who had ever been married right in a rainbow before!

Somebody hastened up to the attic for a great roll of green velvet carpet left over from other days, and they joyously rolled it down the garden walks. So in the soft colored mist of a gorgeous rainbow the garden stood waiting for the bridal couple. Through a bejeweled pathway the bride and groom walked down the velvet path and stood in the vine clad bower where late roses still graced the garden wall. Dew-gemmed blooms smiled under their bedraggled petals in the sunshine and rainbow lights played over the faces of the guests. The flowers were steeped in rainbow colors and Angus softly whispered to his bride, "We are walking under the arch of God's covenant."

The guests had to be careful about getting close to the flowers in their dewy decorations, but it was a lovely sparkling wedding, and most unique.

The twins had been just a little disappointed that they were not to wear the gorgeous Paris creations that they had brought home with them. But Sheila had elected to have her whole wedding party in white, so they all looked like a train of angels, walking down the way to heaven, as they trod the old green carpet among the flower beds.

It was just like Jacqueline to come roaring up in her big red car at the very minute, with Damaris playing the wedding march upon her violin, and the children scattering late roses over the way, and all the lovely chrysanthemums nodding their heavy dewy heads along the path.

"For Pete's sake, what on earth is going on here now?" cried Jacqueline coming noisily in at the wicket gate and accosting some of the summer people who were close friends of Grandmother.

And then she looked up and saw Angus and Sheila coming down the steps of the house, arm in arm, and heard the soft strains of the wedding march.

She saw the radiance of Sheila's lovely face, and the look of deep devotion that her bridegroom gave her as they turned down the garden walk, and her heart contracted sharply. Jacqueline lingered only a moment, long enough to hear the first words of the wedding ceremony, then she turned and stole out the garden gate and into her car, and softly, without the cut out this time, went flying up the beach.

When she had put a good ten miles between herself and the wedding she said aloud:

"Well, there goes the only man I ever really loved!" Then she flipped her fingers and drove hard away, seeking pastures new. She knew in her heart that he never would have loved her, and she never could have stood his quiet ways, yet her heart contracted painfully whenever she remembered.

Angus' wedding present to Sheila had been McCleeve Castle, about whose purchase he had begun making negotiations as soon as he learned who Sheila's mother was. Moira McCleeve's daughter should own the castle where her mother was born and brought up if she would accept it, and so he bought it long before he dared to tell Sheila of his love.

The evening star was just beginning to shine when Sheila and Angus set sail into a silver sea of sky on their way to the far west, to visit Moira's grave, and make arrangements for her body to be moved to the great Ainslee lot where Andrew was buried.

They were going to travel wherever they liked after they had completed their errand, and then come back in time to get Grandmother and sail for McCleeve Castle where they were to spend most of the winter.

It was all wonderful, and life looked bright and sweet to Sheila, even though there had been losses and sorrows mingled with the sweetness. But just now she and Angus were alone together in a sea of silver moonlight flying happily into the years that were ahead.

"Oh," said Sheila, after they had waved good bye to the dear ones watching below, and Sheila had thrown her bridal roses from the plane to the waiting bridesmaids, and even the silver sea in its evening opalescence was far behind. "Oh, I wonder if it will be like this when the Lord Jesus comes. Can't you think how wonderful it will be looking up to see all our dear ones coming with Him in the air? What if it were to-night while we are up here together!"

Then they streamed away into the silver night, and as he softly pressed her hand Angus was humming under his breath a bit of a song he had learned since he came to the States,

> *Jesus may come to-day,*
> *Glad day, glad day!*

About the Author

Grace Livingston Hill is well known as one of the most prolific writers of romantic fiction. Her personal life was fraught with joys and sorrows not unlike those experienced by many of her fictional heroines.

Born in Wellsville, New York, Grace nearly died during the first hours of life. But her loving parents and friends turned to God in prayer. She survived miraculously, thus her thankful father named her Grace.

Grace was always close to her father, a Presbyterian minister, and her mother, a published writer. It was from them that she learned the art of storytelling. When Grace was twelve, a close aunt surprised her with a hardbound, illustrated copy of one of Grace's stories. This was the beginning of Grace's journey into being a published author.

In 1892 Grace married Fred Hill, a young minister, and they soon had two lovely young daughters. Then came 1901, a difficult year for Grace—the year when, within months of each other, both her father and husband died. Suddenly Grace had to find a new place to live (her home was owned by the church where her husband had been pastor). It was a struggle for Grace to raise her young daughters alone, but through everything she kept writing. In 1902 she produced *The Angel of His Presence, The Story of a Whim,* and *An Unwilling Guest.* In 1903 her two books *According to the Pattern* and *Because of Stephen* were published.

It wasn't long before Grace was a well-known author, but she wanted to go beyond just entertaining her readers. She soon included the message of God's salvation through Jesus Christ in each of her books. For Grace, the most important thing she did was not write books but share the message of salvation, a message she felt God wanted her to share through the abilities he had given her.

In all, Grace Livingston Hill wrote more than one hundred books, all of which have sold thousands of copies and have touched the lives of readers around the world with their message of "enduring love" and the true way to lasting happiness: a relationship with God through his Son, Jesus Christ.

In an interview shortly before her death, Grace's devotion to her Lord still shone clear. She commented that whatever she had accomplished had been God's doing. She was only his servant, one who had tried to follow his teaching in all her thoughts and writing.